Come Watch *the* Nighttime Breathe

a novel by

JEFF GRAY

This Novel is dedicated to my Mother

Chapter I

If I was asked to look back and to do so without bias, I would say that I experienced what most considered being a typical childhood in suburbia America. To avoid overwhelming one with a great amount of details when it comes to a day in the life of a middle class child, or at least at this time in which it would prove to render itself pointless, I will stay with the basics. Although cliché, it is worth stating that I grew up in a much simpler time. The streets were deemed safe, children spent the long summer days riding their bicycles, playing hide-and-go-seek or other childhood games. At night, the echoes of innocence, joy and laughter could be heard throughout the neighborhood as children chased one another playing tag or dancing around in their yards chasing fireflies. The neighborhood yards would be littered each weekend with pitched tents where ghost stories were told deep into the night and dreams of what we would do in the real world once we were older would be shared. The lurking panel vans were rare to see, the newspapers lacked grim headlines and the backs of milk cartons were solely for advertisement and nutritional information. Yes, it was a much simpler time. As a result, parental supervision was minimal, with no fears or concerns; the parents were tucked away, fast asleep inside the home. Yet for myself, the boundaries, the perimeters of exploration were still greatly limited. I was raised and surrounded by the unconditional love of blue collared, conservative parents, within a simple home that practiced traditional Catholic values. Therefore, I spent most of my free time within a stone's throw of this home.

Although, as previously mentioned, times were simpler, I was the baby of the family and as a result, when I wasn't safeguarded by my parents, I was closely monitored by at least one if not all three of my siblings. Whether it was the curiosity caused by these limitations, the fact that I knew there was a whole other world out there that existed, anxiously awaiting for me to explore it, or if it was just embroidered in my nature, I found myself migrating to these boundaries quite often, and with the aid of my friends who waved me on to follow, I was sometimes brave enough to push through these boundaries. These actions would rarely go unnoticed and as a result, the hard hand or belt of discipline would come down swiftly and correct this deliberate display of delinquency, rebellion. In the beginning, this strict discipline did nothing more than buy time, and would eventually be out-weighed by the curiosity that continued to rise to the point in which I felt consumed, overwhelmed. Perhaps it could even be argued that the severity of the discipline fueled my curiosity and desires. As a result, the boundaries began to be visited on a more frequent basis, crossed and explored. My exploration deepened each day and with it, the discipline was adjusted accordingly. Eventually, the punishment and threats became so severe, that the rewards of my curiosity were outweighed and I eventually decided to adhere. Although I was unable to calm the curiosity that continued to grow, my innocence for the time being was at least spared.

In addition to this innocence being closely monitored and maintained at home, it continued to be safeguarded within the sacred walls of a parochial school, church and schoolyard that were fenced in from the public. We were observed by the watchful eye of the Monseigneur of our parish in addition to the stern discipline of aging nuns who walked the halls with ruler clinched in hand. Here, I would spend eight years of my childhood receiving the finest of education while the cornerstone of my faith was established through the repetition of kneeling, praying the rosary, the admission of sins and the rigorous toll of the church bell while serving as an altar boy. Even with the distractions of the real world that often caused me to peer out the classroom window or lured me away from my game of hopscotch during recess and over to the fence to observe, it seemed as if life was typical, evolving nicely, accordingly as planned.

Then one morning, which seemed like any other morning, I made my way into class. I greeted the teacher as I passed and made my way to my desk only to stop as my greeting was reciprocated in a tone that just seemed different. I turned and looked at the teacher who with head down, sensed that I was looking at him. He raised his head slowly, his stare was full of awareness, of empathy. It was a stare that was not shared by me at this time. The silence between us was only for a moment as the room began to fill with my classmates. However, this silence seemed like an eternity and induced anxiety that I was unaware even existed. I once again continued to my seat. Class began like it did any other day with the exception that on this day, the teacher seemed to avoid looking in my direction. However, this would change once the door opened and the school counselor stepped into the room. After a few words were shared in whisper between the counselor and my teacher, I was called upon. I sat there as if I was unable to register my name being called. The second time I was called, the counselor motioned for me. I slowly got up and made my way to the front of the class and followed the counselor out the door under the watchful eyes and whispers of my classmates. As the door shut behind us, I could hear the teacher quickly resume his teaching to regain the class's attention. The counselor asked me how I was doing but said no more as he walked me down a hallway. I followed the footsteps that only the most unruly students of our school had taken. The walk seemed long as we passed numerous faculty members that greeted the counselor with a friendly smile. Their smiles disappeared quickly once they saw me, their facial expressions became similar to that of my teacher or was completely void of emotion, I was unsure which was worse. Then as my anxiety began to grow, the walk paused momentarily in front of a door that myself and others had passed often, a door that was always closed and as a result always sparked everyone's curiosity. The mystery of what was behind the door was no more as he opened the door and a long and narrow stairway was exposed. We walked up the stairs and then proceeded to another door which opened to a small room with two chairs. It wasn't long after he motioned me over to the chair and I took a seat that he began to ask me questions in a tone that seemed very similar to that of my teacher. The questions seemed pointless, so much so that they were forgotten soon after they were answered. Yet they continued. There was no clock on the wall but eventually the laughter from outside would start to be heard. It was recess, which took place mid-morning. Soon after the laughter gave way to silence, the questions came to an end. The counselor led me out of the room and back down to the bottom of the stairs. Once the door was closed behind us and I was led back to my classroom, the school day once again resumed as any other day. However, I realized that something had changed, drastically changed.

Was it the conversation that happened within the four walls of the counseling session that morning or the many mornings after that initiated this change? Had this change already taken place, unbeknownst to me, until my answers to the counselor's questions were jotted down, filled every line, every page of his notepad, shining light, exposing the reason behind the change? When exactly the change took place remains uncertain or at least blocked from the consciousness at this time. There seems to be complacency in the answers that lie dormant. However, now as I am older, there are also times in which this complacency becomes taunting. I am currently unwilling to try and have it unraveled by a professional counselor or shrink as I envision them frantically jotting down their notes while watching me with a concerned stare and nervous smile as I pace the floors like a madman, throwing my hands in the air while randomly revealing with reckless rambling. When I do find myself pondering, I seem to revisit the possibility of it being the age in which I first experienced loss and perhaps just as important, the time leading up to the loss which also coincided with the initial counseling sessions that left me so vulnerable and humbled. Although educated on death within the walls of school and church, this education focused less on loss and sorrow, viewing death as a time of celebration, the homecoming for one's soul. As a result, the celebration aspect failed to allow one to prepare, especially at such a young age, for the loss, the grief and all the other raw emotions that accompany death. This event and the frequency with which death would occur could definitely manifest or stir an uneasiness deep within my soul, my psyche, my being, much more extreme than what those around me would experience once they encountered the same events for the first time, typically at a later stage in life and with less frequency.

If that is the case and death is the culprit, then I must consider myself somewhat fortunate. After my first experience, there was a lull. This lull caused the uneasiness that made its presence be known at such an early age be forgotten or at least tucked away from conscious reach. However, in time, as loss reappeared and became much more frequent, the inability to fully grasp what was happening seized me. While my family seemed numb or indifferent, I struggled and suffered silently. Perhaps it was nothing more than maturity that aided them in their coping that I failed to recognize. What was to be recognized was the uneasiness from deep within me that reappeared stronger than before and began to take on a much uglier form: voices. At first, I was fooled into thinking that these were the voices of logic, reason. However, it wasn't long before I realized it was much more. These voices are the ones that are rarely referenced, seldom spoke of. These are voices that haunt, torment oneself. These voices have now become my personal demons and have continued their torment as I've reached adolescence. While my friends and others begin to plan their future, attempt to make their childhood dreams a reality, I find myself at a standstill, trying to awaken from what I hope is nothing more than a nightmare. With this reality I face, I realize that I must find a way to alleviate the torment, salvage my sanity and bring forth the end of samsara.

With the possibility of the reason that drives me now having some light shed upon it, even if only a flicker and narrowing the search to what I believe to be the meaning of life and my meaning in life, I still find myself at times wondering, is this not something that we all seek to a certain extent? So why is my search so intense? Perhaps this is a search that has spanned many lifetimes, always coming so close to finding the answer, but falling short and as a result, cursed to start again. Then again, could it be something as simple as my pursuit itself that proves to be different? Perhaps the fact that I stray from the popular path, the path of Buddha, taking the alternative routes, the roads often overlooked and typically for good reason, to get to the same destination. Is it just a heightened curiosity as a result of my years of confinement that created a more adventurous side, a deeper desire for answers? If and when I find these answers, will all that I seek be attained? An awakening, inner peace as a result of finding the missing pieces in this puzzle of life? The deeper connection between life and death? The mystery of death to finally be solved? Could I reach enlightenment? The cycle of samara finally be brought to an end? These questions, riddles, koans, are what needs to be explored; they must be explored. This alone may take a lifetime or several to successfully achieve. With such an investment, so many roads to venture, paths to follow, I cannot afford to stray from the map and yet with the uncertainty, the unknown that surrounds this search, the possibility, or probability to do so is not just likely, but justified, is it not? With this being said, I consider the following nothing more than an example of one of the before mentioned stumbles I experienced as my journey began. A wrong turn as I approached a fork in the road. Yet, a path that could one day be looked back upon as an essential path in finding my destination. As a result, character built while a stronger emphasis placed on the task at hand. I do feel an injustice as I abbreviate the following, which could be a novel on its own or at least more than just a story within the story. At this point, it is shortened into a couple of paragraphs so the example can be provided. Perhaps I will one day be forgiven as these words are read. Perhaps one day I will come back, revisit and devote the attention it truly deserves.

Chapter II

As stated earlier, I was raised by my father, mother and three siblings. All three siblings were girls, which could explain why I often drifted from the many boys I befriended, no matter how involved we were in what we were doing, for the opportunity to spend time with any of the few girls in the neighborhood. I was only nine years old when my father passed from a long battle with cancer. With his passing, the connection I had with females strengthened. A need developed towards the opposite sex, perhaps sooner than what most experienced. I was mesmerized by the pursuit which seemed to be as rewarding as the capture. To say the word girlfriend, to be referenced as a boyfriend, created a sort of identity and empowerment. To pass notes, to walk side by side, to have our hands brush against one another until we figured a way to allow the fingers to interlock strengthened that identity. As I reached my teenage years, girls demanded more of my attention. The pursuit became much more complex, the rewards substantially greater. As a result, the voices from deep within that had already begun to plague me so were reduced to a whisper. The voices no longer haunted me and as a result, I became lost, lost for the first time in love, lust. The only words these ears heard was the whispering of "I love you." These precious words, this rare proclamation, became more common as the weeks passed and we became bolder with our actions, to express these feelings. It wasn't long before the same ears that were cupped so often to ward off the voices were now being cupped by her inner thighs as I tasted drunken vulnerability, lust for the first time. I looked away from my search and up from the triangle of hair with hungry, determined eyes. I looked past the pulsating hips, obsessed over the soft belly that quivered, the beads of sweat on her chest that began to make their way towards my hungry mouth as her breathing became labored. I looked up, into eyes of ecstasy that slowly rolled back into sweet surrender as she struggled to say my name. Here I am, for the first time feeling as if I mattered. It was easy to ignore the lust-drenched sheets that we lay in, that she clinched in desperation. The sheets that would serve as a constant reminder of this day until they were washed away. I fought back a smirk as I looked down at her, the sweet surrender she gave with a small whimper as I took what I thought to be mine and claimed victory, a victory that falsely fulfilled my needs by stealing that, from which I, myself, had been protected so long, my innocence.

After the fact, it is easy to wonder how one could allow themselves to be deceived so. This question although valid, proves not to be as complex as first thought. The voices, silenced. My thirst, driven by youth, inexperience, was thought to be quenched as I drank from her lips. My hunger seemed to be satisfied by the forbidden flesh that I feasted upon for the first time. The key words are first time. The first time experiencing this would cause many to become complacent. So, is it not better to ask the question, how could one not be deceived? How could one not be led to believe that they had found some sort of meaning? Although the meaning of life still eludes, could it not be argued that to truly live, once must truly love and be loved? If so, couldn't it be argued that those who are fortunate enough to experience love and recognize it as true have found some meaning? Perhaps this will be revisited at a later time. What needs to be recognized at this point in time is that I had become content in this courtship, this conquest of mine. Perhaps I was even a bit awestruck in knowing that Ovid and Capellanus would have been proud of my quest, of my rewards.

However, foolish boy, this search that became aesthetic in nature was not to be, nor was it ever meant to be. My curiosity proved to be catastrophic. The heart that proved my existence, pulsated a newfound warmth that indeed fooled me. Yes, foolishly forfeited, abandoned. As young love runs its course, the remains, once regained, is now filled with coldness. My heart continues to pump but once again pumping the bitter poison that I've become far more familiar with. The poison flows stronger through my veins, far worse than last remembered. The demons from deep within quickly reestablish their dominance, more vicious than before, wrath not worthy a word to define what I am forced to succumb to. In a meager attempt, I cast aimlessly the finger of blame. Have I not fallen victim like every other hungry boy has during this stage of life? However, this can no longer be a defense for my innocence was not lost; it was thrown away, carelessly. The Demons look not with sympathy, they let not the wounds be healed. I am persecuted by voices who serve as my peers. I scream a muted plea, "If nothing else, can sanity not be sacrificed? Can sanctity not be salvaged?" The deliberation takes only a moment, my sentence is simple, yet stern, I must continue this quest.

With what these young eyes have observed, it seems that most are content with life being spoon fed to them one small bite at a time. For myself, the incentives are much higher. I realize my sanity and possibly more are hanging in the balance as I try to find these answers, attain this enlightenment. Although very young, too much time has been wasted, time will not allow the opportunity for me to stand idly by. In knowing that time is of the essence and that tomorrow is never promised, I will not let another minute pass in vain. The voice of reason could argue that with my young age, there is no need to rush. After all, you are too young to recognize your mortality. However, would this not be the same voice that would one day say, "what if" or worse yet, "If only I were able to do this all over again." With this being understood, if this voice does show its presence, which I am certain it will, it will be quickly drowned out by the voices that refuse to compromise. The cost of being an old soul is now consequential. I must silence the voices, prove myself and prove that my epitaph may one day be worthy enough to be read amongst the many that matter not, or as just punishment. I return, retry; Samsara continues.

Chapter III

I walk around through the alleys and streets of my neighborhood aimlessly, almost daily. The weather brings out many to enjoy it. To an onlooker, I am nothing more than a young man taking a casual walk during the late afternoon, enjoying the moment, preferring his alone time, taking in the last remnants of what the green days of summer provide, prior to the arrival of the Midwest autumn foliage. However, little do they know, there is nothing enjoyable for me. These walks have become much more customary than one would prefer. With no certain physical destination in mind, I wander the streets for something that I fear, almost certain, is hidden deep within. If this is the case, then these walks will serve nothing more than to exorcise the demons until the answer I seek may be found. The wandering may perhaps provide more in the psychological sense. I, Tristan Wallace, walk where my feet take me, time is never lost, possibly questioned for its validity but never lost. The distance travelled is often overlooked and without the occasional sound of a train approaching, children's laughter nearing or a dog forewarning me that I need to watch where I'm heading, the walks could last for hours. There are times in which I lift my head after my attention is captured, the hopes of possibly finding myself now forced to be reduced to an attempt to familiarize myself with where I've drifted. I reflect, once more looking back at my youth, and ask the reoccurring question although slightly phrased differently. Should one, this young, only a year removed from twenty, be so lost in his attempt to seek enlightenment, to find himself? I fear to bring this question forward, I fear the answer, instead I throw both my hands towards the heavens in despair and let them drop in frustration, drawing unwanted attention, that I can't afford to entertain.

On this day it is no different. I continue to walk, the many voices from within, which in the beginning of the walk seemed so boisterous, slowly begin to be drowned out by some classic jazz that I have playing in the back of my mind. "April in Paris" by Count Basie and his orchestra is the jazz of choice as my feet keep pace to the trumpet's improvisation that has begun blasting. A smile appears on my face as the last note is played and I stop momentarily to envision the ending. In doing so, I come back to the world around me and observe my surroundings. I look around in an attempt to find familiarity, I have walked much further than normal. I continue to walk and look for the next intersection. Instead, I find an alley that invites me to enter through the friendly laughter of children playing hide and seek in a back yard, I catch a glimpse of a young child as he scurries to safety in the confines of a back porch, another attempts to hide out of sight behind the garage. I remember the days in which I played these games well into the summer evening. I can still hear the faint cry of my mother forewarning me that it is time to finish my game and head home. I pause momentarily as I look past the children playing and see the faint silhouette of my mother making her way to me with purpose. If only I could return. I become anxious to once more be a child, to hide behind my blonde locks, dimples and eyes that have yet to be exposed to the troubled times that patiently await me. To know you can run away from all your problems, and run into the safety that only a mother can provide with her open arms, her reassurance that there is nothing to worry about and that tomorrow is a new day. However, this desire, this daydream is rudely interrupted by the strategic sound of an elderly man who had become weary of my presence clearing his throat while he prunes his bushes. I look over, our eyes meet. The smell of fresh cut grass fills my lungs and broadens the smile on my face that he looks uncertain of. He continues to stare at me as he begins to cut through the air more than the bushes he was once focused on.

I entertain the idea of saying hello and asking him the exact whereabouts that I have wandered into, an effort to make my way back home. Although, his eyes are uninviting, his movements serve as a forewarning that he feels threatened by my presence. I pause momentarily, then decide to begin my walk casually over to him; he watches every step cautiously. I open my mouth to say hello but I'm interrupted by the sound of a car making its way in the alley and pulling slowly into a driveway. The car is driven by another elderly man, near the same age as the man pruning his bushes. He steps out of his car, looks over at me and then walks his way towards his neighbor. The two of them share pleasantries and then turn their attention to the unwanted stranger that has stumbled his way into their neighborhood. Their faces are expressionless, their once audible conversation has now turned to nothing more than a soft grumble as they look me over and plot a way of freeing themselves of this intruder. Now they have numbers, I decide it is best to leave well enough alone and continue to walk towards the end of the alley. As I arrive to the end, I take a moment to look back, the two men continue to look my way although now with less animosity towards me. I raise my hand high into the air and wave at the two of them, leaving it for them to decide if the gesture is to reassure them that I would see them again soon, or that I respect their wishes and will not return. They look at me unimpressed before turning away and turning their focus back to their conversation. I turn towards the road and survey my surroundings.

I was in the middle of a road that provided a faint memory of my whereabouts. I watch the flow of traffic and decided to follow the heavy stream to the next stop sign. As I reached the stop sign I began to take in my location. I could now confirm my previous observation that in all the walks I had been on, this was by far the longest. Not certain whether to relish the accomplishment or sigh in the disappointment that my problems are worsening and causing these walks to lengthen, I turn and begin to head home. I walk a while, subjective to the public eyes that pass me on either side of the street, those eyes that peak through their living room blinds. I begin to feel paranoid, anxious. I look for an alternative route to present itself. I find it once I come to the railroad tracks which will take me all the way to the backside of my neighborhood, away from the rest of the world to see. These once busy tracks now provide the much needed solitude prior to the inevitable confrontation that soon awaits me. As I make my way down the tracks, I can faintly see the intersection ahead that will lead to my neighborhood. I slow down my walk by stepping onto the rail, once again reliving my youth. I attempt to walk the rest of the way while keeping my balance. It wasn't long before my concentration was interrupted by the faint whistle of a train approaching. I stop, carefully turn my body, attempting to stay upon the rail as if my life now depended on it. I can see the train. It is nothing more than a light. This faint light leads me to believe it is far enough away from me to allow me to make it to my destination. I slowly turn back around, resume my tightrope along the rail, slowly picking up some speed and turning my attention back to keeping my balance.

As the train came closer I could feel the faint rumble underneath my feet that grew more and more in strength. The horn began to blast louder and with more urgency as I was now in sight of the engineer. Unbeknownst to the engineer whether I was being defiant, was deaf or had possibly decided that I had reached my breaking point, the blasts became longer. I quickened my pace until I lost balance on the rail and could no longer stay on. I turned and found the train bearing towards me much closer than I had expected. I could look up and see the engineer's silhouette in the window. I took a couple steps away from the track to avoid the swaying cars behind the engine and watched as the train neared. I received a loud blast of disapproval as the train flew pass me. I attempted to gain focus on the cars that passed but was unsuccessful, with the train so close and being at too high of a speed to cooperate. This, unfortunately, eliminated any possibility of hopping the train in efforts to avoid the confrontation that was closing in on me as I made my way closer to home.

Once the train passed, I found myself in front of the crossing that assured me that I had reached my neighborhood. I lowered my head in defeat and exited the tracks to head home. I looked once more towards the train that now seemed to slow itself down in efforts to tease me before it slowly faded from my sight. I walk on and make my way to an underpass that was straight ahead, that I sometimes scaled and sat at the top when there was nowhere else to go, nothing better to do. I make my way up the embankments of the underpass and took in all the graffiti that stretched from beginning to end. Most of the graffiti lacked an artistic touch to it; some was hindered by the presence of paranoia that the artist encountered from the oncoming traffic that occupied the area throughout the evening. As was the case, most of the graffiti showed little or no creativity, made little sense and by no means represented anything well thought of or done by a talented hand. As I made my way back out from the underpass, I took notice of a few familiar names and phone numbers etched on one of the pillars that guaranteed anyone who was desperate a good time if they called. I continued on, now looking to find anything and everything I could to slow down my arrival home.

I found the delay in a huge oak tree that stood proudly on the outskirts of a neighbor's property. Its enormous size, most likely feared, less likely to be appreciated, was a testament of its survival against all of the ongoing development that had and continues to happen around it. Its roots stretched out and unearthed the sidewalk proving civilization to be no match to Nature's strength, leaving jagged edges to what once was uniform with the rest of the sidewalk going down the street. Yet, I found the beauty in it all. I walked over to the tree and looked up to its peak. As I slowly brought my vision back to its base I began to notice the tree had one time been popular. All over the side of the tree that hid from the property owner was the remnants of love that once was. A good ten feet up the tree marked the love of A.M. + T.S. the initials etched broad and deep into the tree. A few feet down, R.M. + M.S. proved their love even more by including a T.L.A. next to it. I couldn't help but wonder if R.M. was the sibling of A.M. If so, what was the possibility that M.S. was the sibling of T.S.? Could these initials possibly be the initials of the children of the first defacers? The thought of this was interrupted at eye level as I found the last of the young lovers initial's, J.T. + E.G. These initials although much newer than the previous were still aged. The initials were carved deep into the tree, the bark around the initials dull and rounded. I took my finger and traced my way through the initials as I continued to wonder who the people were behind all these initials, were any of these lovers still alive? Were any of them still together? Were any of them still in this area? If so, did they visit this tree often, possibly on their anniversary? Had I ever walked passed them on the streets? Did they even remember that their undying love is forever enshrined within this magnificent tree?

I continued to take my finger and pass it through the initials until I heard the closing of a screen door that snapped me out of my concentration. I looked around the tree to see the owner of the property observing me from the safety of his porch, although he chose not to speak, allowing his glare to do the talking, I began to realize that this guy would feel much better if I moved on. I took once last look of the tree, and then, not to antagonize him, I obliged and headed on. As I cleared his property line I looked back to see the man leaving his porch and making his way over to the tree, most likely to ensure no new initials had been added. He observed carefully the area I was in, taking his hand and passing it over the initials that he could reach. He looked down to the ground, back up to the tree before turning his attention back to me. Once his eyes met mine, I entered the alley leading to my house and turned my head towards my destination.

The alley seems much shorter than normal as I seem to find myself nearing the end no sooner than I had entered. The surroundings that were once inviting no longer seemed to welcome me. I could see my car now which provides one last opportunity to escape or at least provide me with some additional time to prepare more. However, I'm not one to run and preparation cannot lessen, nor remove. I continue on and find the house with the front door shut, the curtains drawn. This adds to the mystique of what lies ahead. My mother's car is parked in its regular place. I walk past the front of the car, put my hand on the hood as I pass and notice by the warmth that she hasn't been home for very long. I walk up to the porch, the first signs of life present themselves as I hear voices from within. Upon opening of the door, I will find my mother sitting in her favorite chair watching television after a long day of work.

Chapter IV

As I walk in the door, I know the scrutiny that is to follow through the repetitious pattern that is no fault other than my own. My mother, who has raised me since I was nine and has provided the best she could since then, will be sitting in the front room playing solitaire. During the commercials, she'll pause her game after laying down her next three cards and ask where I've been, with the answer I give, the game will resume. The next three cards will be driven into the coffee table with a little more aggression. She will then ask if I have been out looking for a job. Once that answer fails to satisfy her, she will stop all together, put her cards down and remind me that she won't be around forever. Then the scolding will broaden, not limiting to the reminder that I'm twenty-one years old and most men at twenty-one are finishing college or already have a job and are providing for themselves and their parents. This conversation has become as much of a habit as my walks. However, today was different. As I walked in and anticipated the questioning, she chose to never look up. Her reaction or lack of, made we wonder if she had even realized that I had walked in the door. I stood still for a moment, she finished out her stack of cards, gathered them back up and looked at me briefly or through me before returning to her game. I went to say something but thought better of it and headed out to the kitchen. As I passed her, I realized that all the days, weeks, months of scorning from her was far more tolerable than the one day in which she chose to be silent. With silence came the realization that all hope has been lost. She had accepted the fact that I am an underachiever. The fight in her is over or at least wavering, where we go from here is uncertain and yet certain to be unpleasant.

I opened the refrigerator and looked for a beer. I dare not grab one of my mothers, instead I found a few of mine tucked away in the farthest corner of the bottom shelf, strategically placed so they may be overlooked by any guest who is thirsty and offered to help themselves. I opened the beer as I stood at the refrigerator and took a drink. The much needed drink served as a reward for such a long walk that I had just completed. The question now was, do I dare return to the front room to deal with the silence, the mounting tension, that was certain to grow until there was no way of avoiding an argument? I took another swallow and went over to the counter where a portable stereo was and turned on some music, I looked for something I could listen to that could in return, lighten the tension that I was feeling coming out of the front room. I put on the Statler Brothers, one of my mother and father's favorites and one that I was personally fond of. I listened to the first couple of songs while I stood leaning against the counter, continuing to drink. The music took me away momentarily to a more innocent time that I missed so. However, as each song ended, I found myself once again in the midst of the troubles I face and the confrontation that awaits me, if and when I return to the front room. I finished the first beer and went back to the refrigerator to grab a second. I was close to being done with the second, nothing had yet happened.

I could feel myself becoming restless. I couldn't avoid her forever. I grabbed a third beer and decided that it was time to go into the front room and allow her to open up so I could begin to try and rationalize with her. As I began to head in, I stopped and asked her if she would like a beer. She waited for a moment before she finally said yes. I grabbed her a beer and some newfound optimism as I slowly made my way back in. I went to hand her the beer but she never looked up, I placed the beer on the coffee table which she picked up almost immediately and placed on the table beside her. I took a seat on the couch and sat in silence. She finished her game then opened up the beer and took a big swallow. She placed the beer back down and then turned towards me. "What all did you do today?" she asked in a voice that seemed to be solely for entertainment purposes only. I took a big swallow realizing that it may be the last I took before the argument started. "Well, I headed down to the library for a little while, did a little researching, did some writing and grabbed a few books." She looked at me for a moment and then reached over and grabbed her beer. I matched her drink and awaited the next line of questions. "Were you able to go out and look for a job at all?" The conversation was now becoming the more standard line of interrogating that I have grown used to. "Not really, I looked around a little but didn't really find anything that interests me." I dared not look up at her with the answer I provided, instead I put my beer to my lips and emptied what was left. "Oh bullshit, Tristan! You don't want to work. If you wanted a job you would already be working! I can't afford you, you understand that don't you?" Her approach was taking on a new form of assertiveness. "I understand, I am trying. I don't want to get a job which I will hate and not last. I would like to find a field in which I can excel in ... would you like me to grab you another beer?" I thought

JEFF GRAY

for a moment that my diversion may work. She took the last swallow of her beer and handed me her empty. I walked out to the kitchen, the music was now the only sound in the house as she had turned off the television to focus completely on the conversation, and yet even with the music, the house seemed too quiet. I grabbed us both a beer, now having to get into hers which was sure to provide support to the whole argument on having to support me. I waited a moment before heading back in, I listened to the rest of the song that was playing, hoping the delay would cool her down.

I had yet to make my way into the room before she yelled, "Are you bringing me a beer or not?" I walked in and handed her the beer. I made my way over to the front door, looked outside, longing for a way out. With my hand finding its way slowly down to the doorknob, I knew it wasn't an option, so I made my way back over to the couch, took a seat and waited for her to say something. A few minutes passed. We both just sat there and drank. I thought that maybe she had decided to let it go for the night, give me another day to see if it all sank in. I looked over at her cautiously, trying not to instigate another interrogation. However, the silence was becoming unbearable. "I took a long walk, it's pretty nice out. I think I may bring the music out to the porch and drink a few more while I am out there. Are you interested?" She took a long drink before she looked over at me. Her stare drifted quickly from my eyes to the beer I was holding. A smirk of disgust appeared on her face. My mother was very animated and over the years, I had become used to each and every expression she owned. "I see that you have helped yourself to my beer." The comment was rhetorical. She paused before continuing. "Well, before you head out there, I might as well tell you now," she said. With that comment, the tension in the air thickened.

This was never an intro that would amount to anything I would approve of; I dropped my head without answering her and waited for her to

24

finish what she was going to say. "I talked to Judith today. Do you remember Judith?" It took a moment to place Judith. My mother and I had met her around the same time, she had already served her purpose in my life, and as a result, she had been released from the ties that bound her to my existence. The faded memory only revisited by name drop, as it did now. My mother on the other hand, had remained friends with her and had kept close contact. I already knew where this was going. I took a drink, looked up at her and answered in a dry tone "Yes, I remember Judith" It was now her turn to take a drink before continuing. "Well, we were talking and eventually she asked about you. I told her that you had been struggling to find a job. She asked if you had any experience in anything. I told her no but you learn quickly and that beggars can't be choosers, you just need some work. Well it just so happens that her father owns a flooring company right outside the city and they could use some help in the warehouse." She paused momentarily to see if I was listening or if I needed to respond. I continued to stare at her, motionless. "Tristan, you need work. They like you, and they'll work around any schedule conflicts. Sure, it might not be what you want but it's a start." I sat there and continued to stare till she was done. Once she paused to take a drink and reach for her cards, I stood up, headed back out to the kitchen, and grabbed a beer. I passed back through the living room and walked outside to sit on the porch. I sat out on the front steps, watching the cars slowly go by, attempting to let it all soak in. I continued to sit there until I was out of beer and began to contemplate whether I should go back in to grab another. The door opened, my mother made her way over to me with a beer in her hand, hoping for a truce. After I took the beer, she sat down in one of the many chairs on the porch. I could feel her staring at me the whole time she sat there. I never made eye contact with her.

Once she realized I had nothing to say, she spoke up. "So what do you think?" she asked in a manner as if my opinion would play a part on whether or not I would take the job. However, we both knew it didn't, so I chose not to entertain her immediately. After a few minutes had passed and a couple drinks of beer I responded, "When exactly would I be starting?" I looked at her defeated through exhaustion. She looked at me, unable to hold back her smile and took a victory drink. She paused, "Well, I told them you could start tomorrow, they said to just have you start next week, which would give you some time to get things done before you start. I told them you were fine to start immediately, that you have had half the summer to get things accomplished, but they insisted." I looked at her half disgusted, the thought of lashing out consumed me, I opted to take a long drink instead. I lowered the can after it was emptied and in a less than enthusiastic voice responded, "Well that was grand on both of your parts." I got up and headed towards the door. "So you'll give it a try, Tristan?" An answer wasn't even needed; she knew I couldn't refuse. "Sure, I'll be there on Monday, now if you will excuse me, I believe I will get drunk and get some of those things of mine accomplished." She went to say something but I swung the door open and walked away.

I found myself in the kitchen with beer in hand, leaning on the counter. I decided to change the music to accommodate a more somber mood. As I looked around I found some Billie Holiday that seemed appropriate. As I put the music on I could hear my mother's car start and her leaving. I thought little of it as I continued to stand there, shaking my head in disbelief. I stood in the same spot for some time, slowly becoming immersed in the music. I finished my beer and headed to the refrigerator to grab another, I noticed that at this pace, we would be running out of beers quickly. I grabbed one of the last ones and tried to figure a place to go to with the little money I had to continue this binge I was doing so masterfully. I didn't pay any mind to the front door opening, which caused me to be startled out of my contemplating as my mother entered the kitchen with a case of beer in hand. She placed the case on the table, and grabbed a beer, I could feel her look up at me briefly as if she was offering the beer as a consolation. With no reaction. She slowly walked away. I stood there and waited to hear the front door open before heading over to the table, grabbing a beer out of the case and placing the rest in the refrigerator.

Chapter V

Monday morning came much quicker than anticipated but then again isn't that always the case when you are about to face something you know you will dread? I was lacking sleep, fighting off a hangover as I left the house slowly, quietly. I made my way to the shop, uncertain on what to expect. The carpet shop was tucked away nicely just outside the city, beside a road that I had become all too familiar with. I slowed down and entertained the thought of skipping my first day before turning onto it. I had driven this road a thousand times over the last year or so, amazed by the scenery. However, the road had significant meaning that existed amongst its rolling hills, winding bends and picturesque background. One day, not so long ago, as I drove the road, I stumbled upon a magnificent elm, one of many along the roadside. How it had ever eluded me only added to its magnificence and its mystique. This elm was unlike all the others. The tree seemed to reach out to me, calling my name, offering salvation, especially during the more difficult times I had recently been tormented with. I was more than aware that with each and every pass I made, my car seemed to inch closer and closer to this impenetrable elm. The voices from within became louder, overwhelming, as they seemed to dare me to try and silence them as I passed with a tightened grip on the steering wheel. There was some consolation knowing that a solution did exist and was pondered more times than not. Now knowing I would be working beside this road daily, I couldn't help but wonder whether or not this was a good thing. I passed the road ever so slowly, a smile appeared as some sort of acknowledgement and then I made my way into the carpet shop's parking lot.

Once parked, I sat there for a moment wondering whether I should stay or leave. Without any interest in the job, the position served as nothing more than an obstacle in my search. I was here for one reason and one reason only, to please my mother. As I continued to debate, weighing out the options, the overwhelming feeling of being watched crept up on me; they knew I had arrived. I took a deep breath, turned off the car and made my way up to the door slowly. I paused once more as I grabbed the door and entered. I made my way into the front of the showroom, managing a smile as I did so. In all my years of driving by the business, I had never stopped in to take a look around, never had a reason. The business was just opening for the day and there was no one to be found. I made my way forward, following the voices that became audible as I reached the middle of the store. Upon hearing the laughter I knew that Judith had already arrived. I walked in the office to find Judith and who I would soon learn was her younger sister, her sister's husband and their mother sitting there sharing the adventures that had taken place during the weekend over some coffee. Judith smiled and said "Hello" right away as did her mother, Mildred. The other two who I could tell were unaware of my arrival studied me for a moment and then carried on with their storytelling. Judith could see that I wasn't very comfortable and got up from her desk and came around to meet me. She spoke in a low voice as she told me to come with her. I followed her as she passed me and headed out into the showroom, stopping where she felt no one could hear us.

Judith looked me up and down as if I was a prize she had just won at a fair with the last dollar she had. "Tristan, how are you?" she asked in an excited voice as she reorganized some Berber samples that had been looked through on a waterfall display. "I'm not bad, thanks for asking." She looked at me and smiled. We shared very little in common and it showed with the awkward silence. However, it wasn't her fault; she had come from a sheltered life that her religious mother and father were responsible for and continued to try and bestow onto her. Judith, now in her forties, was still very conservative, still had the traditional long hair that her fellow women of her church wore, still had most of her traditional values. However there were times in which she showed her independence, her defiance. This typically came by incorporating a curse word here and there and refusing to wear the long dresses that the women in her church were notorious for. We stood there searching for something to say when her mother made her way out of the office and looked for us. "So Tristan, you are going to be our new warehouse man?" her mother asked in a loud, stern voice to ensure everyone present was able to hear. I looked over and replied, "Yes, ma'am," as I could see that this announcement didn't settle well with the younger sister who became wide eyed as she watched us through a glass partition that separated the office from the showroom. She looked over at her husband who chose to drop his head and shake it in disbelief. The news had either come as a complete surprise or they completely disapproved.

The reaction from within the office didn't go unnoticed as Mildred looked in with a scowl before turning her attention back towards me. Judith seemed particularly pleased with her mother's action as she giggled. "It's an easy job, Tristan, rest assure. Harold will be here at any time and he'll show you around and help you get started." Harold was Mildred's husband and the owner of the company. He had taken this flooring company, one of many that saturated the small city, and had arguably become the most successful. Up until my arrival, he had kept it all within the family. I was the first outsider, an intruder. This is what I figured to be the justification for the cold shoulder that I had received from his daughter and son-in-law. As Helen had promised, Harold pulled in, his face was already showing stress as he hobbled into the store. He looked completely unaware that I was going to be there as the door closed behind him. His attempt to mask his surprise failed miserably behind a salesman's smile. He walked over and greeted me with a handshake. Mildred looked over at him with a stare that spoke volumes, a stare that he must have become familiar with way too often. "What Mildred? What?" he said nervously as he began to fumble through his keys. "Tristan is here to start today, remember? I told you he was going to be the new warehouseman." The silence became a bit uncomfortable as he seemed to be unaware of what Helen had just said. He continued to go through the keys until he found the right one. Judith and I shared the same look of concern as we observed Harold. In less than five minutes of being there his face was already red, sweat had formed on his forehead and was beginning to stream down his cheeks. "Okay, Tristan, I'll take you back, show you around and we can get started," Harold said in a shaking voice. I couldn't tell whether or not Harold was aware of my hiring; if he was, he had no clue that I was starting today.

I followed Harold back into the warehouse. Once I entered and took a look around, I saw the reason he needed help. The warehouse was small and had become congested. On one side, there were rolls of carpet jammed into shelving much too small to house them. The other side had linoleum remnants rolled up and standing on end, next to carpet remnants that were in disarray. We made our way back to a more secluded area, away from customers. On one side, a mountain of carpet rolls were piled upon one another from the floor to the ceiling. The opposing wall was much the same but these rolls were in actual racks. In the middle of the floor was an old forklift that I would soon become used to. It was obvious by the mess left on the floor that the area only received attention by the carpet layers who came in during the morning to pick up their work for the day. At the far end, there was an overhead door that led to an outdoor loading area and a garage where additional carpet rolls and padding were stored. It seemed as if the warehouse had been in disarray for quite some time. "Your main responsibility will be to unload shipments, take work orders, cut them, roll them and have them ready for the carpet layers when they arrive so they can get back on the road in a timely manner. Of course, you'll also need to tidy up the area." The job seemed easy enough but it didn't stop Harold from having a look of doubt. "That shouldn't be a problem," I answered with confidence. "We would need you in here daily between the hours of eight and four, possibly five; you would get a half hour lunch. We also have an early shift on Saturday from nine to one; it wouldn't be mandatory but you're welcome to it as well. I almost forgot, we don't pay overtime." I knew right away where this would be leading us next. "I'm willing to pay you eight dollars an hour to start, which is pretty fair for starters, especially since you don't have any experience." Harold would have continued to try and sell the position and justify the pay if I would have allowed him. Instead, I answered with a smile, a handshake and a simple "Yes sir, I'll take it." Being the salesman he was, Harold couldn't help but smile knowing he had just secured the better end of the deal.

Harold walked me back up to the front and showed me where I would be clocking in. As we approached the front of the warehouse, Judith opened the door with a smile and asked "So, did it become official? Are you our new warehouseman?" Judith already knew the answer but I went ahead and played along, "Yes ma'am." I answered with a smile as Harold kept a watchful eye on me. "That is great, now I can take you back up front and introduce you to the rest of the family." We walked up and entered the office; everyone was still sharing stories which led me to believe that this was the norm each morning. "Hey everybody!" Judith spoke up loud enough to drown out the conversation and annoy everyone. "I want you to meet Tristan Wallace. He is going to be our new warehouseman. Tristan, this is my younger sister, Ann; she is in sales." I looked over at Ann and smiled. She glanced at me and greeted me with a simple "Hello." Judith moved on quickly to avoid the awkwardness. "Tristan, this is William, Ann's husband. He goes out to the homes, measures and provides quotes." William stood up quickly and reached out to shake hands, his grip was strong, stronger than it needed to be during a handshake. I returned the tight grip as he tried to establish the alpha male role. "Welcome," he said as he released his grip and sat back down. He took a pipe out of his shirt pocket, pulled out a match that he studied before striking and then proceeded to light the pipe while allowing the flame of the match to continue to burn towards his fingers. With the introductions complete. Judith now made her way around the desk and sat down. Once seated, William waved out his match and exhaled his first cloud of smoke towards Judith who grabbed a customer's file to wave off the smoke. "You jackass!" Mildred said with her arms folded and a disgusted look on her face. This brought a mighty roar of laughter from William. Ann hurried and took a customer's file and put it over her nose in preparation of being the next victim of his bullying. "Oh, come on my sweetest, I wouldn't even think about doing that to you! You are going to make the warehouse boy think I'm an asshole." William made his way over and put his hand on the back of Ann's neck as he attempted to kiss her. This caused Ann to cringe as she waved him away with the folder. "Get away from me, go on, get! Don't you have a measurement to go to or something?" Ann tried to make her plea playful but it was easy to see that she was annoyed and it was easier to see why. "No I don't have a job to go measure, my next one is at 11:00. I am going to go back to the back and make the cuts needed for the next job." William made his way out of the office. I stepped out of his way to let him through but he broadened his shoulders enough to brush by me. "Hey, take Tristan with you so he can learn what to do," Judith yelled, still behind the folder she had resting against her face to block all airways from the smoke that lingered. "I guess I can do that. Come on, Tristan, time to earn your keep." I went to follow William to the warehouse. Harold, who had been standing out of harm's way in the showroom, waited for the two of us to pass before he headed into the office and took a seat. William looked over his shoulder as he opened the door to ensure I was coming. As I made my way towards him, he continued on letting the door shut behind him. I grabbed the door handle and stood there for a moment. I could see William and I having issues.

By the time I closed the door behind me, William had already taken a seat on the forklift and was looking over the work order. He started the forklift after several attempts and swung his way towards me. Without saying a word he continued to come right at me. As I stepped back out of his way, he swung the forklift around quickly and entered the carpet roll effortlessly on his first attempt. He lifted the roll, and backed it out. After lowering the roll to where it was barely off the ground, he turned off the forklift, jumped down, pulled a carpet cutter out of his pocket and cut the rope that held the roll together. He grabbed the end of the carpet and unrolled a good portion. He studied the carpet for a moment and then grabbed his tape measure out of his utility belt. He measured both sides, got down on his knees using his carpet cutter to cut a near perfect square of carpet. He then rolled the piece he cut and used the rope that he had cut from the original roll to tie it up. "That's how you do it, Tristan. Any questions?" His arrogance was getting worse. He grabbed the roll of carpet, hoisted it over his shoulders and walked past me. "Tie her up and put her away. Bring the forklift back here and I'll show you what we do next," William said as if I had been working here for weeks.

I was clueless where the rope was, and had no experience driving a forklift. I didn't want to provide him with any arsenal for his verbal attack that I was certain to hear once I admitted to these issues. Instead, I scrambled around to look for a box of rope which I was unsuccessful in finding. I began to walk towards the door to go to the office and ask Judith where it was stored when he peeked around the back room and called out to me. "What are you doing? We don't have all day." I stopped and looked back at him; he was well aware of the situation. I entertained him anyway. "I couldn't find the rope." William dropped his hands in disgust. "Oh Jesus Christ, he didn't show you anything when he was back here, did he?" William made his way up to the front, took a turn prior to reaching me and went to a door half hidden by the carpet remnants. He opened the door and pulled out a box of rope, he then walked over to me and handed me a cutting knife. "Here, you'll probably need that too, don't you think?" I chose not to say anything, instead I took the knife and followed him over to the roll. "Have you ever driven anything like this before?" I shook my head which caused him to roll his eyes in disbelief as he began to mumble. He quickly tied the carpet up and then turned his attention to me. "It's pretty simple, step on the clutch, turn the key, shift it into gear, let off the clutch and go. When you don't have anything to do, drive it around, learn how to operate it. When you leave at the end of the day, turn the handle on top of the propane tank to shut it off," William said in a voice that made him sound pained having to talk to me.

William drove the forklift back to the back, jumped off and showed me where to put all the jobs I would cut for the next morning. "Follow me," he said with a wave of his hand as we headed back up to the front of the warehouse. He showed me where all the supplies were kept and then asked if I had any questions as he made his way towards the office. I had yet to answer him by the time he had swung the door open. By the time the door shut, William had already begun complaining how green I was. I stood there for a moment, taking it all in until I became bored. I then headed to the back to survey the area. I spent the rest of the day in the garage where they kept all the padding and smaller rolls of carpeting. I began organizing it and continued work on it until Judith found me. "I wondered where you were. Tristan, both myself and my mother called out for you but you never answered. We were worried that maybe you had already had your fill of William, decided that this job wasn't for you and snuck out the back and left." I gave her a smile. "No, it takes more than that to scare me off. I just decided to work back here and try to straighten this area up." Judith looked my work over. "You are doing great, Tristan! I'm glad you didn't get discouraged by William or his wife. She may be my sister but she can be a handful at times." I nodded, "No problem, thank you for this opportunity, I appreciate it." I wasn't sure if Judith was buying what I was selling, but she smiled as she made her way out of the warehouse. "Tristan, we do have a couple cuts when you are done. Just come up and get me and I'll help you out. I'm going to lay the order on your forklift seat." The fact that she laid the order down on the forklift seat was a clear hint that she was hoping I would take ownership and get it done. I made my way to the warehouse, grabbed the work order. I looked around the warehouse in an attempt to find everything I was needing to cut. Once done, I took the jobs back to the drop off area, stacked it and then cleaned up the floor where I was cutting. An hour passed before Judith returned with another work order. "Tristan,

I hadn't heard anything from you so I thought I would check on you while I was bringing back another order. The front of the warehouse is looking nice and tidy, are you ready to cut the job I left on your seat?" She gave me an optimistic smile, hoping to hear the best. "I already have that cut." She looked at me and smiled. "Not bad at all for your first day!" Judith handed me the next order. "Once you are done, why don't you come up to the office? We just ordered some pizza for lunch." I looked at the clock as Judith walked away. It was already past lunchtime so I decided to skip lunch, get the cut done, clean up and get out of there a half an hour early.

Although I was far from happy with the job, the paychecks would give me enough to get by, allow me the opportunity to get out on the weekends and most importantly, keep my mother happy. The days soon became weeks and the weeks became months. The job although uneventful wasn't too bad. I showed up, put in my hours, had to deal very little with the public or those I worked with. Sometimes, there was nothing more than a "Good Morning" and "Have a great night" shared between us. Yet, there were a couple days each week in which I had human interaction with the interesting characters that were responsible for bringing in our weekly shipments. These men were typically loners, who spent most of their waking hours on the road, driven by destination, driven by amphetamine. After hours and hours of being on the road, they were desperate for someone to speak to and I was always ready to listen. The opportunity to not only speak but enter the lives of those with unfamiliar faces, those which have no names. This was the kind of interaction I desired, gravitated towards while the others at the shop avoided them. Through these men, and their fast paced storytelling, I visited places that I had often thought of but my eyes had yet to see. Once they left, they no longer mattered, I no longer mattered. It was onto the next stop for them and onto the same monotonous day for me. Throughout the work shift I found plenty of time to read, write and listen to the radio. When the day came to an end, I made my way home, tired, ready to go to bed. But, as I walked in the door, I was greeted with the aroma of dinner being prepared and a refrigerator that had plenty of beer. By nights end, I was exhausted, ready to sleep but often found myself staring at the ceiling, once again thinking of the open road, revisiting the conversations I had with the truck drivers and entertaining the possibility of doing it for a living. Unfortunately these thoughts became stymied with the realization of the work demands this job demanded. The additional time I needed to invest in the adventures I longed to experience simply wasn't possible. So instead, it was back to the same monotonous routine, something that I feared would have terrible consequences. However, the voices that I had been battling were soothed down to a manageable whisper and with it, I became complacent. However, this complacency was about to change.

The business saw its share of visitors. The city was small, but it was a competitive market. It wasn't unheard of for the store to see more representatives from the carpet suppliers than customers on any given day. They came in, showed off their newest and most popular lines, gave their sales pitch, took the order and then sat in the office gossiping for a good portion of the afternoon or until the next representative walked in. Typically the visits went unnoticed by me. Unless it was getting late in the day and I was risking the possibility of having to stay past my shift. Then, I would come up to see if there were any jobs pending. More times than not, just my appearance would cause Judith to realize the time, jump up in a panic, grab a customer's folder and begin to scribble down the cuts. As I waited, most of the representatives would extend their hand and make my acquaintance. I wasn't good with names, never had been, they came and they went, it was business. It was rare to see the same representative from the same company more than a few times. For the girls up front, the different faces presented different stories to learn. However for myself, I struggled to share their interest. There was a difference between the representatives I met in the office and the truck drivers I spoke to. The truck drivers were raw, spontaneous and full of life while the representatives that visited the office were tamed, as if the conversation they engaged in came from a well-rehearsed script. It took numerous interactions from a representative before I started to become curious and possibly entertain the opportunity to dig deep, learn more about them.

The man who instantly sparked not only my curiosity but concern was Dick Messmer. His first few visits were uneventful. As with most representatives, he chose to converse with only the potential buyers, wowing them with his charm and intellect. He rarely ventured away from the office. He didn't have the time to involve those who weren't part of the equation. This was something that never bothered me, I understood the business. However, with this guy, something was different, I wasn't sure exactly what it was, but there was something there that I couldn't let go of. I could tell whenever he arrived, Judith and Ann would act like they were back in high school. The laughing and carrying on became so loud that it leaked out into the warehouse. They competed fiercely for his attention like no other representative that visited. At first glance, it was easy to see why. Dick, by typical standards, was a younger businessman, late twenties to early thirties. He was handsome, his sandy blonde hair looked as if it was cut weekly, his face always clean shaven, showing off a jawline that looked as if it had been chiseled from marble. These features were all brought together with a hungry, determined look in his eyes and a smooth, charming tone in his voice .Judith and Ann were by no means gullible. However, they had fallen for his charm. Something that reinforced the uneasy feeling that I had. But then again, who was I?

Our initial meeting was by chance. The laughter that I had become used to during his visits seemed altered, somewhat forced. It was already past three and I still hadn't received any cuts for the afternoon shift, not to mention the jobs that should be making their way back to me for the following morning. I had finished all of my side work and with nothing left to do I made my way up front. It just so happened that as I opened the door, Dick was on the other side reaching for the handle. "Oh, excuse me" he said as he fought to keep his balance. "Sorry, about that." I quickly responded. "No problem, I need to watch where I am going." He smiled innocently as he passed. Once he entered the warehouse and was no longer within sight of the others his smile went to more of an arrogant grin. Any other time, I would have continued on my way. However, I remained there, my eyes following him all the way to the restroom where he paused, turned and took one last look at me prior to shutting the door. I turned and made my way to the office. I was surprised to see Harold, who hadn't been around for a month or so. Harold sat in the office, his face was pale, he possessed a trance-like stare that was in the direction of William who sat across from him. William's stare was more like a glare towards Harold. He packed his pipe, looked as if he was struggling to keep whatever it was to himself. Mildred stood next to Harold, her head down, with a look of concern. Judith sat in her chair, licking envelopes and sealing billing statements one right after the other before placing them in a pile. She continued to stare down towards her desk, without blinking, in deep thought. Ann was sitting with her legs crossed, leaning back as far as her chair would allow, her arms also crossed in the traditional pouting position. The battle to fight off tears was beginning as her eyes became glassy. My entrance into the office doorway came without being noticed. Whatever it was that had made them all laugh was now missing with the absence of Dick. I stood there for only a moment, realizing that the warehouse door would be opening at any time and Dick would be coming back into the office. There wasn't enough room in the office for all of us and I didn't want to deal with him again. "Judith, do you have any cuts for me?" At first, my question went unanswered, unnoticed. I stepped further into the office which caught the attention of Harold and William as I entered their line of vision. Judith came around as if startled and looked up as if she was torn between despair and elation. "I'm sorry, Tristan, what was that you were saying?" Judith's tone was no longer her own. I wasn't sure what had just taken place but I could tell by the look in her eyes that I would know soon enough. "Do you have any jobs I can take back and start on?" Judith sat there in silence, the energy in the room caused me to slowly back away. By the time I had backed out of the office entirely, she spoke. "I'm sorry, I'll bring them back to you in a moment." I nodded and headed back to the warehouse. As I opened the door, Dick was making his way back towards the office. As we approached one another, the glance we shared had more meaning, our pace slowed down, the glance became a glare. Behind that glare, there was a story. A story that seemed eager to be shared. Dick smiled, looked me up and down and continued on. Once the door shut behind him. I slowly made my way to the back.

The uneasiness that was in the air had settled deep within me. I found myself pacing, which I quickly brought to a stop. I looked towards the front, looked at the clock, looked at the door and then took a seat and waited. My mind continued to wander; I became restless. However, there was consolation knowing it wouldn't be long before Judith would make her way back and ease my curiosity. By the time I heard the door open an hour had passed. I had grown tired, was preparing to leave for the day. Judith made her way back and stood there motionless; I continued to grab my stuff. She started to sniffle; it wasn't hard to realize that she was doing what she could to get me to look over at her. Her sniffles became louder, more consistent, more annoying. I looked over and found her with tissue in one hand, her glasses in the other while staring at me with a trembling lip. I played the part and asked her what was wrong. She dabbed at both of her eyes with the tissue and attempted to gain her composure. By now I had all my belongings to head home, but knew I wasn't going anywhere, so I walked over to the forklift, put everything down and leaned up against it and waited. Judith walked back and forth a couple times and then cleared her throat. "You've probably recognized the guy up front, his name is Dick Messmer." She stood there, continuously dabbing her eyes, regaining the composure she lost while waiting for a response. "Yes, I know who he is." Judith took a deep breath and continued. "Well he has been talking with my dad now for quite some time about the business. Meanwhile, Dad has been throwing some hints that his health is getting worse and there is a lot of things he would rather be doing than running a business. The talk has gone from just a typical conversation to an actual business proposition." Judith became more and more distraught as she furthered into the conversation. "Okay," I said to show her I was still engaged. "Well, I guess Dick is in the process of starting his own family and is wanting to get out of the representative side of the industry." Judith slowed down the conversation, awaiting for me to take over at any time I obliged. "So he put out an offer? Or is this a done deal?" I awaited the answer. I was hoping that it was a done deal and that Dick would make some major adjustments. The job had become old and I was wanting to get a raise or to gain back my freedom. "It's practically a done deal. They are finalizing everything and it looks as if starting the first of the month the shop will be his." Judith's sobbing was getting less contained. "I see, so what does this mean for you and the others?" I asked, taking it for granted that by the actions of everyone up front that the team could possibly be looking for new jobs. "Well, that is part of the deal, everyone here is guaranteed job security. It's just the point, this has been a family business for more than thirty years, I don't know what to do."

Judith acted as if all was lost when in fact, the business was almost destined to improve. The name would stay the same, new blood that was in touch with all the trends, technology and the motivation to succeed would be leading the team. Not to mention, the selling of the business would lower the stress that her father endured and would most likely add years to his life." I was lost on what Judith was so distraught over. "It sounds like this may be the best thing for your father, he can finally rest, finally focus on enjoying life." I tried to act as if I cared as I pointed out what we both knew was obvious. "I just wonder what is to come of this place. I have a family; with my father I can get out of here in time to spend quality time with them. I can tell by the way Dick talks he is going to overwork us." I now realized what was actually bringing Judith to tears, the fear of her actually having to work for the pay she was getting. "I'm sure it will be alright. You'll have to give him a chance before you start thinking the worse." My attempt to show that I cared was becoming more and more transparent and Judith realized it. "Yeah, well I know you are wanting to leave, I'll get the jobs cut and see you in the morning." I grabbed my belongings and headed out the back door to avoid everyone that was congregated in the office.

The following week brought Dick around on a more constant basis, as the end of the month neared. Judith had gone from being concerned and bitter to the all-American employee. As soon as Dick arrived, Judith could be found hovering over his shoulder, going out of her way to assure him that she was the best at her position. William and Ann followed suit. When it came to our interactions, I refused to play along with the others and Dick continued to keep his distance with me. I wasn't certain if that was by choice or because he couldn't free himself of Judith. Then one morning, while Judith was discussing the day's work with me in the middle of the warehouse, the door opened and Dick hollered playfully, "Hello, are you open?" Although playful, there was a point to his greeting that seemed to go unnoticed. Dick made his way back and for the first time he brought with him his wife, Jeanine. As Dick proudly introduced his wife to Judith, I could see why he was so proud. As Jeanine entered a room, her appearance not only gained but demanded everyone's attention. Jeanine had long blonde hair that flowed down past her shoulders. Her eyes were bright green and seductive, her smile was perfect and inviting. She was tall, slender and looked as if she was an athlete. She carried herself as if she had come from a family that had never experienced hard times and with Dick as her husband, chances were that she never would. Judith looked and smiled at Jeanine but it was easy to tell that she felt threatened by her. Before the introduction was even complete, Judith began to rant about how she had heard so much about her. Everyone including Jeanine knew that this wasn't the case. Dick didn't even try and sell it as he interrupted, regaining control of the conversation.

It wasn't long before Ann overheard the commotion and joined the rest, ensuring she wasn't missing out. With Ann's presence and the introductions once again starting, I casually backed away and focused on my work. Moments later, Dick and Jeanine and the others made their way towards the office. I looked over as Dick began to point out to his wife the changes he planned on making. She looked around and then glanced over at me with a smile before turning her attention back over to Dick. Judith began to interject with some of her own suggestions. As Judith and Dick began to share their ideas, Jeanine made her way over. As she approached, Jeanine extended her hand and smiled. "Hi, we didn't really get the chance to meet. I'm Jeanine and you are?" Jeanine's voice was ideal for her physical attributes: professional, a bit raspy, somewhat seductive. "I'm Tristan; it's nice to meet you." I looked over her shoulder to meet a cold glare by Dick that he attempted to mask with a smile. "How long have you been here, Tristan? Are you a member of the family?" The end of her questions brought my attention back to her as I looked deep into her eyes, eyes that I could explore all day and night and never grow tired of. "No, not related, just a friend of the family. I have been here for a few months, give or take a week." Dick made his way over and placed his hand on Jeanine's shoulder as she prepared to ask her next question. "Jeanine, we should let him get back to work. Besides, I want to show you where your office is going to be." Jeanine smiled once more and then followed Dick and Judith back towards the front of the store. Judith was the first to glance back at me and gave me a smile that assured me that she knew the thoughts that I had going through my mind. As they were about to leave the area, Dick took one last look over his shoulder and gave me a glare that served as a warning. I smiled and went back to work.

The next morning I was graced with Dick's presence as soon as I opened the warehouse door. Dick was over at an old soda machine tucked away in the corner, checking to make sure everything still functioned. Off to his side, he had numerous cases of soda, a brand that I had never seen before. He looked over his shoulder and we made eye contact; he slowly turned his head but stood there motionless, cautious as if he anticipated a possible attack. There was no greeting as I made my way past him and continued to my area, I could see through my peripheral vision that he had turned to be certain of my whereabouts. I was greeted at the forklift with a clipboard and a long list of tasks to get done; this was by far the longest list that I had seen since I had started there, not to mention, the list didn't include any of the prep for tomorrow's crews. I knew immediately that there was no way it was going to all get done. Instantly, I sensed that this was premeditated, that this was a way of ensuring my failure and potentially ridding himself of me. I looked over the paper, smiled and placed it to the side. I walked over, grabbed the broom and swept the floor of the mess that had been left behind by the morning crew.

Dick came strolling back; he approached me for the first time with the new title of store owner, my boss. With a smirk on his face, he spoke. "Have you ever heard of this?" he extended his hand with one of the sodas. "No, I haven't." Dick seemed amused but not surprised by my answer. "I didn't figure that you had. It's popular in Cincinnati; try one." He extended the soda further towards me. "No thanks, I'm fine." The smirk on his face slowly disappeared. "Awww, go ahead and take one, I want to talk with you." I reached out, took the soda out of his hand cautiously, thanking him as I did so. Dick opened up his can, looked at it as if he was studying a fine piece of art and took a swallow that seemed to satisfy him far more than any typical soda should be capable of doing. "That's good stuff, Tristan, what do you think?" I took a swallow and was unimpressed. After a second sip, I decided to patronize him. "Definitely not your typical soda, but not bad at all." We both stood there and took a few more drinks without saying anything; it was getting to be a bit awkward. I awaited his conversation but he never started it. I finished my last swallow as I heard the door open. "Tristan, have you seen Dick?" Judith asked in a tone which was borderline desperate as she made her way back. Dick poked his head around the corner. "Yes, Judith, do you need me?" Dick's glare stopped Judith in her tracks. "Oh, I was unaware you and Tristan were talking, no nothing big, it can wait." Judith turned and headed back to the office. Dick once again turned his attention towards me, completely aware that his window of opportunity was shutting quickly as it was only a matter of time before Judith would return to see what exactly was going on. "So, Tristan, what are your thoughts on Harold selling the company to me?" Dick stopped for a moment, went to open his mouth to continue and then decided that he would give me the opportunity to speak. "I don't really have much thought on it. He is getting older, is wanting to be able to enjoy what is left of his life, you were looking for an opportunity and it presented itself." Dick smiled, hoping for more of a comment that he could attack. "Yes, it was a good opportunity for both. This store has much more potential than what he is aware of. Things are never going to be the same as they were; we are going to be busy. I need strength, I need hard workers, understand?" Dick finished his speech by taking his last swallow of soda and then waited for a response. "I understand." Dick looked for more; I gave him nothing. "I see that you got my list, shouldn't be any problem, right?" He asked, fully aware that two people wouldn't be able to get it completed by the end of the day. "No, not an issue at all." Dick was unable to get the resistance he had hoped for and looked to be growing impatient. "I promised Harold that no one would lose their job. However, I have high expectations that I expect to be carried out. You see, that promise will mean nothing in a month, understand?" Dick delivered his point with a smile on his face that I wanted to remove physically. However, I chose to play along. "Not a problem," I answered him with a smile. Dick gave me one last glance before walking away.

Dick was true to his words. In the next couple of weeks, the business picked up. On good days, I was able to get done by day's end. However, on most days this wasn't the case and it didn't go unnoticed. With the inability to stay on top of the demand, I knew it was only a matter of time before I would have the conversation that most dreaded. Each time the door opened I paused and waited. However, the conversation never took place. It was early one morning, as we started a new week, that I heard the door open, and could tell by the walk that it was Dick and he was in a hurry. "What are you doing, Tristan?" he said quickly as he looked at me with a smirk. His question went unanswered. "I wanted to take a second to explain what is going to be happening here instead of you walking in and being surprised." He now had my attention as I looked up at him. "I am not sure if Judith told you or not, but I just landed a major project. This is just one of many that

I plan on landing in the near future. With that in mind, in the next week or so you'll have some help. During my last visit home, I spoke to Stephen, the youngest of my brothers. He is in between jobs right now, and is going to come down for a while. He has been in the carpet industry for years and will be a valuable addition here." Dick took a moment to pause and see if I had anything to say. I crossed my arms, and continued to stare at him. "We are going to be busy and you could use the help. Stephen is easy to work with, he is a lot like you, you are going to like him." I nodded. Dick looked at me for a couple more moments and then turned and walked away. "If I don't see you by day's end, you have a good night, Tristan." It wasn't the conversation I was expecting, quite the opposite actually. I could use the help. When the day was over, I made my way towards the office somewhat relieved. However, I opened the door to a much different energy. There was an eerie silence. Everyone was in the office, but no one was talking. It was obvious that the news of Dick's brother arriving was unsettling.

The following day, I passed the office and with a quick wave, made my way to the back. Dick was already out doing measurements; Jeanine's car was there but she was already in her office. I had barely got started on the list when I heard the door open. I was surprised to see Jeanine making her way back. "Well good morning, Tristan. So you've heard the news?" she asked full of energy and with a smile. "What news would that be?" I baited her. "That we have some help coming." She could have continued but she said the minimum to provide an opportunity for me to interject. "Oh yes, its Dick's younger brother, correct?" Jeanine smiled. "Yes, Stephen. Dick told me that you seemed somewhat indifferent with the news." I stopped the cut that I was about to make and looked up. "Well, I really have no opinion about it, it's not my decision on who comes and goes." Jeanine studied my answer carefully. "Well, Dick was worried that you weren't going to be receptive to him coming so I told him that I would talk to you about it." I stood up and made my way closer to her to avoid anyone who may be sneaking around to listen. "Jeanine, I come in and I do my job. As far as I know, I do it well. If Dick thinks that Stephen can come in here and help me out then that is fine, he is the boss. It has nothing to do with my enthusiasm or how receptive I might or might not be. I have no worries, I cannot speak for anyone else but as for me, I could care less." Jeanine's expression seemed to take on a more defensive look. "The business is falling behind. It isn't just on your end. Stephen isn't coming just to help you out. Stephen has a great background with the industry. He knows what he is doing. He may help you out one day, Dick the next and myself or one of the girls the following. He is a good guy, I want to make sure his visit, however long it may be, is one in which he feels welcomed and everyone works productively with him to make the most of his time here." I smiled. "You have nothing to worry about on my end, Jeanine, I can work well with anyone." Jeanine looked relieved. "So tell me, Tristan, how old are you, twenty? Twenty-one?" I wondered where she was going with this. "I'm a young twenty-two." Jeanine looked deep into my eyes, studied her thoughts and then continued. "Stephen is twenty-five, I believe. I think you guys will get along great. He is quite the card, a real ladies' man. He is always up for being crazy and likes to get out. I think that this could be an opportunity for the two of you to make a new friend, and give you an opportunity to go out and show him a good time." I was always up for a good time. Entertaining the thought of including Stephen all hinged on whether or not he was anything like his older brother. There was absolutely no way I was going to be able to hang out with him if he resembled Dick. "Yeah, we can do that, Jeanine." Jeanine looked at me with a big smile as if victory was now hers. "That is great, Tristan. You will have a blast. Oh my god, he spoke about possibly bringing some of his buddies up here to help out on the weekends. God save us all if he does! He has some crazy ass friends—Sal, Robert and Hal. They are all as crazy as Stephen, if not more! You will have the time of your life!" Although a bit leery about the idea, I nodded with a smile "Sounds like a plan, I'll look forward to it." Jeanine smiled; her job was now done. "Well, Tristan, I better let you get back to work," Jeanine said as she turned and walked away.

Chapter VII

There were numerous days mentioned in which Stephen was to arrive. However, those days came and passed with no arrival, which seemed to create more anxiety than anticipation. Then at the beginning of the following week, shortly after I had arrived, I could hear a warm welcome take place up front. Once the laughter and greetings subsided I awaited the door to open and be introduced to Stephen. Quite a bit of time would pass before the door finally opened. Once it did, I could hear Dick talking and knew that it was most likely Stephen on the other end of the conversation. I finished tying the piece of carpet I had just cut and placed it down. I decided to make my way over to the forklift to look over the task sheet so I would be prepared for any questions once they made their came back. I looked up front and could see Dick standing at the soda machine with his back to me. He grabbed a couple of sodas and yelled. "Tristan? You back in the back?" I rounded the forklift and made myself more visible. "Yes."

Dick looked over his shoulder to better project. "Would you like a soda?" I slowly made my way towards him; Dick's company was still out of my sight. "Sure, thank you." Dick turned his back to me and mumbled something as he bought another soda. Whatever it was that he said, the response he received, which was also inaudible, caused the smirk that I had grown to loathe appear on his face. I slowed down my walk as I approached to allow time for him to face me for proper introductions.

There he stood before me, Stephen Messmer. Although there had been little said about Stephen's appearance, there wasn't much surprise as I took my first glance of him. Stephen was about five foot eight inches tall, His sandy blond hair, which was styled professionally, was thinning and receding. His eyes, although piercing, told little of his story. His jaw was much like his brother's but that is where the similarities ended. His chin had a clef in it that was deep and even more distinguished with his chubby face. His thick neck gave way to his broad shoulders. The overall husky, athletic build led me to believe that he had spent much of his spare time in the gym. Stephen was sharp dressed, with a dress shirt that accentuated his muscular torso and his pleated pair of dress pants and designer shoes. Steven possessed the all-American college boy look and yet was far from cliché. Stephen looked me up and down a few different times as I made my way to them. The inability to read his eyes caused caution and intrigue. Dick handed me a soda as he introduced the two of us. We shook hands and in a cliché gangster voice he asked me how I was doing. I returned the greeting and turned my attention to Dick, who already had a smile on his face from our initial meet and greet. "This is our warehouse boy, Stephen, maybe you can show him the ropes a bit." There was no response. Dick continued. "Let me show you what we have going on." Dick walked him around every square inch of the area, then took him back to the other warehouse where the padding was. He began to talk to him with all the ideas he had for the area. I looked at him in amazement since I had never heard any of these ideas when we were back here one on one. Stephen pointed out some of the opportunities that he saw, agreed on a lot of Dick's plans and stepped up and questioned anything he didn't seem to approve. Not once was I ever involved in the conversation. I actually stood there and listened to their interchange in disbelief. Half of what was being spoken between the two of them were ideas that I had come up with weeks ago and had already shared with Dick or Jeanine. Finally at the end of the conversation, Dick looked over at me with a smile. "What do you think, Tristan?" I just simply nodded and stepped aside as they went back to the warehouse; I followed.

Once we were back in the warehouse, Dick surveyed the area once more before turning his attention to the two of us. "I'm going to go ahead and finish my appointments. Why don't you stay here, take the measurements we did earlier and help Tristan with the cuts?" Stephen nodded. "Aye, aye, El Capitan," Stephen said in a lazy voice. Dick walked away and Stephen stood for a moment surveying the carpet pile. Without saying anything, Stephen walked over to the forklift, looked at the tray of tools that I had on a box laying loosely next to the seat. The area was far from organized—there was a utility knife, a carpet cutter, a chalk line and a bunch of pens, of which half were no use. Stephen grabbed a pen and went to write something down on his notepad. When the first pen didn't work, he flung it over his shoulder; the second pen he grabbed also didn't work which caused him to shake his head in disbelief. "Are you fucking kidding me?" He said as he once again flipped the pen over his shoulder. The third pen worked but not to his satisfaction causing the pen to experience the same fate as the others. "This is fucking embarrassing! How long have you been here?" He looked over at me in disgust. "A few months, not sure of the date." He shook his head in disbelief. "It doesn't matter. You telling me that this is all the shit you have to work with? Nothing is organized." For the first few moments of our interacting, Stephen was coming across harsh and yet, it was in defense of me. "Yeah, that is pretty much it." Stephen picked up the chalk line and let it fall from his hands back into the box. "This is pathetic. My brother knows better than this; he should be taking better care of his employees. How much are you making? You know what, don't even tell me, let me guess, nowhere near enough?" I looked at him and grinned. "Right," Stephen said as he evaluated the forklift. Stephen grabbed a utility belt that had not been used since I had worked here and put it on. After grabbing the clipboard off the seat he climbed up and sat down. "Let me get on this old girl if you know what I mean and show you how to handle a lady!" Stephen spoke in an ornery tone that was topped off with a devious laugh and a wink.

Stephen pulled a list of cuts from his shirt pocket, glanced at it so quickly that one would question if he had enough time to actually read it. Stephen then whipped the forklift around in the tightest surroundings, making me cringe in fear that he would end up hitting something or tearing something apart. And yet, no matter how close he came, he never slowed down, never doubted his judgment. Stephen got a roll of carpet from the middle of the pile and swerved it into position quickly. In what seemed to be one motion, he jumped from the forklift, reached into his utility belt, pulled out a knife and cut the string. He twirled the knife like a gun, placing it back in the belt and pulled the carpet out, before dropping it on the ground effortlessly. "We need eighteen feet, Tristan. You wanna measure it or just trust me that I have it nailed perfectly?" Stephen looked at me hoping for me to challenge his eyeing of the distance. "No, it looks good to me." Stephen took his tape measurer and extended his hand as he offered it to me. "I can see you have some doubts. Go ahead, I won't be offended. Try and prove me wrong," I decided to entertain him and took the tape measure. The carpet measured eighteen feet two inches. He looked over and smiled, I didn't get a chance to open my mouth before he spoke up. "Just a hair over eighteen feet, just the way we like it, always leave a couple inches so there is room for error. Now, one side son, as I make this cut." Stephen went through the cut quick and precise; he had the carpet rolled, tied and the remainder back in the pile in the amount of time it would have taken me to get it down and measured. "Now that is what I am talking about!" Stephen was cocky but he also had the skills to back it up. Stephen looked over the task list once more and went back to work. He continued this rhythm for the next hour, cutting everything by eye, rolling it up by himself and placing it in a pile. I stood back, out of his way and watched.

At the end of his final cut, he looked over at me and then over to his work that he had completed, he wiped the sweat of his brow and said. "Not too bad, Tristan, eh? Do you have any questions?" If I did, I didn't feel as if I wanted to ask, so instead I chose to use a safety, "How long did you say you have been doing this?" Stephen looked at me, looked down towards the ground, nodded with a smile and then looked back up at me. "Let's put it this way, I've been doing it way too long. I actually started like you did and made my way up to a service representative before quitting. If it wasn't for my brother needing me, I would never pick up a knife again." He looked over to me as he finished the comment then continued. "So what exactly is the deal here?" I really didn't know where to start. In the short amount of time in which I was able to observe him, he seemed carefree, rebellious. What I chose to share and what I held back would not affect the way he slept tonight. It seemed as if he was simply trying to spark conversation, I appreciated that. "Well, your brother has definitely fallen into a nice opportunity. This place has more potential than what the end results show. It's been treading water effortlessly for a long time and yet is still one of the best flooring shops in the area. It needs direction, leadership. Your brother should strike it big here." Stephen rolled his eyes and then looked at me with a smirk. "Listen, Tristan, you didn't tell me anything I didn't already know. I know my brother; he'll polish this turd till it's nice and shiny. He is a Messmer, and we Messmers are bred to succeed, you see?" Stephen looked at me long and hard as if he wanted to ensure that I had digested all that was just fed to me. I really didn't care, so I chose to return the stare. Stephen made his way around the forklift and took a look towards the front of the warehouse. In noticing that no one was around, he looked at the clock to make sure there was enough time to entertain the next conversation and then looked at me and through the side of his mouth spoke. "So, what is the deal with everyone here?" I looked at him and we both smiled at one another. "Well, what do you want to know?" Stephen looked at me as if I was choosing to be defiant. "Tell me their story, Tristan." I then looked over his shoulder at the clock to make sure I had enough time. "I'm still not sure if I know where you want me to start, but I will tell you this. Harold and Mildred were the owners; it's been a family business since it opened. Judith does most of the work. Ann is Judith's sister and is married to William. They have been around as long as Judith. The understanding is as follows: Dick is to keep the name of the company and guarantee job security for the employees." I could have continued but Stephen had rolled his eyes almost every time I finished a sentence and I knew he was anxiously awaiting to share his views on what I had said. As I paused, Stephen interjected. "First off, Dick would be an idiot to change the name, it's been here what, thirty years? I can tell by being here for only half a day that this town is afraid of change. Second, there is no legal binding when it comes to that kind of a promise. That is nothing more than a false sense of security. Dick can fire anyone at any time. So tell me, what is Judith's problem? It is no secret that she doesn't want me here; that is obvious in the way she acted towards me, I can only imagine how she truly feels about Dick and Jeanine. There seems to be a lot of drama." I looked at Stephen, who was studying my movements, my reactions to everything he was saying. "Yes, there is drama. I don't think she is as dumb as people think she is. She is quite aware of her job being in jeopardy. In my book, she is a valuable asset to the store, I think it would be foolish to get rid of her." Stephen gave me a look of disgust. "You don't have to try and sell me that, Tristan. Who in the hell said she is going to get fired?" I looked at him without answering, he continued. "As for William, I only met him for a moment; I don't like him. My brother and I have seen his type a million times over, and I assure you, Dick will eat him for lunch. William and his wife are the ones who I would get rid of. However, if and when Dick chooses to do so, he will most likely try and bring me on and as I said, I don't see myself getting back into this profession."

We continued to talk the rest of the day about the history of the store, where it was going, what changes needed to be done and the best way in Stephen's eyes of getting it done. I had quickly become bored; I was intrigued to learn more about Stephen, something that we either didn't find time to explore or he chose not to share. The following day I saw very little of Stephen; he spent almost the whole day with Dick and when he wasn't with Dick he was up in the office or sitting back in Jeanine's office sharing stories. Their laughter stayed consistent and allowed everyone to know where they were. Judith took advantage of this and headed back to catch up on what all had been going on with Stephen and me. She hid her intentions poorly with a task list. Judith looked at me cautiously as she handed me the list; she seemed uncertain if I had changed sides. "So, how is it going back here?" I looked at her, I could see the anxiety of Stephen's visit was wearing her down. "You know, not bad at all. Stephen is different but seems to be a pretty good guy." Judith looked at me as if she had possibly just lost an ally. "Watch yourself, don't get pulled in by the Messmer charm. I can see them befriending you one day and turning their backs on you the next. Be careful, Tristan, I mean it." I looked at Judith and saw the concern in her eyes. She looked back towards Jeanine's office after taking notice that there hadn't been any noise coming from that direction and then became relieved once a hearty laughter was heard. She looked back at me, not sure where to go with the conversation. "Judith, I understand your concerns, I'm not ignorant, I'll be fine." Judith heard nothing that I had just said, she was already beginning to continue "Well, what else? What all did you talk about." I looked at Judith, she was becoming more and more restless. "Stephen and I talked about the history of this shop, his background, the employees here and their backgrounds, where I fit in, what my intentions were." Judith interrupted before I could say anything else. "Oh brother, and what did you say?" Judith was on the verge of a panic attack. "I told him what I know, which really isn't much about the history of this shop. I mean, I could state the facts that this has been a family business since day one, that it is one of the more successful flooring businesses in the area but outside of that, my knowledge is limited. I will tell you this, Judith, I had nothing but praise for you. I told him how valuable you are, how "you" are this company, what kind of loss it would be if you ever decided that you didn't want to stay here. He seemed to agree. I really don't think you have anything to ever worry about when it comes to your job security or your future here. If the day comes where you are no longer here it will be as a result of you making that choice, not them." This seemed to relieve Judith. She smiled although with caution. "You don't say?" Judith said on the verge of a nervous laugh. "I do. You can count on that." Judith took one last look over her shoulder towards the office, the laughter had subsided a few minutes ago. "Well, I better be heading back up. Thanks, Tristan, I really mean that." I gave her a smile and she headed back up front.

The next morning I went back to the back and was greeted with the biggest list in my short time at the store. I knew it wouldn't be long before help would be on its way. However, when the door did open it was Jeanine that came back. She failed to look my way as she headed to the restroom, so I thought little of it and began looking for the first roll of carpet to cut. Once she stepped out of the restroom she headed back to my area. "Good morning, Tristan, how are you?" I gave her a smile and took a moment to study her eyes. "Not too bad, how are you?" With the formalities all but out of the way, Jeanine could get to the real reason she was back to see me, "So, what do you think of Stephen?" The rest of the conversation seemed to hinge on what my answer would be. "He seems like a pretty good guy from what I could tell. We kept it pretty professional." Jeanine's face lit up as she gave me a big smile. "He is pretty straightforward. I imagine he kept it professional because it was the first day here and all. I think you guys are going to get along great." Jeanine awaited confirmation. "I imagine so," I entertained her. Jeanine continued to smile. "Stephen is a hoot! You probably heard us in the office yesterday. If we were too loud, I do apologize." I decided to bait her a bit with my response. "Oh, that was Stephen in the back making you laugh?" Jeanine didn't hesitate to seize the opportunity to share their conversation. "Stephen was just sharing his adventures over the last weekend. He is a wild one! You aren't dating anyone are you?" I wasn't sure where she was going with this. "No, not currently." Jeanine looked relieved. "I know that was somewhat of an odd question. However, I ask because Stephen is a playboy. There is never a dull moment with that man! I was thinking, you should give some thought to going out with him this weekend. I know he is eager to go out. Maybe you could show him around. If you don't, he'll hit Dick up on it. I cringe to think about two Messmer boys being out and about in this or any other town. What do you think, Tristan? Do you have anything planned this weekend?" I could see in her eyes that keeping Dick off the streets was a major concern especially with Stephen in town. I was in need of getting out and this would provide the opportunity to possibly learn more about Stephen. "If he wants to go out,

I could show him around the town." Jeanine's excitement almost made her giggle. "Thank you, Tristan, I appreciate this so much, you don't even know!" Jeanine looked as if she had just had the weight of the world taken off of her shoulders. "No problem, I'm glad I could help." Jeanine smiled and walked away

With the conversation Jeanine and I had, I had fallen behind quickly. I expected Stephen to open the door at any moment. However, it was after lunch when he finally opened the door and headed back. Stephen started off all business: he walked over to the forklift as I was making a cut and took the task sheet and matched up the cuts off the sheet to the ones that laid on the floor. He waited till I was finished cutting and rolling my piece of carpet before he shook his head in disappointment. "Tristan, you are way behind! What the hell you been doing back here? Sleeping? Reading?" I looked at him as I made my way past him with the carpet in my arms and awaited a smile or some kind of tip that he was just having fun with me. It never came. "No, I haven't been reading or sleeping. A lot of the carpet I needed was near the bottom of the pile." Stephen looked at me as if he didn't believe a word I was saying. "Here, Tristan, I'll help you, you can't be here all night and if Dick makes it back before you leave I can guarantee you he'll have at least a couple more jobs to cut." I wasn't one to turn down help so I pointed out the next piece of carpet as he hopped on the forklift. He had the next piece out and cut in no time and awaited direction for the next piece. This continued until we were caught up. Stephen did the work; I gave him the directions. Stephen said little, staying focused the whole time. Once we caught up, he seemed to loosen up. "So tell me, Tristan, are there any women in this town worth looking at or are they all fat and ugly?" I looked at Stephen and gave him a smile which was reciprocated with a dirty glare. "Yes, Stephen, as a matter of fact, there are a lot of beautiful women in this city." Stephen looked at me as if he didn't believe me or took it for granted that my taste was very poor. "You don't say, eh? I imagine our taste in women is a bit different. You probably fuck anything with a hole, right?" Stephen gave me a big smile as if I was as easy to read as the others at the shop. "Actually, my taste is impeccable, I would rather go home empty handed then settle for less." Stephen's rebuttal was very quick. "I see, I see, said the blind man to the deaf man!" Stephen said with an Asian accent that needed work. Stephen continued, "The fact is, I run a no skank program and yet, I never seem to go home empty handed." Stephen looked for approval as he had now turned all his attention to our conversation. "I see, well then you should be fine here." I could tell Stephen was dropping hints, looking for a way to get me to go out with him. Unbeknownst to him, Jeanine and I had already talked. I decided to keep that hidden to observe his approach a little more. "Where are some of these places you are talking about, Tristan?" The fact was, there were plenty of places in the city and in the neighboring town in which good times were to be had. The biggest thing was whether he would be able to lower his bar standards from what he was used to seeing in Cincinnati. "Well, do you like social gathering types of bars, dance clubs, what do you prefer to do?" Stephen looked at me with the same disgusted look on his face that I was becoming quite familiar with. "I am a simple man. I like the bars where the pussy outweighs the cock! I want primo pussy, you understand? So tell me, what exactly are you planning on this weekend?" I looked at him as if I was surprised, he didn't seem to buy it. "I'm not sure, I was thinking about possibly running around with some friends." Stephen rolled his eyes, unimpressed. "Are you serious? A fucking sausage fest? Fuck that, you need to take me out and about. I'll show you how us Cincinnati boys spit some game! I'll have pussy crawling out of your ears by the end of the night!" I looked at Stephen who was full of confidence. "You don't say? Okay, I'll change my plans. Take us out, I'll drive, and you buy the beer, sound good?" Stephen nodded with confidence.

Chapter VIII

The next couple of days I saw very little of Stephen. By Friday afternoon, I began to think that maybe Stephen had forgotten that we had plans for the night or perhaps had come up with something else. I was totally fine either way; the high volume of work that I was putting in was keeping me pretty grounded around the house each night. I typically spent my evenings drinking at the house or going to bed early, which was causing me to second guess what exactly I was doing with my life. It was getting late when Jeanine made her way back to the back where I was. She looked around the room and then brought her attention back to me. "Looking pretty good, Tristan, how is everything going?" Jeanine was stunning, she had a glow about her that was different than other days. I looked up at her and we smiled at one another. I was totally lost within her eyes and had totally forgotten that she had even said anything. Jeanine continued, "It's been crazy around here, I'll tell you what, Tristan, it's nice to have the business but it definitely can cause some stress as well. Thank God Stephen was able to free up some time and come up to help. He has meant the world to Dick and I. Tonight will be a much deserved break for Stephen. I think it'll be nice for you to be able to get out as well. Have the two of you decided where you are going to be going?" Jeanine's remark confirmed that Stephen had not forgotten. "You know, we haven't really talked about it since earlier in the week. I wasn't even sure if Stephen was still looking forward to going." Jeanine looked surprised by my comment. "Tristan, he has talked about it every night. I am sure he'll bring it up to you when he gets back today. If he does get back! Does he have your number?" I pondered for a moment before writing it down and handing it to her. "Thanks, Tristan, I'll be sure and give this to him. You guys are going to have a great time, just stay out of jail. Although you don't need to be here, he still needs to be here first thing in the morning." I looked at her with a smile after the jail comment. However, she looked very serious as she turned to walk away. I went back to work and contemplated what we should do tonight. With Stephen being from a big city, should I take him to Columbus? A strip club? Stay in town and hit some of Newark's finest? Although they were all good options for the first time out, the way Stephen boasted about his adventures, I had a feeling that none of them would suffice to Stephen's expectations unless he was able to take someone home with him.

As my shift came to an end, there was still no sign of Stephen. I went home and found the house empty. I made my way to the refrigerator and found an open case of beer. With plenty left, I grabbed one, turned on some music and took a seat in the kitchen. The beer was much needed as was the seat. I sat and contemplated where I should take Stephen tonight. Time passed with no real plan. The trip to Columbus was losing its appeal by the end of the second beer, as was any desire to go out tonight. Soon, I became caught up in the music and my train of thought, not to mention the time.

As I finished my third beer I got up to grab a fourth when the phone started ringing. I looked at the clock it was a little past 7:00. I had yet to eat, yet to shower and with drinking on an empty stomach, I was feeling no pain. I contemplated whether or not I should answer the phone. I opened the beer and took a long drink. Whomever it was calling, they were determined to talk, as the phone continued to ring. I headed back over to the kitchen table, was about to sit down when I finally decided to go answer the phone. I made my way into the room slowly; I knew it was Stephen. I decided to wait for a few moments to give him one last chance to give up on the call. He didn't.

I slowly picked up the phone and answered it. "Hello?" I said in a less than enthusiastic tone. "Is this Tristan?" Sure enough, it was Stephen, I could tell he was wound up and ready to go. "Yes, it is. Who is this?" I knew who it was without asking but decided to play the game anyways. "It's Stephen. What the fuck are you doing? Sleeping already?" I could sense that we had a long night ahead of us. "No, I am actually on my third or fourth beer, just waiting on you to call." Stephen chuckled, "You've already started? Nice, well don't go and get all shitfaced before we get a chance to get on the road." I stood there for a moment, took a drink before I answered. "I'm just getting started, are you still at the shop or are you home yet?" I had no reason to believe they would still be at the shop; the store stayed open late on Fridays but the measuring was always done by six on any given night. "I'm still at the shop. We have a couple of cuts to still do and then I'm heading home to shower. You know the area better than I do. What time do you want to head out? Ten o'clock good?" I knew if we waited till ten I would already be drunk and passed out. "Let's plan on getting out on the road around nine. That will give us enough time to check out a couple different spots. Is that cool or do you need more time?" Stephen laughed. "I'll be home by eight; I need fifteen minutes to shower and get ready, I'll be ready by nine." I returned the laughter. "Nine it is. Where exactly do Dick and Jeanine live?" Stephen gave a sigh as he provided me with directions. Dick and Jeanine had bought a house in one of the wealthiest manors in the city which shouldn't have surprised me but actually did. "That works, I'll see you at nine sharp." I was about to hang up when Stephen interrupted. "Tristan, make sure you pack some condoms. You are going to have more pussy than you know what to do with! Hey, by the way, don't be drinking anymore; you are already starting to slur and I don't need to be babysitting your ass tonight." I was far from being drunk but decided to just go ahead and let him voice his concern so I could get off the phone; I was in need of another beer. I didn't say anything else as he waited for a response, instead I hung up and headed to the kitchen.

I sat there with beer in hand and thought about the night that lay ahead. As I finished the beer and grabbed another I decided to make my way to the bathroom. As I left the kitchen, the front door opened. I looked into the room and saw my mother with a bag of groceries but more importantly a case of beer. "What time did you get home?" she asked as our eye contact came to an end and with her focus drifting down to my beer. "It hasn't been long, maybe an hour or so." She made her way into the kitchen, opened the refrigerator to put the groceries away and surveyed the current beer situation. "That long of a day?" she asked as a result of the beers that were missing. "Not just a long day, it has been a long week." She looked at me, well aware of this by the hours I had been working. "If you want, I'll grab us a couple, we can go sit down and talk about it?" The offer sounded good, and provided an opportunity to drink more without any type of scrutiny. "Sure, I can do that." My mother grabbed us both a beer and walked towards the front room. I followed her and took a seat across from her. We went through the first beer quickly and put down another as we took turns talking about the challenges of the work week that had just finished. As she inquired more on my work, I told her about the arrival of Stephen;

I described the minor details of Stephen but said enough to attract her attention to want more. As I finished my beer and considered heading out to the kitchen to grab another, I realized that I had completely forgotten about the time and in doing so, conveniently forgotten about our night out. It was now 8:15. I told my mother that I better get going, I was supposed to go pick up Stephen and show him around Newark. This seemed unsettling as a concerned look appeared. She turned her eyes to me but I refused to entertain the stare, the glare, knowing the consequences. I knew it was only a matter of moments before she opened her mouth and addressed her concerns. Before she could begin, I assured her that all would be well and then continued onto the kitchen grabbing us both another beer. I walked into the front room, handed her a beer while keeping mine out of sight, then made my way to the bathroom. As I took a shower, I began to realize that I was closing in on a good drunk. I stayed in the shower a little longer than normal to try and bring myself back. However, as I stepped out of the shower I realized it didn't help.

As a result, I took longer than normal to get ready. I looked down on my watch that was laying on the sink and saw that it was 8:45. There was absolutely no way I was going to be able to make it on time. I finished getting ready right before 9:00 and headed into the front room to call Stephen. My mother had already made her way to the kitchen to be closer to the music and the beer which provided me an opportunity to talk to Stephen without her hearing any of our conversation. Stephen answered the phone at the end of the first ring as if he had been expecting my call. His tone not only verified that he was expecting my call but let me know that he was already frustrated with me. "Is this Stephen?" I tried to act as if I didn't know it was him who answered. "Yes, Tristan, where the fuck are you? Are you still drinking?" I knew that my speech was getting slurred; I had earned it. "Yes, it is me. I had some complications; my mother came home and I started talking to her. However, I just finished up so I just wanted to let you know I will be on my way, should be there in about fifteen minutes." Stephen let out a big sigh and interrupted me before I could finish the sentence uncontested. "Whoa there, Tristan, you are not talking to an amateur; you are fucking drunk. I'm not going to get in the car with you while you're slobbering everywhere and swerving all over the place. Just forget it, I'll just see you on Monday, all right?" The thought of Stephen getting off the phone and telling Dick and Jeanine that I was too drunk to go out was very sobering. I went to tell him that I would be all right but he hung up. I hurried up and called him back. The phone rang several times before Jeanine picked up the phone. I tried to be professional, keep it short and just ask for Stephen; he must have already told them. "What is going on, Tristan? Are you okay?" I cleared my throat in an attempt to also clear my slurring. "Everything is fine, could you tell Stephen I'll be there in fifteen?" Jeanine put her hand over the phone and said something, she got back on a few moments later. "Tristan, have you been drinking?" I stood there for a moment until she called my name again. "I had a couple of beers, I always do when I first get home, I wouldn't say that I've been drinking." I heard the hand go back over the phone for a moment. This was already getting old; I could vaguely hear her say "Why don't you just talk to him?" I could tell that it had grown old with her as well. Stephen took the phone from her hands "Yes?" Nothing more. I could tell that Stephen was holding back because Jeanine was still in the room. "Stephen, everything is fine, I am coming over, getting ready to leave right now." Stephen sighed. "I told you it was fine, I would just see you on Monday." I could now hear Dick in the background telling him he should just go and Jeanine supporting Dick's view. "It's fine, I'll be on my way, give me fifteen." Stephen began to say something as I hung up the phone. With the fact that I was slurring I decided not to say anything to my mother and just leave.

I took my time in heading over to Dick and Jeanine's. The way there wouldn't be too bad with police but the manor was the neighborhood in which all of the city's elite lived and everyone knew it. The area was safe guarded by police patrol and those with nothing better to do than perch themselves at the window, looking for cars passing that they were unfamiliar with and reporting them. The manor was winding, I wasn't exactly sure where the street was. I drove into the manor cautiously. It felt as if I had been through the manor two maybe three times with no luck when I came up to an intersection I wasn't familiar with and saw the street just ahead. I pulled in and saw someone look out the window. I sat there and waited but no one came outside. I started to wonder if they had given me the right address or if I had possibly gone to the wrong driveway. I got out of the car and went up to the door. As I went to ring the doorbell, the door opened slightly and Stephen gave me a dirty look. He looked over his shoulder as if contemplating whether to let me in or not then opened the door the rest of the way. "Come on in." He said in a drawn out voice. I walked in and found Dick there with a sandwich in hand and an import beer on the counter. Jeanine was standing across the counter greeting me with a smile. "What were you doing, soaking in the scenery?" Dick said without looking up while still chewing his food. I looked at him blankly when Jeanine interjected. "We saw you drive by a couple different times." She smiled. "This manor has always confused me at night with its winding roads and poor lighting." No one seemed to buy my excuse. "If you come in through the end of the manor and take the first right we are right there," Dick said with attitude. "I'll have to remember that the next time." Dick got up and walked by, taking his plate over to the sink without looking in my direction. Jeanine looked uncomfortable; Stephen was restless. "Well, are we going to go or are we going to hang out here tonight? It would be nice to get a drink before last call." Jeanine gave Stephen a look of disbelief and then a sympathetic look my way. "Where all are you boys planning on going?" Everyone's attention turned towards me. "I was thinking we would probably head to Heath; there are a couple nightclubs there that I think Stephen will like, Parkinson's and possibly Truman's then head back to Newark before last call and hit a couple bars where everyone likes to congregate before calling it a night. "That sounds like a plan, Tristan, let's go hang out with some middle aged women and then a bunch of guys." Before Stephen could finish his sentence Dick was already laughing. Jeanine gave him a look of annoyance. "I think it sounds like a fun time. Tristan, please be safe tonight." I looked over and gave Jeanine a smile, the smile faded quickly as I glanced towards Dick with a cold glare. I made my way to the door with Stephen following with some reluctance. Stephen shut the door behind him and caught up with me. "Hey, are you fucking drunk? If you are I'll just drive us." Stephen put his hand out to collect the keys which I ignored. I opened up the door and took a seat. Stephen paused for a minute next to the door to possibly weigh out some options and then got in. I had some music on that he instantly turned down as he reached into his pocket. "I figured you wouldn't mind me bringing some music for our ride." Stephen was already putting the music in before I could answer him but I said something anyways. "No problem at all, I'm always up for some good tunes." Stephen looked at me like a maestro and nodded his head. "Are you familiar with Harry Connick Jr?" he asked with a devious smile on his face. "Yes, I am, love his work." Stephen acted surprise that I had even heard of him. "This right here is the music to put you in the right mindset when it comes to a night of patrolling the streets for honeys." Stephen turned the volume up as soon as the first horn blasted and then eased back into his seat, closing his eyes as he began to tap his leg to the rhythm of the music.

We spoke no more until we were in Heath and I passed by Parkinson's which I had planned on going to first but with the lack of cars that were in the parking lot, I decided differently. Stephen who had recently opened his eyes to take in the surroundings, caught the neon of the club. "Hey, where are you going? Isn't that the club you wanted to hit?" Stephen turned and looked at me as if I had just committed a crime. "Yes, it's dead though, too early. Let's check out the other club, it is just up the road a ways, perhaps it is happening there. We can always come back here a little later. Stephen gave me a look of doubt before allowing himself to ease back into the music and turn his attention out the window where he continued to watch the scenery as it passed. We pulled into Truman's. The club didn't look much better than Parkinson's, Stephen was sure to point this out to me. "So what do you call this if the other bar was dead?" Stephen shook his head in disbelief. "It's early, most bars don't start happening till 11:00 or so. Did you want to try something else?" Stephen's look of disbelief quickly turned to disgust. "I haven't been drinking all night like you, I would like to get somewhere and have a drink." I pulled into a parking spot. Stephen, although expressing his desire to start drinking, wanted to listen to the rest of the song so we sat there and took in every last note. "Now that is how you get the night started, my boy!" Stephen said with a devious grin as he slapped my leg. We got out of the car and headed towards the club; Stephen looked around at the cars that were scattered throughout the lot. "Are you sure this is a bar or a used car lot?" Stephen shook his head. I chose not to say anything and continued on. The music was loud, the club poorly lit by design; there was, however, enough light to notice through the window the little bit of movement that was going on at the dance floor. "Jesus Christ, Tristan. You've done well," Stephen said sarcastically. I glanced over; Stephen had paused, looked as if he was contemplating heading back to the car. "Just give it a chance, you might be surprised." Stephen trudged forward saying no more.

When we entered the club, we were immediately greeted by a bouncer at the door who had plenty of attitude as he asked us for our identification. I watched Stephen as he looked the bouncer up and down before pulling his identification out and handing it to him. We made our way past the bouncer, down a tight path that separated us from the dance floor. During the day, Truman's was a restaurant that served food and drinks until 10:00 p.m. At that time, they closed off the dining area that was located on the east side of the bar, cleaned out the lower dining area which became the dance floor. The restaurant was spacious and the whole late evening dance club was pulled off rather nicely. I had decided not to tell Stephen this since I figured it may tarnish his expectations of the night before the night actually began. We headed towards the bar, Stephen worked his broad shoulders in between some young kids and looked back at me as I stood complacently behind him. "What do you want? I've got you covered as agreed upon." Stephen observed the bar and its surroundings as I told him what I wanted. "I'll just take a bottle of beer." Stephen looked at me a bit disgruntled and then turned and was greeted by a good looking barmaid. He placed the order, provided a wink. Once the barmaid walked away, he took a moment to observe her ass and then looked back at me "What is this? A fucking eighteen-year-old and under club? Half these kids still shit there diapers, Tristan!" Stephen stated loud enough to cause those around him to give him a dirty look. I looked around, there was a young crowd out tonight but I only looked at this stop as a place for us to get started. "It's not that bad, Stephen, we can drink one or two and head out. By that time, the other club should be happening." Stephen grabbed the beers, tipped the barmaid generously as he gave her a smile, followed by another wink. As she walked away, her ass seemed to have developed a little more shake than earlier. He handed me my beer and leaned in to ensure I could hear him over the music. "Well, worst case scenario, we can always grab a booth and order a couple of entrees if the dance floor doesn't pick up!" Stephen gave me a smirk, tapped the top of my bottle with his and walked away. I watched him walk away with a strut that guaranteed everyone in the bar would know he was from out of town and then followed him over to the dance floor.

As I looked around, I couldn't help but notice that most of the women who were here were with their boyfriends. I figured this would be pointed out at any moment by Stephen who continued to walk over to a corner before grabbing a seat. Once seated, Stephen reached into his pocket and pulled out some gum. He tossed a couple of pieces into his mouth and then in a smooth manner, he tipped his beer back and cleared half the bottle on his first swig. After he surveyed the dance floor he spoke. "There isn't shit going on in this bar. I might have to go up and show one of these boys how they should dance with their woman before it's over with." I could tell by the comments he was making after his first drink of his beer that by night's end we could end up having our hands full. I chose not to say anything; instead, I looked the floor twice over to see if there was anyone worth talking too. Stephen stood up, reached into his pocket and handed me a five. "Why don't you go get us a couple more beers? While you are up there, find out the barkeep's name. See if she wants to head out to the bars with us after she gets off work. I think I will make my way over to the far corner and see what that woman looks like once a little light hits her face." I took his five and walked away. The line was growing as I approached the bar. As I waited for the barmaid to get done with some of the other customers and make her way over to me, I turned my attention to the dance floor. Stephen was working his way behind some of the women that were on the edge of the dance floor conversing; he looked most of them up and down and then moved on. He had just made his way out of sight when the barmaid approached. I placed my order and awaited her to return. She was definitely cute, although the power that one possesses behind the bar has always seemed to attract me. She had what I needed and took her time in bringing it back to me. As she placed the beers on the bar top she gave me a smile. "Where is your buddy at? Is he making you come and get the beers?" I was surprised she had remembered us. The tip he had left her must have made a pretty good impression. "He had to go to the restroom. He did however want to know when you would be done tonight and if you would like to join us elsewhere when you are free." She gave me a smile as she took the five out of my hand. "Oh yeah?" she said as she put money in the register and gave me some pouty eyes with the change that was left over as she hovered near her tip jar. I gave her the nod to keep the change and she smiled as she made her way back over to me. "It sounds wonderful, but I close. Maybe next time." She shrugged her shoulders as if it was out of her power. "Well, we plan on shutting down the city tonight. When do you get off?" She gave me a smile in regard to my persistence. "Honey, I won't get out of here till probably two, then I need to get home to my baby. I'm sorry but tell him maybe next weekend." She gave me a wink and walked away; her ass was amazing as she provided just enough shake to lure you in. Once she was across the bar waiting on another patron she took a moment to look over her shoulder at me to make sure I was watching and gave me a smile. I smiled and walked away.

I looked around but was unable to find Stephen. I made my way back to the table and continued to look for him, knowing he would sooner or later return. As I was looking I noticed a couple women about twenty feet away who smiled at me as our eyes met. At first glance, they didn't seem to fit the description of what Stephen was looking for. Nonetheless, I headed over to their table. As I introduced myself, I could tell that one was definitely interested. I turned my attention to her. The other woman was slightly older and would be good for Stephen once he returned. The older woman looked at both of my hands and asked me if I had a drinking problem since I was two fisting it. I hadn't even given the thought of having both beers in my hands as I smiled and explained that my buddy was wandering around and it was his beer. This brought on further conversation on where I was from and questions about this so-called buddy. As I told them more about myself and Stephen, I noticed Stephen standing back where we had originally been sitting waving at me to try and get my attention. The women who had their backs to Stephen noticed I had become distracted and turned their attention to where Stephen was. The older women raised her beer towards him. Stephen looked uninterested as he waved. Once they turned back towards me, he once more began. He was aware that I was in the process of hooking the two of us up. I was also aware that he had absolutely no interest in either of the women. I forgave myself for a moment and headed back over to Stephen. By this time the floor was becoming crowded with more filing in.

Upon arriving, Stephen greedily took the beer out of my hand and swallowed half of it effortlessly. "What the hell took you so long at the bar?" He said much louder than he needed to. "I've been back for a while; I just couldn't find you." Stephen looked at me with an ornery smile, sweat was beading onto his forehead. "You like that huh?" He expected me to be able to decipher what he meant. "What happened, did you hook up? Seems like you worked up a sweat." Stephen gave me smile. "That I did my boy, that I did!" I looked Stephen up and down not certain whether he was telling the truth or not. "Well, I was trying to hook us both up right now when you waved me down." Stephen rolled his eyes as he took another big drink finishing off the beer and squinted across the room at the two women I had just left. "So you were, huh? Which one was you planning on hooking me up with? The woman with the club foot or the one with the fucking moose knuckle?" I couldn't help but laugh at the serious tone in Stephen's voice as he asked without breaking a smile. "Stephen, they aren't that bad." Stephen gave me a look as if he was dumbfounded. "Are you fucking serious, kid?

You need to take your beer goggles off, son. If that is what you consider a primo piece of ass then do us both a favor and don't do me any favors, you dig?" I laughed once more although Stephen didn't find the amusement in it. "Stephen, they aren't that bad, you have to trust me. Besides, you can't see them with the lighting in this place." Stephen reached down into his pocket, I expected him to pull out another five but instead he pulled out a napkin. He opened the napkin and showed me a name and phone number in woman's handwriting. "Yeah, I'm doing fine, Tristan. You say you were wanting to help me out, well, what happened at the bar with the hot little piece of ass?" I went to answer him after I finished my last drink but he didn't allow it. "You fucked it all up, didn't you?" as he reached down in his pocket to put the napkin back in, he pulled out another five dollar bill. "I guess I shouldn't send a kid to do a man's job." There was a part of me that didn't want to say anything, let him go up to the bar and let him make an ass of himself. That could possibly be what we needed to get the night back on track. However, I felt as if I needed to defend myself. "Stephen, she seemed flattered, I had you halfway home. She just doesn't get off till close, she said maybe next weekend." Stephen reached his hand out towards me "Okay, well give me her number." Stephen knew I didn't have her number as he waited patiently for me to hand it over. "You didn't get the number?" Stephen looked at me as if he was amazed by the missed opportunity. "No, she was busy waiting on other people, it's pretty crowded up there, I was happy just to be able to talk to her as long as I did." Stephen started to turn to the bar. "Here, just stand back and watch the man work his magic." Stephen walked away, his strut oozing confidence which attracted everyone's attention.

As Stephen made his way effortlessly through the crowd, I followed. As we approached the bar, the barmaid turned and gave him a big smile before making her way over to him, ignoring others that had been there longer. This didn't go unnoticed as many gave Stephen a dirty look, Stephen didn't care. Stephen put his hand up on her shoulder and pulled her near as he leaned over and talked in her ear for a few moments. She shook her head, began to blush, and followed it with the cutest of giggles. She attempted meagerly to pull away, only to be pulled back in, which was all part of the game. She once more laughed and then walked over to the bar. After grabbing a piece of paper, and scribbling on it, she went to the cooler and grabbed us a couple of beers. All the while, Stephen continued to lean on the bar top, staring attentively at her ass which she was completely aware of. As she began to make her way back over to us, Stephen looked at me and raised his eyebrows a few times before he winked. After a few more things were said between the two of them, she placed her hand with the piece of paper into his. She withdrew her hand slowly, smiled and walked away, Stephen watched her as she made her way to the next customer and then motioned for me to follow him as he walked away with our beers in hand.

Once we were away from the crowd, Stephen handed me my beer and gave me a smile. "Did you see how the Sensei works?" His confidence was growing by the second. "Yes, I observed. So what all did she have to say?" I entertained his question since the chemistry couldn't be overlooked. "You see, it's all about how you deliver the goods, my boy. She gave me that lame ass excuse about having to get home to her baby. I explained to her that the baby would be fast asleep and wouldn't be missing her until the next morning, I also assured her that I would set the alarm early enough for her to make it home. I then closed the deal by telling her that I was from out of town and wasn't for sure if I would be back next week. So if she wanted to hook up tonight, it would be the perfect night to do so and it would be our little secret." Stephen took a big swallow and continued. "I can promise you that she'll be meeting up with us later." Although it was borderline arrogance, I liked Stephens's confidence. It was a sight to be seen in this area. "Do you think?" I took a drink to avoid Stephen from being able to see my smile. Stephen shook his head, reached deep into his pocket and pulled out a piece of paper with a phone number on it. "Yes, I do think." Stephen forced the paper back down into his pocket, took another drink of beer, and made his way to the dance floor.

Stephen and I observed the dance floor that continued to fill as we finished our beers. The selection of women was improving considerably. However, when it came down to getting another beer, Stephen motioned for us to head out. It was all part of a game with the barmaid. He didn't want to show too much interest. Well played, I thought. We made our way to the door. There were a lot of women paying as much attention to us as we were towards them as we walked out. Stephen led the way, each step with more swagger than the previous. As we headed to Parkinson's, little was said as we both chose to listen to music rather than converse. I was getting quite drunk and knew that this would probably be our last stop for the night. If everything went well, we would get in, have a drink, grab some women, get out and take them back to Dick and Jeanine's. As we pulled in, I had little doubt that we would have success, the lot was filling up quickly. Stephen navigated us through the lot to try and find a parking space. Once we were parked, Stephen disposed of his gum and pulled out some new. He handed me a couple of pieces, turned off the music and without saying a word, got out of the car and stretched as he waited for me to join him. I got out and surveyed the situation. Parkinson's was like night and day in comparison to Truman's. Truman's attracted the younger crowd, the twenty-something to the mid-twenties while Parkinson's attracted a crowd between their mid-twenties to mid to late forties. Most of the women we saw walking towards the club looked to be in the late twenty to early thirties range which brought an ornery smile to Stephen's face. "Tristan, I can tell you before we even walk into the club that this is much more to my liking than the other dive! We should have no problem picking up some primo babes here. If we meet anyone while we are together, let me do the talking. If by chance we separate and one of us hooks up, we make sure they have a friend. Oh, and by the way, no fat skanks and no married women, understand?" Stephen was setting up the night in a way that assured me that he had done this a million times before. "That works for me," I said slowly to avoid a struggle and possible expose the state I was in. Stephen gave me a smile. "Alright my boy, let's go and get laid!" Stephen moved ahead of me and walked us to the door; he held the door open to allow a couple women in ahead of us. They all shared smiles with one another. As they passed, Stephen gave me a smile and arched his eyebrows.

Parkinson's wasn't just different with the crowd it attracted; it was a whole different format. Parkinson's was a true nightclub. When you walked in, there was a bouncer that seemed to share the same attitude as the bouncer at Truman's awaiting you. However, behind his darkened glasses there was no threat: we knew, he knew it, everyone knew it. He was nothing more than an overpaid host. Once we made our way past the bouncer the floor was wide open; there were a few tables and chairs on either side of the dance floor. A full size bar was to the right that attracted as many patrons as the dance floor did. There usually was one to two more bouncers that hung around the bar insuring that the bar stayed free of hassle; this also provided quick access to the dance floor in case of help being needed. Past the bar were some tables and chairs. The dance floor continued on towards the back and ended where the restrooms started, which were also on the right hand side. In the very back were a couple of pool tables that always seemed occupied by the boyfriends of the girls who were on the dance floor. For myself, this area was rarely visited. It seemed the further you went in the club the shadier the people became.

Stephen looked the club over once we got past the bouncer. All the optimism he had as we pulled into the lot had seemed to have faded as he looked at me and shook his head in disappointment. "What the fuck is this? Do you think there is enough bouncers in this place? Did you bring me to a hangout for felons?" Stephen's demeanor let me know that he was ready to leave before he finished his sentence. I knew there were opportunities if we just stayed. "It's not as bad as it seems, Stephen. Besides, we don't have to stay here very long, let's just get some honeys and we'll head out of here." Stephen refused to move forward as he looked the club over for a second time. "I tell you what, Tristan, stay the fuck away from the pool sharks in the back. Stay away from any skanks who have a wedding ring on or a nice tan line where the ring usually is. I swear to God if you get yourself in trouble you are on your own, understand?" I completely understood, I just couldn't believe what I had heard. I looked Stephen in the eyes, I wasn't sure whether this was the way they handled themselves in Cincinnati or if we just weren't tight enough for him to have my back. Either way, I knew that wasn't the way I played. "Yeah, I understand. I have your back if a problem arises, you on the other hand have no issue with turning your back on me." Stephen looked at me with a smirk. "It isn't that, Tristan, I didn't fucking come here to bloody my knuckles, I came here to get laid. You misunderstood." I still wasn't in agreement as I nodded my head and then surveyed the dance floor. "What do you want to drink?" Stephen asked to get us on a different topic. "Just get me a bottle of beer." Stephen headed to the bar, I continued to look around at the dance floor for potentials. Stephen came back and handed me my beer. "Do you see anything?" Stephen asked as he took a drink of his beer and nodded at a woman as she walked past. "There are plenty of women here; it's all about finding the right one." Stephen looked at me and sighed. "Jesus Christ, Tristan, you're not trying to marry them, you're just going to have some fun and forget about them. The criteria is simple: cute, no ring and no camel toe large enough to hold their cigarette as they drink. Oh, and by the way, no sores around the mouth!" Stephen gave me a smile, winked and then tapped the neck of my bottle with his as he walked onto the dance floor and made his way in between a couple of women that were dancing together; he gave me once last smile before he turned his attention to the prettier one of the two. It seemed as if Stephen has dropped his guard rather quickly. I kept an eye on him for a moment to make sure no jealous boyfriends or husbands were making their way towards him. By the time the song came to an end, my attention had shifted to surveying the area for myself.

I ended up walking the perimeter of the dance club. As I started to make my way around for the second time, Stephen caught a glimpse of me, he motioned for me to grab him a beer as he held his empty up high and began to shake it back and forth. I headed up to the bar, grabbed a couple beers and headed back over, he nodded with his head to come join him and then nodded towards the other woman as if she was some sort of sacrificial offering. I shook my head as a friendly refusal as I made my way through the people on the dance floor and headed over to him with his beer. Stephen took the beer and motioned for me to come closer; he leaned in and began to say something in my ear. There was no way to hear what he was saying over the music. I shook my head to let him know I was clueless on what he had just said. He seemed aggravated as he leaned over once more and tried to be a bit louder and yet not so loud that anyone else could hear him. Once more I had no clue what he was saying. At this time, he shook his head in disbelief and turned his attention back to the woman he was dancing with. I took one last look at the woman he was offering, who at this time was now looking at me with an inviting smile. I turned to look for the easiest way to get through the crowd and off the dance floor before I was committed to entertain.

I made my way down through the far end of the floor, heading towards the area in which Stephen feared the most. En route, I found several women that caught my attention. However, there was one that really seemed to pull me in. She stood alone, standing off the side of the floor looking as if she was waiting for someone to ask her for a dance. I stepped away from the rest of the crowd in an effort to stand out and then observed her for a while to make sure that there was no boyfriend. I looked on the ring finger and saw nothing. She was exceptionally good looking, tall, tan with long dark hair. She looked as if she was in her mid to late twenties. Her body was nice and tight. There was no reason for her to be standing alone. She looked over my way and we caught one another's eyes. It was nothing more than a glance as we both turned our attention back to the dance floor and the game of cat and mouse began. I waited for a moment and turned back towards her. She had a smile on her face as she brought her beer to her mouth. She was aware that I was watching her. Once she took her drink she began to move her hips and dance in place; she looked over and we once more made eye contact. She gave me a smile and then turned back towards the floor. I gave it a minute and then took a drink and headed over, just like she knew I would.

I slowly walked up to her and stood beside her, she continued to look forward, the smile on her face began to grow, in return exposing her hand. I took a drink. My concern that she was not alone caused me to take one last look around before I made my move. With no one approaching, I leaned in. "How are you doing tonight?" She took a drink and leaned in close to my ear. "I'm fine, how are you doing?" Once again the music was so loud that I could barely make out what she was saying, after trying to piece together what it was I tried to answer appropriately, "I'm not too bad, it's quite a night here. Are you from around this area?" she looked at me with a clueless look. "What is that?" she answered in a scream as she was unable to hear anything I had just said. I attempted to keep the conversation a bit shorter just to get us acquainted. "It's quite a night here." She looked at me and smiled. "Yes, not too bad." This wasn't a good place to try and pick up a woman with casual conversation, I put my arm around her shoulder and with my beer hand motioned towards the dance floor. She smiled and walked ahead.

I am not much of a dancer. When I do dance, I prefer something slow. However, slow songs were not an option at this club unless it was closing time. This club was all about the dance music that was popular at the time. We made our way out to a corner of the dance floor which turned out convenient, since we wouldn't have to worry about interruption and began to dance. I had strategically walked slow enough time to ensure that when we finally began to dance the song was nearing its end. Once the song finished, I leaned in to ask her if she would like to go and sit down and talk over a beer. Unfortunately, she continued to dance as a song came on that she seemed to like. We made our way through another song; I was really liking the way she worked her hips. I could tell that she enjoyed to dance and I was drunk enough not to care anymore, so we continued. Once we finished a third song, I was out of beer. I quickly leaned into her before the next song began and asked her if she would care for a beer, she smiled and nodded her head. I told her I would be right back right. About this time, the music started to play, I wasn't sure if she had heard me so I put my finger up to let her know to give me a minute and walked away.

I made my way to the bar quickly. Someone of her looks and how she was moving her hips wouldn't be alone for very long; I needed to get back over to her. I realized while I waited for the barmaid to make her way over to me that Stephen would be ready for another. Since he had taken care of me most the night. It would only be right to return the favor again. I looked out onto the floor to try and locate him but I had no luck. I looked around for a little longer and couldn't find him or the woman he was dancing with. I looked the area over around the bar and towards the door where the tables were, still no luck. By this time the barmaid had made her way over. I ordered a couple of beers and then turned my attention to the dance floor where the woman I danced with was at. There were two guys standing in front of her talking. My window to get back over there was shortening. The barmaid put both beers on the bar top which caught my attention. I put a five dollar bill on the table and walked off without getting any change. I made my way back through the crowd. I could see the two guys struggling to talk to her as I did earlier, although they were all laughing. As I neared, she looked over and saw me coming and gave me a smile. I extended my hand with her beer which she gladly accepted as the two men took notice. They were somewhat reluctant to accept their invitation to move on as they looked me up and down, sizing me up. Then with a nod, they looked over to her, tipped their bottle of beer towards her, and slowly walked away. I put my hand on the base of her back and motioned us towards the tables.

We walked past the first row of tables that were taken and went further towards the back where it wasn't so loud and we would have the opportunity to converse. Unfortunately, the further back we went, the darker it was and the closer we found ourselves to the pool table area. I knew if Stephen was looking for me, it would be a struggle. We grabbed a seat and pulled our chairs tight towards one another. We looked, shared a smile as we both took a drink and waited for the song that was playing to end so we could talk. As the song came to an end we both turned to talk at the same time. I pulled back and allowed her to start. "I want to thank you for the beer." She said with a smile. I tapped the neck of her beer with mine and took a long drink. "Don't mention it." She was already starting to speak as I finished. "I also want to thank you for asking me to dance. What made you to decide to do that?" I knew right then that she was interested. "It's not a question what made me decide to come over and ask you to dance, it is a better question on why exactly no one else had approached you?" She gave me a big smile and then spoke up louder as a new song came on "Well actually, those guys that you may or may not have chased off were coming up to ask me to dance." I returned her smile "Well I'm glad you chose not to and I am glad to have obliged." She winked at me as she slurred, "Well, I've been known to be a bit picky with my men. Not to mention, they didn't offer me a drink. I was getting thirsty!" She was clever and was getting drunk. I realized that I was in there. Now it was all about the timing on when I could get her comfortable enough to leave with me and if I could find Stephen. I tried to buy some time. "If you don't mind, I am going to go grab me another beer and hit the restroom. Can I grab you a beer as well?" She gave me a smile as I started to stand up and motioned for me to bend towards her. I obliged. "I don't even know your name," she said with a devilish grin on her face. The grin caused me to contemplate whether or not I should give her my actual name, "Forgive me, my name is Tristan." She reached her hand out to shake "My name is Tammy." I knew right then that she had entertained the same thought and chose not to share her actual name. I took her hand and held it softly "Tammy, it is a pleasure. Can I buy you that drink." She nodded her head in agreement as she took a drink of her beer and turned her attention to the dance floor to giving me the opportunity to leave. I disposed of my beer and then headed to the restroom. I was beyond the point where I didn't need any more beer. However, I needed the opportunity to survey the club once more and try to find Stephen. Although he had assured me that he didn't have my back, I was getting concerned that he may have been dragged outside and needed my help.

Once I stumbled out of the bathroom, I made my way to the bar and surveyed the area as I waited for the barmaid. There was still no sight of Stephen, nor the woman he had been with. Upon the barmaid's arrival, I placed my order and then continued to look around, still nothing. I took a glance at the table in which Tammy was sitting, only able to see her silhouette. I turned my attention back towards the barmaid who was now placing my beers onto the bar. I once again gave her a five, this time she took it for granted that the rest was hers and dropped it into her tip jar. I stood there for a moment and contemplated going outside to look for Stephen. I looked over at Tammy who sat there waiting. There was the uncertainty with the window of opportunity I had with her that I needed to contemplate if I took any more time away from us to go look for him. The more I thought about it, the more I could hear him forewarning me not to get myself in any kind of trouble because he wouldn't have my back. After letting that echo in my head a couple of times I found it much easier to make my way back over to Tammy. It looked as if Tammy had rummaged through her purse in an attempt to freshen herself up before I made my way back. I handed her a beer, sat down beside her and took a moment to inhale the perfume she had recently sprayed, and admire the freshly painted lips. I pulled my chair closer to hers, I brushed my leg against her prior to returning my leg and settling in, she didn't pull away. Instead, the two of us became content sitting there, listening to the music and staring into one another's drunken eyes in between our drinks.

I was unaware of the time, unaware of my surroundings. My attention was totally towards Tammy. I was wanting to lean over and kiss her; she seemed eager for me to do so. I was slowly making my way towards her when she turned her attention to someone walking towards us. I didn't have to look up to know who it was. I could see Stephen through the corner of my eyes as he clumsily pulled the vacant chair from the table and threw himself down in it. I continued to look at Tammy but she was transfixed with the man unbeknownst to her that had just sat down. I looked over at Stephen. He didn't look as if he had been in any fights or anything. He just looked like he was drunk. I tried to figure a way to gesture for him to get out without saying anything. If the eyes can speak a story, mine spoke an epic novel. However, Stephen played dumb rather well as he smiled at us both. "Man, where the hell have you been?" Stephen tried to turn the tables as if I was the one that had gone missing. "I've been here all along, what about you?" Stephen leaned back in his chair, folded his arms on his gut as he attempted to keep his eyes open. "I've just been dancing." Stephen smiled at me in a way that let me know that there was much more than dancing that he had done. Stephen's eyes that had been struggling to stay open all of a sudden opened wide; he looked over my shoulder and then back at me. "So are you ready to head out?" he asked in a rather sober manner. I looked at him, still trying to get him away from Tammy and me. He looked over my shoulder and then back into my eyes. "Actually, I was just getting to know Tammy a little bit here. Do you want a beer?" Stephen looked at Tammy and forced a smile that was somewhat cold in her direction and then turned towards me. "No, I'm actually pretty drunk and have to be at work in the morning, I am ready to call it quits for the night." I looked at him for a moment with disgust and then turned my attention back to Tammy with a smile. I was hoping that eventually he would get the hint and leave the table. I at least wanted to get her phone number if I wasn't going to get anything else. Stephen just sat there. He began to tap on the table with his hands in rhythm to the beat of the music. It was as if he was purposely trying to be annoying. I went to speak to Tammy but she was focused on Stephen and his antics. I attempted to lean in and ask her if she wanted to go out and dance. She just looked at me and smiled. "I think your friend wants to go." She looked sympathetic about the situation. I nodded my head; I wasn't going to be able to get her to enjoy herself when she looked at it in a way that her enjoyment would result in his misery. I nodded my head in defeat. "You are absolutely right, if it wasn't getting so late, I would drop his ass off and come back. Maybe next time." She smiled and then looked over at Stephen and smiled. "Yes, there is always next time." Stephen perked up as he sensed that we would be leaving soon. I looked over at Stephen and gave him a glare. Then stood up and drank the rest of my beer. As I put my beer down, Tammy slid a napkin over to me. I picked it up, chose not to look at it prior to placing it in my pocket. I gave her a smile, leaned over and told her how nice it was to have had the chance to meet her. She returned the smile and nodded. Stephen was now standing, his chair was pushed in and was ready to walk away.

We walked away, I never looked back. I knew as we left that the odds of me seeing her again were low, probably as low as the odds of me actually calling her. We never said a word as we fought our way through the dance floor and towards the exit. I walked quickly, leaving Stephen behind. Once we were outside and away from the music Stephen picked up his pace and cleared his throat. "Hey, you can thank me later." I stopped in my tracks, I wasn't sure if that was a comment to actually get under my skin or if he actually meant it. I gave him a glare and then turned and headed towards the car. "What was that all about?" he asked as if he was actually clueless on why I would be upset. I couldn't believe him, I stopped again and turned towards him. "Are you fucking serious? I mean, really?" Stephen's mouth dropped as I lashed out at him, he looked as if it was unjustified. "You have no clue, do you?" Stephen retorted in a defensive tone. I turned and continued towards the car. Once I got to the car and to the driver's door I looked over at Stephen who was now at the passenger's door with his arms draped onto the roof, awaiting for me to unlock his door. "I have no clue, enlighten me!" I finally answered the question that I had almost forgotten that he had even asked. I was now to the point of wanting to climb over the car and go after him and for a moment, I looked him over and considered it. "Did you not notice the way I kept looking over your shoulder and back at you while you were sitting there next to that skank?" he continued. I had remembered, but chose to stand there and wait for him to continue uninterrupted. "You had two guys in the pool table area, talking back and forth, staring at you, sizing you up. If we would have stayed there any longer, you would have gotten your ass beat." I was certain that Stephen was too drunk to actually know what he was talking about. "Stephen, the pool table area was poorly lit, you said it yourself when we entered the bar and looked around. They could have been staring at anyone, they could have been looking past us and onto the dance floor for all you know. I had been dancing with Tammy, we had been sitting at the table before you came and was getting to know each other. You actually think that two guys who could have taken me out numerous times when I was alone with her were now contemplating beating my ass now that you were sitting at the table?" Whether or not there was anyone actually sizing me up I wasn't certain but I definitely had a point and Stephen knew it as he looked down at the ground. "I know what I saw, Tristan. Besides, she was a skank; there is no reason for you to get your ass beat over some skank." I looked at him, and shook my head in disbelief. I looked back at the club, contemplated heading back in to rejoin Tammy, but instead, got in the car.

There was no reason for me to even think about driving in the condition I was in. There were usually a couple of the city's finest hidden between the parked cars. However, it was still a little too early for them to be there. They would arrive closer to last call to ensure that they would be able to bust at least one or two drunk drivers. I turned on the car for a moment and tried to collect my senses. We were still supposed to head over to another hotspot, this one in Newark and closer to Dick and Jeanine's. However, I was ready to call it a night and as I sat there with the car on contemplating everything that had just went down, Stephen broke the silence. "Hey, I saw what I saw. I was looking after you, nothing more, and nothing less. Listen, I am feeling pretty good, let's stop through a drive-thru, grab something to eat, I'll buy and just call it a night?" I looked over at Stephen and just stared. He smiled and arched his eyebrows at me. I drove across the street to the nearest drive-thru and we ordered a bunch of food which we couldn't possibly eat. Stephen turned his music on and sat there nodding his head to the rhythm. Once we got our food, he tore through the bag until he had everything he ordered. He shoved a fry in his mouth, smiled at me and handed me the bag. As I drove up to the exit a cop drove by us. "Are you sure you are okay to drive?" Stephen asked as if he cared but it wasn't as if there was an alternative, Stephen sure in the hell wasn't going to drive. "I'll be fine, I have done this a million times before." Stephen looked at me with another french fry hanging out of his mouth. "This city seems small, can't be more than a couple cops out on the streets, why don't you follow that one if you can without taking us too far out of the way. I would rather have them in front of us than in back, ya know?" Stephen made sense for as drunk as he was, so I pulled out and followed the cop. I stayed far enough back to allow a little room for error.

We followed the cop for a mile or two before they turned towards another bar. I continued on while Stephen focused on eating. I could tell by the smile on his face that he had a great time. As far as I knew, the barmaid from Truman's was a no-show but then again we had left a little early. She was probably still at work. Nonetheless, I was curious on why Stephen was smiling so much and what had actually happened to him when he had disappeared. "So tell me Stephen, did you have a good time?" Stephen washed down his bite with some soda and looked over at me with a wink. "It wasn't bad; I've had worse nights." It was obvious that Stephen was hoping for me to prod him for more information, so I decided to entertain. "Well, I went to the bar to grab us a beer and it seemed as if you had vanished. I looked everywhere but to no avail. What happened?" Stephen finished off his sandwich. I looked over to see what was taking him so long to respond and found him smiling as he arched his eyebrows. He slid his straw between the corner of his lips and took a big drink to help wash down his food. Stephen began with a naughty giggle. "Well, you see, my boy, that skank I was dancing with, she was all about me. I stayed there for a moment but was losing interest fast, I was just wanting to get the old wiener wet. She was talking about maybe hanging out some time and I told her we were hanging out now. Rule of thumb, you have to keep them in check. A skank is a skank. I asked her if she drove here but she had hitched a ride with her friend. It didn't take me long to talk her into getting her girlfriend's keys. We went out to her car, climbed into the back seat, and the rest is history my friend!" I looked over at him as he turned his attention straight ahead and took another sip of his drink. "Are you fucking serious?" I was uncertain if I was more appalled that he might be trying to fill me full of shit or that he got a piece of ass and then kept me from doing the same. Stephen finished his soda and then gave me a lazy, drunken look as he shook the ice violently around in the cup. "What do you think? Hold on, if you don't believe me. Let me check my fingers, there still maybe a little rot remaining." Stephen took his right hand and held it to his nose, he looked at me with a smile on his face and crossed eyes and extended his hand towards me. "Ah, she lingers on, smell this!" I turned my head away from his hand. "I'm not smelling nothing." Stephen pulled his hand back, smelled it once more and then put his hand down. "Suit yourself, I have no reason to lie. You see, I was planning on burying the boy in that hair pie until he was ready to spit, but she filled the back seat up with so much stink, that I began to have second thoughts. So instead, I decided to cut the losses but figured I owed her something, so I ended up letting her drink from the nozzle. Oh, by the way, I will give credit where credit is due, she swallowed like a champ!" Stephen finished his story with a hearty laugh and then turned the music up louder and started to tap his leg in rhythm to the song.

I drove the next couple of miles letting everything he said resonate. I found myself shaking my head in disbelief. We were closing in on Dick and Jeanine's and my frustration was building. I waited a little while longer and then turned the volume down "So you are telling me you were sucked dry by that fat skank in the bar, then came back in, found me and then cock blocked my ass on a woman that at least was worth looking at?" Stephen looked at me with a disgusted look on his face "Are you fucking serious? How drunk are you, Tristan? I thought that chick was a dude when I walked up. What did you find so attractive about her? Was it her mustache? Her unibrow? Was it the Adam's apple that was bigger than mine? Seriously, even with the poor lighting it wasn't hard to pick up on her five o'clock shadow!" Stephen knew that his woman didn't even hold a candle to mine. "I think it was the clubfoot actually that turned me on; it made her moves on the dance floor much more inviting!" Stephen looked at me and smiled. "Nice call on the clubfoot, if I would have known that, we would have both tagged her ass!" I looked over at him and shook my head. "Well, I don't see us getting together anytime soon, I guess as long as you had a good night that is all that matters." Stephen looked at me as if he was appalled. "Are you fucking serious, Tristan? If that is your best attempt at a guilt trip you might have to work a little harder at it. One of these days, you'll thank me, I promise." I knew that if we kept on we would end up in another argument. With being moments away from Dick and Jeanine's, I turned the music back up and kept quiet.

I pulled into their driveway and noticed that all the lights were out. I was surprised that someone hadn't stayed up to wait on his return. Stephen looked at me for moment; I chose to look straight ahead. "You are coming in to stay, right?" Stephen slurred as he turned down his music and ejected the tape. I contemplated for a moment; it was getting late enough that the only people that would be out at this hour would be cops, cabs and other drunks. With being as drunk as I was, I hated to continue to try my luck by driving home. However, once I thought about waking up and hearing Dick or worse yet having to interact with him while on a hangover, I realized that driving home was the only logical thing to do. "I think I'll just head home, I'm alright," I said as I looked over to see Stephen who began shaking his head in disbelief. "You aren't fucking serious? Just come on, turn the car off and come in. You can sleep downstairs where I sleep. Hell, if nothing else you can come down there, eat and hang out until you sober up and then leave." Staying the night was out of the question but actually going in and hanging out till I sobered up wasn't a bad idea. I looked at him for a moment. I could see he was getting impatient. "Listen, I got to piss, just shut off the car and come on." Stephen turned his back to me, got out, and began to piss in the driveway." I went ahead and shut off the car. "I'll stick around, eat my food, sober up and then go." Stephen looked over his shoulder at me and smiled as he rolled his eyes in the back of his head and moaned in ecstasy as he continued to piss. "Now that right there, that is what I am talking about! Holy shit, I kept that in there way too long." I walked around the front of the car and waited on him to finish, as he zipped up, he once again smelled his hand. With a grave look on his face, Stephen slurred in a concerned tone. "Holy shit, this stench is manifesting into something larger than life! I'm not sure whether to go and try and wash my hand or just cut my losses and chop the hand completely off!" I couldn't help but laugh. Stephen never smiled, never broke character. We made our way inside.

92

Stephen turned on the light, tripped over a chair and then looked back at me and whispered for me to be quiet. We wandered through a hallway and over to the basement door. Stephen led the way down.

Once we got downstairs he turned on the light to illuminate a long winding room that was carpeted with the store's finest Berber. To the right of the stairs was the laundry room, and the current storage area for all the boxes from their recent move that was piled up. To the left was a couple recliners, a large sectional couch and a coffee table. A large stereo system, a partially filled bookcase and television were at the end of the room. The room had everything one would need to live comfortably which led me to believe that Stephen would be staying longer than anyone at the shop had anticipated, including Stephen. Stephen looked at me with a big smile and nodded with satisfaction as he kicked off both of his shoes, letting them land where they may and threw himself down on the coach. "Take a seat there, Tristan, just make sure you take off your shoes before you kick up your feet. I looked around at the room a final time, and sat down. Stephen looked over at me as I took my first bite of food and said as he yawned. "Not bad for a basement, eh? You are liking what you see, aren't you? I am telling you something, add a refrigerator and I could fucking live down her. It pretty much has all the necessities. Now, if only there was a door. Then we could scurry off the skanks in the morning to avoid possible humiliation." Stephen turned his attention to the television as he turned it on. This was followed by a long, loud yawn. I said nothing as I continued to eat.

As Stephen's eyes began to close, his head started to lower. Once startled, he looked over at me with a smile and newfound life in his eyes. "I'll tell you what, Tristan, tonight wasn't that bad. However, you haven't seen anything yet, that I can assure you!" His smile turned to a devilish grin. I finished my sandwich and waited for him to continue. Instead, he turned his attention back to the television so I decided to coax him a bit. "Haven't seen anything yet, eh? Why would that be?" Stephen had already forgotten that he had said something. He began to yawn once more "What's that? Oh yeah, you haven't seen anything yet. Next weekend my boys will be coming up and that is when you will see how the big boys do it, if you know what I am saying!" By the time Stephen finished his rant about his Cincinnati crew I was already well into my second sandwich. Stephen looked over at me for a few seconds and then turned his attention back to the television. I continued to feed my drunk until the sandwich was gone, then I looked over at Stephen. "So tell me about your boys from Cincinnati." Stephen was now laying down, staring at the television with a blank stare. "Stephen, tell me about your boys." Stephen still didn't answer. This time I could hear him starting to snore softly. I eased back the recliner, kicked my feet up and continued to eat. I looked around the room as I sat there and checked everything out. Once I finished my food I took a minute to see how I felt. I was still buzzing bad, too bad to try and drive home. I decided to stay for a little while longer, watch some more television with the hopes of sobering up.

I was soon awakened by some muffled noises from upstairs. Dick and Jeanine were up. It was morning. As I opened my eyes, there was Stephen standing over me shaking his head. "Wake up, Gorgeous, it's time to hit the road." Stephen walked back over to the couch and began to put on his shoes. "Obviously, you passed out." Stephen gave me a smile as he looked over. "I went to rest my eyes for a minute, thought it might help and that was it." Stephen shook his head. "You, son, are a lightweight! We'll have to work on that, now won't we?" I gave him a smile as I stood up and started to stretch. "Hey, junior, you parked where no one can get out of the garage. You might have to take that stretching and what not elsewhere. I need to be getting to the shop. Dick is also about to leave and isn't in the best of moods." I didn't want to have to deal with Dick on my day off so I got up, grabbed my stuff and looked around for the exit that eluded me. "Are you looking for the door? Jesus Christ, you really were fucked up last night, weren't you?" I looked over and gave him a smile. "C'mon, the stairs are off to the side, behind you." Steve passed me with a smirk and headed up the steps; I followed him. We made it up the stairs without any issues. There was no sign of Dick or Jeanine so I headed out the door. "I'll give you a call later, who knows, maybe tonight we'll go out to Truman's and see what is going on with my little honey." I walked on without comment to my car, as I turned around to get in, I noticed that Stephen was still standing halfway out the door awaiting confirmation. I shook my head in acknowledgement, got in the car and drove off.

I was fortunate enough when I got home to find the house empty. My mother must have had work and was already gone. I went to the kitchen, took Tammy's number out of my pocket and posted it on the side of the refrigerator to avoid losing it. If last night was a sign of things to come, the refrigerator would soon be full of numbers. I made my way back into the front room and laid down, still tired and hungover. I reflected on the night that was. I wasn't sure if I was wanting to go back out with Stephen tonight or not. If I decided to, I wanted to be rested. I don't know how much time had passed when I had awakened. The opening and closing of the front door had brought me out of my slumber. As I looked up I found my mother staring at me from the doorway. "Aren't you supposed to be at work?" Before I could answer, she continued. "Where were you all night?" she asked while still standing at the door. "They gave me the day off today." The answer didn't seem to appease her curiosity. "Well that is obvious, Tristan, you didn't think about calling to let me know you weren't coming home?" She looked at me with disgust, then headed to the kitchen. "I didn't think I would be out all night; it just happened. I was hanging out and just fell asleep." I got up and followed her. "You went out drinking all night? Let me guess, you were the one that got stuck driving everywhere while you were drunk?" She already knew the answer. I pleased her anyway. "I really wasn't out all night; besides I didn't drink that much. We went back to Stephen's house and hung out and that is where I fell asleep." My mother gave me a stare that assured that she didn't believe me. "You shouldn't have been drinking and driving. I tell you right now, if you ever get pulled over, you are on your own, you can rot in that cell. I won't be coming to get you!" She headed to the refrigerator and grabbed herself a beer. "I told you, I didn't drink that much." She took a long drink before she turned her attention back to me. "It smelled like alcohol as soon as I walked into the house, so don't be telling me that you didn't drink much." There was nothing more to say on my end; on her end it was a different story. "Go get a shower; I'll make some food. I hope you don't have plans to go back out again tonight." I wasn't sure until that moment whether or not I would be going out but after that confrontation I knew that any possibility of going out was now out of the question. My mother had put up with a lot, being out all night long drinking and driving wasn't something that she would continue to tolerate and I needed a place to live

I took a shower and while doing so, I tried to piece together some of last night's events that seemed to elude me. I don't remember how much time had passed but by the time I was finally able to come up with the highlights of the night, my mother was pounding on the door to bring me back to the present and let me know that I had been in there way too long. I stepped out of the shower and was able to leave it all behind me except the thought of Tammy. I didn't buy into Stephen's concerns with Tammy and because of this, I felt there was some unfinished business. I figured if nothing else, I could cancel plans with Stephen in front of my mother and then with her mind at ease go meet up with Tammy once my mother went to bed so we could finish what we started. I sat down with my mother, who was already well into her second beer. I refused her offer for a beer which actually pained me. However, if I had taken up her offer, I would have been stuck at the house for the night. As I ate, and she continued to drink, I glanced at the refrigerator where Tammy's number was posted. I got up from the table once I was finished and casually walked over to the refrigerator, grabbed the number then slowly made my way into the living room. My mother, who seem to be aware that something was going on, got up, grabber another beer and followed me.

The living room currently housed our only phone. With my mother sitting across from me, I had to wait for the right moment to make the call. I kicked up my legs and lay down and waited. The phone rang a couple of times, but it was never Stephen. The shop had been closed for quite a while; I was a bit surprised that Stephen had yet to call. I lay there and continued to wait. The afternoon progressed and was about to surrender to evening and yet, no call and no luck with my mother; she had obviously had a trying day, as the beers continued to flow. I looked at Tammy's number and then up at the time. The window to set my plan in motion was becoming smaller but it still existed. However, I was becoming inpatient. To avoid my mother recognizing this, I closed my eyes and waited. When I opened my eyes the front room light was on but my mother was nowhere to be seen. I looked up at the clock. As my eyes regained focus I noticed it was after ten. My mother was in bed; the night had passed me by. As far as I knew, there was no call from Stephen and no time left to call Tammy.

Chapter IX

Monday came, as did the anticipation to get settled in at work and await Stephen showing up. I headed back to the warehouse to get the day started when the door opened behind me and the familiar footsteps of Judith followed me back. "Well, well, well. How is Tristan this morning?" I knew by Judith's tone that Dick, Jeanine, Stephen or all three had filled her in on Stephen and my night out. "I'm fine, how was your weekend?" Judith gave me a big smile. "That's just what I was about to ask you!" My thoughts were confirmed. "Pretty uneventful, just another weekend." Judith gave me a smirk. "So, I heard that you and your new friend went out on Friday night, how did that go?" Judith leaned against a pile of carpet samples to prepare herself for what she hoped to be a fascinating story. "It wasn't really anything special, just a night out. It was fun getting to show him around the area. That's about it." Judith looked at me with a smile. "They said that the two of you were out so late that you had to stay over." I looked up at

Judith with a sigh. This was what I had expected and had hope to avoid. "Is that so? So what else did they tell you?" Judith was taken aback at my tone and direct approach. "Don't get upset; that is pretty much all they said. Stephen didn't even talk about it, Dick just said that you went out, Stephen showed you how the Cincinnati boys do the town and that you both ended up so drunk that you stayed at their house." I was relieved that Stephen had kept his mouth shut. "Yes, that is pretty much it." I decided not to add to the story that Judith had been told; this seemed to disappoint her. You could see that she wanted more, while I just wanted to let it die down. Judith looked up front, ensured that no one was entering the warehouse and then turned towards me. "Just be careful, Tristan. I don't trust any of them. You can never be too safe, you know? I just don't want to see you getting in any kind of trouble." I smiled at Judith whose facial expression actually showed concern. "I understand, I thank you. Trust me, I won't let them get me in any kind of trouble." Judith looked at me and smiled, then headed back up to the front.

It was later in the day when Stephen showed up. He walked into the warehouse with Dick beside him. They both grabbed a soda and stood near the entrance to Jeanine's office and talked for a moment. Dick ended up going into Jeanine's office and Stephen made his way back to the back. He stood there and watched me make a cut and then belched loud enough to get me to look over at him. "What's going on, Tristan?" I looked at him, then over to the jobs that were cut and then back to him. "Just getting caught up, are there any more cuts pending?" Stephen shook his head no and then went and leaned on the forklift. "What did you end up doing Saturday night? Did you hook up with that skank from the club we were at?" I looked up at Stephen who had his typical smirk on his face. "No, I didn't. How about you? Did you get into anything worth talking about? You said you were going to give me a call. I ended up calling it a night kind of early so I wasn't sure if maybe I missed your call or not." Stephen took a long drink of his soda. "Nah, you didn't miss my call. I decided to go in solo Saturday night. I headed out to Truman's to see if I could get my peter wet with that little barkeep." Stephen's conversation came out too casual to believe him if he did say that he had hooked up. "Well, what happened?" Stephen took another drink, looked up to the front to make sure it was okay to talk and then turned his attention back towards me. "She was there, she jumped my ass about not meeting up with her on Friday night. She said that she went over to Parkinson's and I wasn't there. She was giving me all kinds of grief, too much for someone I don't even know. Now imagine how that would be if I was to get a piece of that ass? I ended up drinking a beer and then got up to leave. However, on my way out I started bullshitting with one of the waitresses. She wants me to come see her tonight." Stephen gave me a smile and arched his eyebrows. "So, are you going to try and get out there tonight and maybe hook up with the waitress?" Stephen looked at me as if I had broken the first law of being a man. "Are you fucking serious? I'll make her wait and maybe go see her later in the week. Then again, maybe not at all. Besides, there are tons of skanks like that out there. I'll keep her in mind in case one of the primo honeys fall through." Stephen's confidence continued to grow with each word that came out of his mouth. "I see." Stephen finished his soda, belched and then looked at me. "Tristan, I think it's time you hang out with the big boys." Stephen gave me a wink. "The boys from Cincinnati are coming up to hang out for the weekend. We are going to turn this town and all the pussy that you could ever imagine inside out!" Stephen looked at me and once again, arched his eyebrows. I could tell that Stephen was waiting for me to inquire about these so called "boys." Unbeknownst to him, he had already alluded to their arrival last Friday night prior to his passing out. I decided to oblige anyways. "You don't say? Who are you talking about?" Stephen gave me a smirk. "Just the baddest motherfuckers in the Queen City, that is all! Tristan, these boys are fucking insane! My best friend Robert and our buddies Hal and Sal. Trust me. They are the epitome of cool. Just ask my brother, he'll tell you!" Stephen was gleaming with the pride he held for his friends. "It sounds great, are you sure you want me to come along?" Stephen just looked at me blankly? "I mean, if they are coming in town to hang out, I don't want to impose." Stephen's expression turned sour. "Tristan, just shut the fuck up already! My boys are coming in on Wednesday to help out the rest of the week and then we are all going out this Friday. It is going to be epic and you are going to have pussy coming out of your ears! Do you dig?" Stephen walked away slowly looking over his shoulder for me to acknowledge him. Once I nodded in agreement he continued on with his typical swagger.

I anticipated "the boys" presence for the next day and a half, if I ever had a moment in which I didn't think of their legendary status, I would be instantly refreshed with the conversations I overhead from the Messmers as they shared their memories. However, Wednesday and Thursday passed uneventfully. The momentous occasion began that Friday morning, when the store opened. I found Stephen in the warehouse already well into the day's agenda. I made my way back to the area; he gave me a quick glance and went back down to his cut. "What is going on, Tristan?" I looked down at the clipboard on the forklift and noticed that he was well into the second job of cuts. "I was just about to ask you the same thing. I figured you would be out with Dick helping with measurements. Is this going to be a slow day?" Stephen finished his cut and looked up. "Not at all, I just wanted to make sure you are all caught up so you can get out of here on time tonight." Stephen waited for me to inquire about the urgency to be done on time; I didn't. Stephen swaggered over towards me and as we faced one another gave me his best John Wayne impersonation. "I'll tell you what, pilgrim, tonight we're going to take over these streets here, and I finally have my backup on the way. So what do you think about that?" Stephen jabbed me playfully in the side with his elbow. "I hear you, are your buddies finally on their way in town?" Stephen's grin grew. "They should be arriving by afternoon; they're going to be here for the whole weekend. I hope you are ready to have the time of your life!" With all the talk I had heard and the constant reminders, I couldn't help but be anxious to meet them. "Now listen, these guys know what they're doing, getting the honeys are their specialty. Just relax and follow their lead, okay?" Stephen had made their status so legendary I really didn't see any way for them to be able to live up to it. I nodded my head before Stephen went back to making cuts and motioned for me to join him. We kept busy to the point that we hadn't heard Dick walk into the warehouse till he made his way back to us. As Dick came to a stop, we looked up and he greeted us with a big smile "So the boys should be getting here any moment, huh?" Stephen stood up and gave him a proud smile. "Yes, anytime. I have been telling Tristan here that tonight is going to be a night he'll never forget!" Dick looked directly over at me as Stephen finished his sentence. "You are going to go out with the boys tonight? You sure he is ready for that, Stephen, you sure he is deserving?" Stephen gave me a glance and then turned his attention towards Dick. "Probably not, but we'll see." Dick busted out laughing. I could tell that Dick took satisfaction with any kind of comment that belittled me. "So when do you think they'll be here, you think they'll be up for lunch?" Stephen gave Dick a look as if he was shocked that Dick would even ask. "I'm sure they'll be here in time for lunch, which will give us all some time to catch up." Dick smiled and started to walk away. "I'll let you and Tristan keep working, I have one more appointment and then I'll be back. If they are here we'll head out." Stephen and I continued to work quickly until we were down to our last cuts. "Go ahead and finish, I'm going to go up and see if there is anything else we need to get done prior to them showing up."

Stephen went up front but didn't come back. I finished the cut and looked up at the clock. It was going on noon. I figured I would do a quick cleaning of the area before heading up to the office to see what was going on with Stephen and if any more cuts had been added.

As I walked up to the front, I could hear some laughter; it was Stephen. He had his hand on the doorknob and was starting to open the door. I backed away and awaited his entrance. When he opened the door he wasn't alone. "Here we are boys; this is where the magic happens!" Stephen walked out with three other guys, the Cincy boys had arrived. Once the door shut, Stephen walked them over to me. "Tristan, these are my boys I've been telling you about!" Stephen's tone was that of a proud father. "This is not only my frat brother but my brother in crime, Robert! These here are my boys from way back, Hal and Sleepy Sal. Gentleman, this is my pupil I was telling you all about, Tristan Wallace." Each one prepared to take their turns in leaning over and shaking my hand. Robert was the first to step forward. Robert's handshake was strong and represented him well. Upon first glance, Robert and Stephen could have easily been mistaken for one another, they were that physically similar. They were almost identical in size and build with Robert possibly being an inch taller and a few pounds heavier than Stephen. Robert had a ballcap pulled tight over some wiry, sandy blonde hair; his green eyes lost some of their intimidating quality behind his wire rim glasses that held thick lenses. A five o'clock shadow accentuated his rock solid jaw which brought out a tough guy quality. However, this almost gave way to the deep cleft in the middle of his chin, deeper than Stephen's, which gave him the similar all-American college boy look. As for the rest of his physical attributes, Roberts's shoulders were broad, his chest was big and his lower body looked as if he had never missed a leg day in the gym. Robert was definitely an alpha male. This brought instant intrigue on which one between Stephen and Robert would give way to the lead when we all went out.

The next to step forward was Hal. Hal paused the quick chewing of his gum as he introduced himself and shook my hand. Hal was about five foot ten; he had jet black hair that was cut and combed professionally without one hair out of place. His dark brown eyes looked almost black, which blended well with his hair. With the way he dressed, Hal looked as if he could have been a lawyer, and his choice of words and professional tone supported that perception. It was easy to see that Hal was well educated. Hal unlike Robert and Stephen was slender and taller than the other two. Yet with the contrasting style of the others he still had the qualities of an alpha male. There was something within the eyes of Hal that caused our introduction to be prolonged. Although the handshake was released prior to it becoming awkward, I continued to look into his eyes. Within those eyes there was an interest to know more, almost a need to know more. Within those eyes, there was a fascinating story to be told, whether it was a story enshrouded in darkness, struggle, perhaps perseverance and triumph, I was uncertain and so would anyone else be that would was fortunate to meet him. Although I wanted to learn more about Hal, I could see within that stare, within the greeting, the handshake, that any attempt would be futile.

As my observation of Hal continued, Sal stepped up last and casually shook hands. Sal was the only one out of the bunch that Stephen had to directly introduce. Sal was the direct opposite of all the other three; his handshake was soft, almost fragile. Sal was the same age as the others and yet his appearance made him look much older. Sal was the tallest of the four and to me, the most interesting in appearance. A little over six feet in height, Sal had a receding hairline; his pale face was shallow; his nose was large, bony, and caused his eyes to look almost sunk in. Eyes hazel in color that never completely opened, which gave him the appearance that he could fall asleep at any time. His lips were thin and his jaw was covered by a well-groomed beard. Sal's neck was long; his Adam's apple looked as if it was about to burst out of his throat. His shoulders were narrow, his torso thin to the point where he looked unhealthy. Sal was quiet; when he did talk, his voice was deep, yet soft. He didn't come across shy as much as he did conservative. Once we were all done with shaking hands, Stephen took the lead. "There you have it, Tristan, the boys who are going to own this town!" We all exchanged smiles and I was about to speak when the warehouse door opened and Dick came running in jumping on the back of Robert. Dick reached out and shook all their hands while giving them all an embrace. Dick had a look on his face as if he had just been reunited with friends that he hadn't seen in twenty years. They all shared pleasantries and then Dick invited them all to go with him to have lunch. They all turned and walked away except Stephen who waited until they were almost at the door and then turned towards me. "What do you think?" I was shocked that Stephen was looking at me for approval. "They seem like a really good bunch of guys!" Stephen gave me a smile. "They're the best. We're going to have a blast. Do me a favor and make sure you get everything done so you can be ready." Stephen patted me on the shoulder. I could tell that Stephen was really looking forward to the night out. I nodded and walked towards the back.

I was surprised when the door opened and I looked up to see Jeanine walking towards me. She smiled and waved as she approached. "Hey, Tristan, Judith just put together a couple of orders, so I thought I would bring them back and while doing so, see how you are doing?" Jeanine looked fabulous. I couldn't help but stand there for a moment and take all of her in. "I'm fine. How is everything with you?" She gave me a smile. "Not too bad. Have you had the opportunity to meet all of the boys?" I looked at Jeanine with a bit of trepidation. "Yes, I met them. They all seem like really nice guys. I'm just not sure if it is a good idea for me to go out with them tonight." Jeanine looked at me as if she was disappointed. "What are you talking about, Tristan?" Jeanine's tone came across as if my comment had insulted the Messmer name, so I looked for a way out. "These are his friends; he doesn't get to see them near as much as he would like; they all came from Cincinnati to see him; I just figured this would be a good opportunity for them to all go out. They don't need me tagging along to have fun." Jeanine looked perturbed. "Tristan, Stephen had a great time with you the other night; he has been talking about all of you hanging out. He has been looking forward to this. Trust me, if he didn't want you to be a part of the night's festivities he wouldn't have invited you." Jeanine was sincere. I smiled and took the order from her. "Alright, I just didn't want to intrude. I'm sure we'll have a good time." Jeanine gave me a big smile "Yes you will. I am about to leave for the day; I'll see you tonight. You might as well plan on staying the night. I imagine you'll be out most of the night and definitely won't be in any condition to drive home. Jeanine walked away and as the door shut I came to the realization that I had some work to do. Not just in the warehouse but at home as I had to try and come up with a way to convince my mother that I wouldn't be coming home tonight.

Dick and the boys came back much later than I expected. By the time they arrived I was finishing up the last of my work. Stephen and his crew came back and took a tour of the warehouse. As he brought them back through he stopped to talk to me. "It's looking good back here, rookie. What do you have left?" Stephen tried his best to look as if he was an integral part of the company. "Nothing, really. Cuts are all done and in order; warehouse is clean. We had a shipment of padding come in; I was just going to get a start on that before calling it a day." Stephen had an underlying agenda and it was about to come out. "Well, listen. Why don't you go ahead and get out of here? The boys and I need something to do before we head back to Dick's to get ready for tonight. Get going so you can be on time." Stephen gave me a wink and then led me towards the front while the others waited. Once we were far enough away from the rest so they couldn't hear, he looked over his shoulder to ensure no one was around and then spoke to me in a voice that was almost a whisper. "Listen, tonight is going to be a big night. The boys and I are going to show you how it is done. Go home and get ready but don't be getting all fucked up like last weekend, okay? I don't need you all sloppy drunk or acting like you are some kind of a bad ass. Can you do that for me?" Stephen had a serious look on his face. I had no intention of drinking before I left, especially since I was going to have to convince my mother that I was going to be out all night. I nodded my head and started to walk away. "Hey, Tristan, I'll call you when we are about ready, I'll have you a beer waiting over at Dicks for you when you get there," Stephen added. I nodded again and headed home.

The whole way home I tried to figure out a way in easing my mother's overactive mind so I could go out and she could rest easy. Best case scenario, I could get home, shower, change and slip out the door leaving her a note without her being there which would avoid confrontation. That hope was short lived once I saw her car as I was nearing the house. I walked in the gate quietly and entered. She was out in the kitchen. I avoided the kitchen and headed straight up stairs to grab some clothes and head to the shower. As I walked down the steps my mother called for me. I headed out to the kitchen and found my mother sitting at the table peeling potatoes. "I figured since I got home early I might as well make us something to eat." By the looks of things she planned on a feast for the two of us. There were pork chops on the stove, frozen vegetables thawing on the counter, the grater, and a head of cabbage was out for her to make cole slaw and of course the potatoes. "You didn't have to do that." She looked at me as if she was already aware of my plans and was trying to make it hard for me to even start a conversation on what I was hoping to do. "It's not a big deal. Now that you are working we just haven't had much time to sit down and eat a good meal." She stopped her peeling momentarily to take a drink of her beer. "Well, I was about to go get a shower; I worked hard today and stink." She looked up at the clock. "Well go ahead and take a shower. This won't be done till six or so; you should have plenty of time." I did have plenty of time as long as she was accurate with her time. I nodded my head and walked away.

I stood in the shower and tried to figure out a way to get out the door without an argument. By the time the shower was over, the aroma of the pork chops crept through the door. I finished up, shaved and headed out to the kitchen. Mom had the music playing, the empties on the table confirmed that she was on her fourth beer. She was finishing up the meal; she turned and was startled to see me standing there at the door watching her. "You scared me. Dinner will be ready in about fifteen minutes. Do you want a beer?" I looked up at the clock; I still had plenty of time. "No, I'm okay." My mother looked me up and down. "Well, if you want to, I could give you some money and you could go and get us a twelve pack if you want to drink when we are done eating." I looked at this comment as nothing more than a "feeling things out" kind of comment. "I don't know, we'll see." Mom turned her back to me and turned her attention to the food. "I see you shaved. I hope you aren't planning on going out all night and running the streets again?" The attempt to make me out to be one that is always running the streets was typical in her effort to keep me contained. "Mom, I don't go out all the time, as a matter of fact, I hardly go out at all. Stephen at work had all his friends come in from Cincinnati tonight to hang out. They asked me to come out with them, I wouldn't have to drive other than to get to their house and then they offered for me to stay the night so I didn't have to drive home later." She took a big drink of her beer. "I can't see why you just can't stay home one weekend." She put her beer down and lit a cigarette. "I haven't drank one beer yet tonight. The only thing you have to worry about is me getting to their house. If I'm not drinking any beer before I leave, you have nothing to worry about." She looked at me with a disgusted look as the cigarette smoke poured out from her nostrils. "Oh yeah, Tristan, I have nothing at all to worry about. Go ahead and do what you want, you always do anyways. Just don't be calling me up from jail." She turned her back and took another hit off of her cigarette. The conversation was over with; she wasn't happy. There was nothing I could say or do to improve the situation so I decided to go outside and sit on the porch. Time seem to elude me as I sat there and waited for dinner to get done. Eventually my mother poked her head out the door and said to come on in a disgusted tone.

I walked in the house and saw that she had brought all the food into the living room. She had done away with any plan for us to sit together and talk over a nice dinner at the table, instead she had numerous coffee tables set up around the couch. She sat down in the chair with the television on, a beer in hand and a lit cigarette on her stand next to the chair. She chose not to eat. I sat there and picked at my food, the food was great but the guilt trip she deliberately planned was working to perfection and I was no longer hungry. I looked over at her numerous times but she never returned the stare. "You aren't going to eat anything?" I asked to break the silence. "No, I can eat later, it's not like it really matters when I eat." She took a drink of her beer and kept her attention turned towards the television. I looked for something to say but couldn't find it. I sat there and waited for her to say something. As I sat there, the phone rang. Before it could ring for a second time, she looked over at me with a disgusted look. "You might want to grab that; I am sure it's your buddies wondering how much longer you are going to be." It was closing in on seven, still too early for them to be calling but for some reason, I knew she was probably right. I got up slowly, made my way to the phone, every ring seemed to get my mother more upset. As I brought the phone to my ear I could hear all the guys laughing and carrying on in the background. Stephen was already impatient and asked for me before I was able to say hello. I gave him a moment to quiet down before I even thought about saying hello. "Is Tristan there?" I could tell that Stephen and the boys had already started to drink. "This is Tristan." Stephen tried unsuccessfully in getting everyone to quiet down as he yelled in the phone. "Where you at? Are you about ready to head over or what?" There was absolutely no reason to go out this early. The Newark area never got started till after ten. I turned my back to my mother and stretched the cord as far as possible and headed into the other room to avoid my mother hearing the conversation. "I am actually having dinner. I figured I would head out around eight, have a couple beers with you guys and then go from there. It's going to be dead this early." Stephen sighed; he put his hand over the phone and mumbled to the others. It became quiet. After a short conversation with one of the guys he came back on. "We have been thinking about heading up to Columbus. These boys are way too big for this small of a town. You need to get over here, like pronto!" There was no way for me to leave this early. There was already too much tension, adding any more could bring forth ultimatums. "I am having dinner with my mother, give me a half hour and I'll hit the road." Stephen sighed once more. "Okay, try and get here as quick as possible, the boys are getting a bit restless." Stephen hung up the phone before I could respond. I hung up and sat back down. My mother never looked over but I could tell that she had overheard some of the conversation by the look she had on her face. I decided not to say anything until she brought it up. I continued to eat, slowing down my pace and taking second servings to show her my appreciation for the meal and that I wasn't in that big of a hurry to leave. She finished her beer and actually looked as if she might let this all pass without any more confrontation.

I finished up my dinner, looked at the clock; it was just about to hit seven thirty. I still had some time since I had no intention of leaving before eight; I sat back and relaxed. A few minutes passed before my mother finished her beer. She jumped up, took a look at what remained of the dinner and then started to gather the leftovers. "I can help you with that," I said as I got up and started to grab a few of the pots. "No, don't worry about it, it sounds as if your friends are waiting on you. You might want to get a move on so you don't make them upset." The tone she used confirmed that she had heard everything in our conversation. I stood there and looked at her as she walked away and headed to the kitchen. She had made her point. However, I had little time to argue. Instead, I walked out with the pots that remained and placed it all on the kitchen table. "Thank you, it was really good." My mother opened the door and grabbed a beer. "Yep," is all I ended up hearing from her. I stood there for a moment as she began to rummage through her cabinets for something to put the leftovers in. She kept her back to me the whole time. I waited a little longer and then gave up the attempt to leave on a good note. I headed to the bathroom, finished getting ready and then made my way out to the kitchen to say goodbye. I found my mother sitting at the table playing a game of solitaire. "Well, it's almost eight o'clock and the guys are wanting to get started so I guess I'll be leaving now, thanks again for dinner." She never looked up, she played the last of her cards, took a drink and then said, "Remember, don't be calling me to come get you out of jail if you end up getting arrested." She didn't raise her voice, but she said it in a tone which let me know that she meant it, was almost hoping for it. I stared at her for a moment. "Thanks again, I'll be safe," is all that I could come up with as a response. I made my way to the door, opting not to call Stephen before I left.

Chapter X

I've never been one to leave on a bad note, especially with my mother. I was her baby; she was all that I had. I knew that she would spend the rest of the night sitting around, watching the time pass, wondering if I was okay and hoping if the phone was to ring it wasn't the police letting her know that her son was in jail or had been in an accident. I headed over to Stephen's unable to clear my mind, thinking the whole time about my mother. In the short amount of distance between my home and his, I thought numerous times about turning around and not going out just to keep my mother from spending the night worrying. However, I came to the realization that this was an opportunity to prove how responsible I am. She found me old enough to go out and get a job, I now had to prove that I was also old enough to go out, run the city and still be responsible. It was little consolation but I was able to ease my mind enough to avoid walking into Stephen's and ruining the atmosphere. As I pulled into the drive, I could see several of the guys walking past the window and saw Stephen who looked out of the window and spotted me. As I walked up to the door, Stephen was already opening it. "It's about fucking time, Tristan! Jesus, what did you have, a four course meal?" Stephen blocked the entrance of the door to let me know that coming in was not an option. "Are you ready to go?" he asked as if we were running late. "I thought the whole idea was to have some drinks before we hit the road?" Stephen looked at me in disbelief. "What do you think we've been doing in there? That's why I called and told you to get over here. We've been drinking since six!" We looked at one another, neither one willing to surrender our ground. Robert came around the corner. "Is that Tristan? What the hell is going on, son? Get your ass in here and have a drink!" Stephen looked back at Robert as if he had been betrayed. "No, fuck that, you boys want to head to Columbus, we need to be heading out now." Robert and Stephen looked at one another. Robert was surprised that Stephen seemed so adamant about leaving that instant. "We need to let Tristan catch up a bit. Come on, Chief, get in here and let's have some drinks. Step aside, Stephen, why don't you let the boy through, he looks a bit thirsty." Stephen shrugged his shoulder and took a step back to the side. I walked past Stephen; I could feel his cold stare. Stephen made certain to keep himself somewhat in my way. Robert reached out and shook my hand and headed me to where all the guys were partying. Once we went into the kitchen Sal and Hal smiled my way and tipped their bottle towards me. Dick was standing there smiling at Sal and Hal as they shared stories. "Dick, grab Tristan a beer would ya?" Dick looked over, sharing the smile with me that he had as a result from the last tale him and the others had shared. "What do you want there, Tristan?" Dick was in a great mood, he was actually being nice towards me. "Whatever you have the most of, I'm not picky." Dick opened the fridge and grabbed me a beer. "I hope you are ready to drink a real beer. We don't do domestics here." Dick handed me an import; Robert nodded in approval. "Now that is what I'm talking about!" Robert changed his tone to one I was familiar with; it was one of the many voices that Stephen used when he was goofing off. Stephen walked into the kitchen looked at the time, looked at me and shook his head in disbelief, which Hal noticed. "Who pissed in your Cheerios there, Alice?" Hal asked Stephen. "No one, I just thought you were all ready to hit the road." Hal looked at him, surprised by the way he was acting. "Lighten up there, Nancy, it'll be alright, have a beer. Let's let Tristan have a couple and then we'll scoot." Everyone in the room was loose, Stephen was uptight and by the way everyone was acting, they were all surprised at his behavior. "I'm already buzzing, I am ready to go," said Stephen. Robert busted out laughing on hearing this and almost choked on his beer that he had just swallowed. "Do you hear this pansy? He is fucking drunk already!" Everyone in the room laughed except Stephen and I. Stephen shook his head and then smirked. "Hand me another beer, I'll show you who is a fucking lightweight!" Stephen seemed to loosen up with this comment. "Now that is what I'm talking about!" Robert hollered as he headed towards the refrigerator and grabbed Stephen a beer. "Drink up, Tristan, are you ready for another?" Robert asked as he grabbed two beers and offered me the second one. I took a glance to see where everyone else was with their drinks so I wouldn't be the one making everyone wait on me, I took a swallow and then nodded my head. Robert handed me the beer with a smile.

As I drank my beer, I found myself quickly becoming one of the boys, with Robert being the one that seemed to take the most interest in me. Hal, who was standing there listening to the interaction between Robert and Stephen, took the time to look over at me with a smile and the kind of stare to reassure me that this kind of behavior was the norm between the two of them. Sal on the other hand was the quiet one even as he drank, standing there with his head kind of hanging in comparison to the others; he was drinking slower than the rest, didn't seem engaged and only occasionally moved to let us know he was still alive. I found him fascinating and wanted to get to know him better. "I'm about done, are you boys ready to hit the road or what? It is going on nine." Stephen was once again becoming restless, with an hour drive to Columbus, his concerns were becoming more justified. "Jesus Christ, will somebody grab him another beer?" Hal said with a smile. "I don't want another beer here, we can take them with us, we need to get on the road" This comment got Dick's attention, who quit smiling. "Hey, you guys are going to be driving my van, I don't think you all need to be drinking in the van as well. I don't have insurance on anyone else." Dick's tone was that of a concerned father to his illegitimate children. "You don't have anything to worry about, Dick. You see, Robert is going to be driving and you know Robert, he'll be fine," Hal said with drunken confidence. "I can drive if you want me to, I am only on my second beer," I offered, which gained Stephen's attention as he gave me a dirty look. "Tristan, there is no way in hell your ass is going to drive, I wasn't sure if we were going to make it home in one piece last week!" Robert looked over and smiled. "You leave a little to be desired when it comes to your drinking and driving?" Stephen looked at Robert and then looked over at Dick. "Robert will be fine with driving, just ask him yourself." Dick decided to call Stephen out on his confidence. "Robert, are you drunk?" Robert looked at Dick and finished his beer. "Yes, yes I am. However, I am still good to go." This brought everyone to laughter. Even Sal, as he dropped his head even further with a quiet laugh as he shook his head in disbelief. Stephen looked over at me and took a quick drink. "You see, Tristan, Robert and our crew have a long ass history in defying the odds when it comes to drinking and driving!" As Stephen finished his sentence, Hal jumped into the conversation and the stories began. "Do you remember that time we were coming home from that party and everyone was so fucked up we had no clue how to get home?" Everyone turned their attention to Hal as he paused for a moment. "It was that party where we met Moose Knuckle and Club Foot and good old Sal here brought forth his "A" game and almost got us all in a fight after hitting on the skank with three teeth." Everyone busted out laughing as Sal shook his head, his cheeks reddened. "Don't even deny it, Sal! Well anyways, Tristan, we were all beyond fucked up and Robert decided he was the only one that could drive. Well, he was all over the road and the next thing you know we saw some headlights in the rearview mirror. Those headlights must have followed us a good four or five miles before they turned their cherries on! You want to talk about the car sobering up real quick! Well Robert looked over and told us all to be quiet. The police walked up and told Robert he noticed that he had been swerving. This motherfucker tells the cop that he has allergies and had just experienced a sneezing fit! The cop asked him if he was going to be okay and told his ass to be careful on the way home! No sobriety test, no nothing!" The room roared with laughter. "The last time I checked, allergies never caused one to slur and slobber as they spoke!" Hal added, as Robert shook his head as if he too was surprised with how lucky he actually was.

There was a small pause at the end of the tale as everyone continued to laugh and digest the memory. "That is nothing compared to the time we were all coming back from the party after the football game!" Stephen began and brought everyone's laughter down to a chuckle due in part of their curiosity. Stephen perked up to continue the story. "I believe it was homecoming. We were one year removed from high school. We all went to the game already half fucked up, the team ended up getting destroyed, no one cared past halftime, so we started focusing on drinking. By the time we got to the party, we were all kinds of fucked up! We must have stayed there till the last of the beer was gone and then decided to head home because we were bored and all the honeys had left." Robert raised his finger to his chin listening attentively as if he was trying to figure out this specific time of the many they had experienced. Stephen continued, "So we were driving home, looking for a place to eat. Robert could barely keep his eyes open and the next thing you know, there are the cherries flashing. We were so fucked it was ridiculous, we might as well have just parked the car, handed the officer the keys and put our hands behind our backs for the cuffing. The next thing you know, Robert looks in the mirror, sees the officer coming up to his window, tosses me his glasses and says to just go with the flow. He rolls down his window and when the cop asks him if he knows why he just pulled him over he comes straight out and says, "Because I was swerving!" I about shit! Then before the officer can say anything else he continues by saying, "Sir, my eyes were getting a little bit irritated by the oncoming traffic lights and when I went to rub my eyes, I lost one of my contacts." I kid you not, he said this so convincingly, that I was about to buy it! I about fucking lost it! The funny thing is, the cop actually looks him up and down then lets him step out of the car, and helps illuminate the floorboard with his flashlight so he can find the missing lens! Robert pretends to find it, acts as if he cleans it off and then pretends to put it back in. The officer fell for it, asks if there was anything else he could do and then told us to be careful on the way home, it was late and there would be a lot of drunk drivers out on the road! As Stephen finished the story the whole room erupted in laughter. There was a newfound energy in the room, the stories were beginning to flow and the rest of the evening could have been spent reminiscing over their drunken adventures. "So you're telling me that Robert is more than able to drive you all around tonight?" Dick seemed to inadvertently bring the storytelling to an end with this question. "Aye, aye, Captain!" Robert answered as he raised his beer towards Dick for a toast. "You guys still need to be careful, maybe you should keep it local since you all seem to be feeling no pain. There is always tomorrow night, you know?" Dick's plea, although legitimate, seemed to be falling on deaf ears. Dick continued, "Listen, whatever you are going to do, you need to decide quickly. Jeanine's in her room, I don't want her to come out here and see you all fucked up and then leaving in our van, she would shit!" Stephen looked even more ready to leave with the end of this sentence. "You're right, someone grab the rest of the beer and let's get out of here," Hal said. Stephen headed over to the refrigerator and grabbed what was left of the beer and in doing so, handed Dick one more as a sort of peace offering, which he gladly accepted. Everyone shook hands with Dick and made their way towards the front door. Dick followed closely behind us like an usher as he reminded us to be careful.

Stephen yelled shotgun as we headed towards the van which earned some negative comments from Sal and Hal. I opened the back door of the van and let Hal and Sal enter first, I ended up squeezing in last and took my place next to Sal, optimistic that I would be able to get him to open up some on the way to Columbus. As we all took our places, Stephen started passing us some beers. Robert took a quick swig and pulled out. "So where the hell are we going to go tonight?" Robert asked. "I think Dick may have a point, maybe we ought to just stay local, there is always tomorrow night in which we could hit Columbus," Hal commented. The persuasion and the fact that the time was quickly passing us by began to wear on Stephen. "You know what, if you fuck heads would have just listened to me when I was saying we should be leaving, this wouldn't have been an issue." Stephen took pride in the fact that he was right. "Relax there, Nancy. It's going to be alright, I promise. We'll still have a good time if we stay local, we'll tear up Columbus tomorrow night, besides, it gives us a little more time to find out where the hotspots are in Columbus before we head out and drive around the streets with our thumbs up are asses not knowing where to go." Robert looked over at Stephen and arched his eyebrows which brought a smile to

Stephen's face. "Alright, let's hit Newark." The news seemed to come as a relief to everyone except Sal who looked as if he was about to fall asleep at any moment. I wasn't the only one to take notice of this. "Sal, you okay back there?" Robert looked in the rearview mirror at Sal with a big smile on his face. "Fuck, he's about to fall asleep already!" Stephen confirmed with a look of disbelief. Robert turned his eyes in the rearview mirror to my direction. "You see, Tristan, it hasn't been medically diagnosed yet but we are certain that Sal has narcolepsy. Sal has fallen asleep every time we've ever went out and I'm not talking your typical nodding off, I'm talking full snooze!" Hal leaned over and poked Sal to make sure he was taking it all in fun, Sal responded with a shaking of the head and a smile. "This motherfucker will be deep into conversation then out of nowhere slam his head back and start snoring!" Stephen said and added a demonstration that brought everyone in the van to laughter, including Sal. This encouraged Stephen to continue. "Remember that time in the club we were all standing there planning out what women we were going to bang and Sal stood there with his eyes wide open sleeping?" Robert smiled as he looked back at Sal and then picked up where Stephen had left off. "Sal, have you ever fallen asleep as you banged some random skank?" The van erupted in laughter once more. "You guys are fucking hilarious, you know that?" Sal exclaimed in a perfect monotone voice. It was one of the rare moments that he chose to spoke, as he shook his head and prepared to finish off the last of his beer. "You are the best, Sal, don't let anyone tell you different!" Hal said as he grabbed Sal by the chin, pulled him close and gave him a big kiss on the cheek. "I'll tell ya what, if we don't hook up with any honeys tonight, you'll be sleeping in my bed!" Hal said as he slammed his hand down on Sal's knee and massaged it. "Whoa boy, here we go already. You just behave yourself back there, Hal, everyone knows that Sal is my bitch!"

Stephen said as he puckered up towards Sal, who acted as if he had heard this a million times before.

Unbeknownst to us all, Robert had been sitting at the stop sign at the exit of the manor that Dick and Jeanine lived in for the last few minutes partaking in the heckling and awaiting directions. Once the laughter ended, Robert spoke up. "In case you all haven't noticed boys, I have been sitting here for the last half an hour or so waiting for a little direction from somebody." Stephen and the rest of the guys looked at one another and busted out laughing. "Well fuck, why didn't you say something there, buttercup?" Stephen looked at Robert in disbelief that he hadn't asked for directions. Robert gave him a glare with a raised eyebrow. "Which way, funny guy?" Robert asked once more. "Take a left, go on down to the stop sign and take another left. Tristan, is Parkinson's going to be happening yet?" Stephen turned to me quickly. I looked at my watch. "It should be picking up." Stephen shook his head in amazement. "Is there any place better to go?" Stephen asked. "I think Parkinson's will be fine." My response caused Stephen to whip back around and as he did, he mumbled, "Maybe that skank you were trying to bang will be there with some of her friends." I faintly caught what he said but knew which direction he was aiming with the comment. Robert on the other hand had heard it all which brought him to turn his head towards Stephen. "Old Tristan has some game, eh?" Robert asked with a smile. "I wouldn't say the kid has any game, he found some skank with four teeth, with two of them being bad and was trying to make her his steady." Everyone turned and looked at me with a smile. "Is that so, Tristan?" Robert looked at me through his rearview mirror and winked. "She wasn't a skank; she was better than the dirty whore that Stephen disappeared with that night." Everyone busted out in laughter and turned their head towards Stephen awaiting his rebuttal. "Hey, hey! Do tell, Stephen, do tell!" Hal joined in as he leaned forward to hear Stephens's response. "Yeah, she was a fucking pig, but she knew how to swallow. I am actually hoping to find her in here tonight, I lost my class ring in that gash!" Everyone laughed except me as Stephen continued. "Besides, I got what I wanted and then told her to get home to her kids. Unlike Tristan here who was asking for numbers and when he could see her again!" Hal turned and looked my way. "Is that so, Tristan?" Hal asked with a smile. "She gave me her number. She was probably the classiest chick in the joint." Hal looked at me and shook his head. "It's all about divide and conquer. Don't limit yourself to one chick. Get out there and mingle, get out there and bang them all. If they give you their number, that's fine. Just as long as you know to drop it in the nearest trash can on the way out the door!" Robert nodded in agreement. "Yeah, you are too young. Bang them all, worry about something serious when you are thirty or so." Stephen looked back at me, "Fuck, I say nothing serious until you're fifty or so and your balls are bouncing off your knees. That's about the time you need to quit being selective." Everyone laughed. Robert looked at Stephen for the next set of directions, Hal kept his attention towards me. "We'll show you how it's done tonight, Tristan, and at no charge! Hey, pass us another round back here. It's time to get this party started." Stephen passed the beers back and we all drank. It was a welcome break from the conversation as we all turned our heads towards the road and took in the scenery.

We arrived at Parkinson's right before the weekend rush came through. However, Robert parked at the far end of the almost empty lot which seemed to raise no one's concern other than my own. The guys surveyed the club from the van; none of them looked too impressed. "Swanky joint there, Tristan!" Hal said with a mortified look on his face. "Now this is what I call a dive! You say this is the best that Newark has to offer?" Robert looked over at me with a smile. "It's not that bad, ask Stephen." I looked over at Stephen for a little support which was definitely the wrong thing to do. "He is right; it isn't as bad as it appears. I think tonight is felon night. All felons get in free and if you haven't heard, tomorrow evening is free admission for teens with multiple children!" This brought laughter from the guys although the laughter seemed a little more reserved than previously. You could feel the apprehension within the group as we got out of the van and made our way towards the club slowly. "Sorry, I parked so far away, Tristan, we have a rule not to park close enough where people can associate us with the car we came in," Robert stated. As we made our way towards the bar we walked side by side, like a scene straight out of the Wild West. I found myself in the middle of line, with Stephen on one side and Hal on the other. All the guys simultaneously reached into their pockets for chewing gum and loaded their mouths with it. The more I observed the group; their gestures, their vocabulary, the more I could see their influence on Stephen or vice versa. He was no longer the unique individual I first perceived him as; now he was nothing more than a typical guy from this group out of Cincinnati. "Tristan, it's the same rules as our last time out. If you find someone, and bring her back to the van, make sure it's a stink we can deal with on our way home. If you decide to get your noodle wet, load up with two rubbers. I am too young to be a Godfather. Remember, no skanks with wedding rings. Lastly, keep your nose clean and don't be picking any fights. Remember, you pick a fight and your ass is on your own, understand?" The comment was more less scripted from the other night. However, that didn't leave it any less abrasive. By the looks on everyone's faces, they were somewhat surprised by the comment. I said nothing as I continued to walk. Hal looked at Stephen and then over to me and then mumbled to Stephen in reference to the comment that sparked a conversation between the two of them. The conversation was short. Once it ended, Robert looked over and motioned for me to step back. I stepped back and we slowed our pace as the others continued on towards the door. "Listen,

Tristan, that was a fucked up comment and that isn't the way we play it. I am sure that is exactly what Hal is talking to him about right now. The fact is, we all like you. I have your back if you get yourself into anything and I guarantee you, Stephen will too." I gave Robert a smile and nodded my head as if I knew. He motioned for me to once again pick up my pace and we closed the distance with the rest of the group. Robert seemed to be a good guy; all the guys had their own unique ways about them that somehow balanced itself into a great chemistry between them all. Although I found Sal the most fascinating, it was Robert who was becoming my favorite out of the bunch.

We headed into the club; the guys tried their best not to look like sightseers from a foreign land. I led the way towards the bar as the rest of them fell back and congregated. As I stood at the bar, Robert came up and stood beside me. "You grabbing us some refreshments, Tristan?" Robert asked as he nudged me with his elbow. "I have the first round; I figure it's the least I can do." I motioned to the barkeep as they made their way past. "Hey, don't take Stephen too seriously, he likes to bust people's chops and can actually be an asshole at times, but he is a hell of a guy," Robert said with passion as he seemed to feel the need to revisit what had taken place outside. "I know, I don't take anything personal," I assured Robert, "Good, because if he knows he is under your skin, the kid will continue to burrow. The fact is, Stephen has talked highly about you. He feels you are a younger version of us. The kind of guy that would fit perfectly in our pack in the big city. That is a damn good thing, you know?" I gave Robert a smile and then placed our order. We headed back over to the rest of the guys and handed out the beers. Robert stepped off to the side, which gained every-one's attention. Stephen nudged me to make sure I watched. At that point, Robert proceeded to tilt his beer back, and drink the bottle of beer in its entirety in two swallows. "Okay, that wasn't bad, I'm still thirsty though!"

Robert smiled and belched before wiping his lips off. Everyone smiled. "This motherfucker is something else!" Stephen said to me with a look of astonishment. "Some old college tricks are hard to shake, what can I say boys? Is anyone ready for another round?" No one had even taken their first drink. Robert looked around for a trash can and a waitress. He found a waitress with a tray of shots walking around and called for her. She came up with a shake much more defined than the one she was using as she walked around aimlessly. She gave Robert a wink and a smile as she approached. "How are you doing tonight, cutie?" she asked in a seductive voice. "Well toots, I would be doing much better if I had a beer in my hand." Robert leaned over towards her in an effort to talk discreetly, instead, the rest of the guys heard it and smiled. "Well we are going to have to fix that then, huh?" she asked as she turned on her charm to a higher level. "Now that's what I was thinking!" Robert started to bring more animation in his voice as he winked at her. "Well, I have to get rid of these shots real quick, but if you can wait on me, I can bring you one back here in a few." She leaned into Robert as she spoke. "What man in his right mind wouldn't be willing to wait on something as precious as you? While you are at it, could you bring the rest of these boys a round as well?" He gave her a boyish grin as he looked her up and down. "Of course, give me a moment, okay? Don't go anywhere!" she smiled as she walked away. "Trust me I'm not going anywhere unless it is home with you," Robert said which brought out a giggle from the waitress as she left. "Fucking skank!" he mumbled looking her up and down as she walked away and he turned his head towards us. Stephen and Hal both were smiling although they weren't overly amused by his charm. Sal just nodded his head. "That, my boys, is how it is done. She is already planning out a wedding dress to become my wifey over there!" Stephen smiled and made his way closer to Robert. "Listen here, Casanova, take her out and bang her but make it quick, the night is young, there is a lot more honeys to dominate." Robert looked at Stephen as if he was disgusted by his comment. "You think I am going to hook up with the first pig that gives me a little attention? Come on, Stephen, I have higher standards than that!" Stephen motioned for Robert to turn around as his waitress was making her way back to him. "Here you go, honey, sorry it took me so long." The waitress's flirtation was becoming more of an interest. She was completely absorbed by Robert's charm and attention to her. "No problem, I'm sure you can make it up later. How long do you work tonight?" This brought a huge smile to her face as he slowly slipped his arm around her waist. "I was supposed to close tonight, but I might be able to get off by midnight," she said with promise. "Well, why don't you look me and the boys up when you get ready to get off and maybe we can all have a drink or something?" Robert said with a wink as he pulled her a little tighter towards him. "That sounds like a plan. If you boys need anything else just motion for me, okay?" She was totally hooked by Roberts's charm. Everyone nodded in agreement that they would and then turned their attention to the dance floor. Robert leaned in and whispered something in her ear that she absolutely loved as her face lit up and she giggled. She began to walk away with a shake, eventually turning back to see if Robert approved. Robert tipped his beer towards her and winked. He then turned and looked over at us as he tipped his head back and once again emptied the beer in two swallows. "You might want to settle down there a bit, Chief, you might already have some snail tracks appearing down in your tighties." Hal said with a smile. "My boy, you haven't seen nothing yet!" Robert assured him. "Well talk is cheap, let's get out on the dance floor and hook up some honeys," Stephen said as he arched his eyebrows.

Stephen turned and headed out onto the dance floor. Hal and Robert followed closely behind while Sal casually walked his own pace. I stood back for a moment to witness the boys in action for my first time. It was amazing to watch them all just walk up on strangers so carefree and so confident. They totally took control of the groups that they joined with their big city charm. Sal stood off to the side, slowly blending in with a woman who was dancing amongst her friends, and did so masterfully. Once Stephen, Robert and Hal had settled in, they looked around and noticed I wasn't amongst them, then continued to look around to find me. Once Robert saw me he nudged Stephen and they both motioned for me to come out and join them. I declined as I motioned that I would join them in a bit. In return, they motioned for me to go and get them another round. I headed towards the bar. The waitress that Robert had been working caught my eye and smiled. I returned the smile but avoided her as I walked over to the bar to place the order. As I stood there I looked around a little bit to see if I could spot Tammy. I looked over at the table we sat at but didn't see her. After I placed the order with the barkeep I looked over to the pool room and there is where I found Tammy. Leaning over a table taking a shot. She stood up, smiled at the guy who walked towards her with her beer and exchanged her pool cue for one of the two beers he was holding. I wasn't familiar with the guy. I vaguely remembered the faces of the guys hanging around the pool table the other night but I began to wonder if indeed he was one of those guys that Stephen swore was sizing me up and if Stephen was on to something when he had intervened. Tammy and the guy seemed cozy, too cozy to just be friends. I could only smile and shake my head. I turned my attention back to the bar. I grabbed the beers and with my hands full, made my way back to the dance floor, trying my best to once again avoid the waitress. The club was filling up quickly which made her a little easier to avoid. However, it also made it more difficult to see where the guys were.

There were a lot of beautiful women on the dance floor, a lot of them alone. I was getting to the point where I was wanting to mingle, I just had to get rid of the beers. As I surveyed the dance floor I saw an arm go up. It was

Stephen motioning for me. Stephen and Robert had stayed together and were working a couple of women that appeared to be in their early thirties. Although average in looks, they both had nice bodies. As I headed towards them, I found Hal off to the side. Hal was up against a good looking woman who was a few inches taller than him. His attempt to dance with her seemed more like foreplay as he grinded against her. Sal was closest to Hal. He had left his first dance partner from earlier and seemed happy to be working a woman much older than him. I walked up to Hal trying to be discreet as I offered him a beer. Hal tilted his head back in his best impersonation of Robert as he finished off his remaining beer, exchanging his empty for a full as he gave me a wink and turned his attention back to the woman without her even noticing my presence. Sal shook his head that he was fine without the beer. I continued on over to Stephen and Robert. Robert yelled over the music for me to join them as Stephen handed me his empty bottle and took both his and Roberts's beers. "I think I am going to check out the club for a little bit on my own. If I don't get into anything worthwhile, I will make my way back." Robert looked at me as if he was disappointed in my decision, Stephen told him to let me go and they quickly turned their attention back to the women.

I worked on Sal's beer while I looked the club over. There were more than enough women in the club to choose from, so I didn't feel the need to hurry. I surveyed the area around the dance floor and then the dance floor itself. I caught Stephen and Robert who both had an ornery smile on their face. I was unsure what they were actually smiling about until I looked over and noticed that Hal and the woman he was working were no longer in the bar. I knew it was only a matter of time before the others followed suit so I decided to pick up my game. I saw a couple of attractive women off to the side that had looked over at me numerous times, sharing some comments after each stare. I made my way slowly in their direction, walking across the dance floor. I looked around before approaching and caught a couple of men heading in their direction with drinks. I paused for a moment and watched the men join the women. It didn't take long to realize that they weren't meeting for the first time. I turned and made my way back off the dance floor. In doing so, I turned and found myself in the middle of a dance with a young woman, I danced for a moment and then slowly backed away with a smile. I continued to watch the dance floor and the areas around it to look for a potential partner for the night. In doing so, I didn't pay attention to the waitress that Robert had been hitting on as she made her way up beside me. "Hey you, are you having fun?" I looked over at her a bit startled as she broke my concentration and then gave her a smile. "Not too bad of a night. How is your night going?" She gave a sigh, "Oh my God, we have been slammed! Don't get me wrong, I love the tips but it pretty much ruins any chances of me getting off early. So where is your buddy?" I could see that she was really into Robert. She seemed sweet, innocent. Most likely unfamiliar with the likes of a guy like Robert. I didn't want her to be the victim of a back seat fling and yet, I wasn't one to sell out a fellow man. "He is around here somewhere. He and his buddy wandered off." She took a quick glance around the dance floor in an effort to spot him but the floor was getting crowded enough that even I had lost track of him. "Well, are you guys planning on going down to the corner after you leave here?" I could tell that she had high hopes of meeting up with Robert. "I'm really not sure what the rest of the night holds for us. I could have him look for you in a little bit when I catch up with him." She gave me a big smile. "Yes, if you would please. I would like to catch up with you all later, you all seem like you're fun. Let him know, just in case we don't catch up here, that I'll be at the corner for last call." She put her hand on my arm as she smiled and walked away. I watched her for a moment and then turned my attention back towards the dance floor. It seemed as if every woman I made eye contact with had a man standing beside her or en route back to her with drinks. As I continued to look around, I caught sight of Sal, as he danced away from the mainstream of the crowd with the older woman. As he continued to work on her, he seemed to be looking over her shoulder at another woman. I then saw Robert as he made his way towards Hal who had returned with the woman he had left earlier with. There was no sign of Stephen. I noticed there were quite a few women beginning to congregate in the area that Hal and Robert were in, so I decided to make my way over towards their area to join them.

By the time I arrived, everyone was dancing. Hal was with the woman he could not seem to shake and Robert was dancing with numerous women. I made my way alongside of Robert and began dancing. Robert seemed completely unaware that I was beside him. I could tell he was feeling no pain. I continued to dance while inching my way close enough to him where I could nudge him. Robert looked at me with a big smile on his face as he leaned over towards me and shouted over top of the music with a slur "Tristan, my boy. How are you doing? Looks like you got yourself a fine looking honey there!" Robert looked over to the woman I was dancing with and gave her a wink. "Where is Stephen at?" I tried to ask without yelling too loud. He shrugged his shoulders as if he wasn't sure and then leaned over. "I am pretty sure he took some skank out to the van. I told him she was a pig but he didn't seem to care. His beer goggles told him something completely different." Hal overheard the last part and gave us a smile. "What is up, Tristan? You land a honey yet?" Hal yelled as he continued to try and figure a way to dump the woman he had been with all night and make his way over to another woman who was now aware of his interests and was returning a smile each time he looked over. "I'm doing alright, you look to be doing well yourself." Hal turned his head to me and winked. "Are you guys ready for a round?" Hal asked as he realized he was running low.

Robert answered for the two of us as he made his way up tight against a cute blonde that looked as drunk as he did. I turned my attention back towards the woman who I was dancing with but she was drifting away. There was another group of women dancing together so I danced off to the side of the one closest to me and tried to get her to focus more on me than the women she was with. After a few moments, she was turned towards me with a smile as we began to dance. I could see the women she was with, leaning into one another and talking. It wasn't long after they quit talking that they came over and tapped her on the shoulder to get her away from myself and what they knew was ultimately waiting for her. She at first ignored the tap but eventually smiled and turned away after the taps became more persistent. It seemed as if I was had become guilty by association. Hal was walking back with our drinks and must have seen what had happened. As he handed me my drink he leaned in towards me. "Fuck them pigs, Tristan, there are way too many of them in here to be sweating them. Get out there boy and land you a honey." Hal winked and headed off; he danced his way past the woman who he had been hanging out with since we arrived and went over to the woman he had been exchanging smiles with. As the woman he had been with watched him talking to another woman, her reaction or lack of confirmed it wasn't the first time she had experienced this and wouldn't be the last. I walked away, deeper into the dance floor with the new drink in hand and looked around for someone new to work. As I made my way closer to the pool tables, I caught Tammy's eye as she danced with her man. I continued on, in the presence of her stare. I glanced over one more time as I made my way past, she looked at me, giving me an apologetic glance and attempted a discrete smile which I did not entertain. As I neared the end of the dance floor, I found another couple of women and made my way over towards them. I danced the remainder of the song with them. As the next song began, I attempted to lure the more attractive woman away from her friend. However, they continued to stay together, inseparable, safety in numbers. By the middle of the song, I faded back into the rest of the crowd.

I headed off the dance floor and made my way around its perimeter. There were mostly couples standing around conversing, awaiting the right song to play before they headed onto the floor. There were a few women here and there, standing around, looking for company. I observed them all but even with the drunkenness that was coming on, I had no interest in any of them. The night was progressing quickly, I was ready to try some-place new and began to head toward the guys. I felt a tap on my shoulder and turned around to see Tammy. "Hey you, how are you doing?" Tammy looked at me with a big smile. She acted as if I was unaware of her boyfriend that I saw her with earlier. "I'm okay, how is your night going?' My tone informed her that I was being courteous and nothing more. She looked for a way to change the mood. "So you brat, you never gave me a call." She took a sip of her drink through her straw looking up at me with an innocent schoolgirl kind of look. "Well that turned out to be a good thing did it not?" I came at her directly. "What do you mean? I was hoping you would give me a call." I was too the point that I just wanted to get away from her, I didn't want to waste any more time. I looked around trying to find the guys then turned back towards her. "Well, I figured I would see you here tonight and we could pick up where we left off. Then again, I'm not one to intrude on someone else's woman." Her innocent look went away quickly as she searched for a response. "Oh, he is just a friend." Unbeknownst to her I had seen them earlier prior to the dance floor and even if he was a friend, I no longer wanted anything to do with her. I looked and just nodded my head. My doubt was easy for even her to read. "Are you needing to go? I see you looking around for someone?" She was well aware that there was nothing left to salvage. "Yeah, my buddies are here, I believe we are about to take off." She looked at me discouraged as she looked around in an effort to find these buddies that she expected to be fictitious. "Well, OK. Do you still have my number?" she asked in desperation. I nodded my head, and turned to walk away. "I guess I'll see you later then. Give me a call sometime if you would like to get together." I took a look back and gave her a wink. She waited for a moment and then headed back in the direction of her boyfriend that I imagined was busy enough playing pool that he hadn't noticed her shopping around. I walked over to the front of the dance floor where I once more caught up with Stephen, who had returned and was now out on the floor dancing between a couple of women; Robert was beside him. A few feet away Hal was leaning in on a woman he was dancing with, their noses up against one another as she placed her hand on his chest, playing with his buttons. It was easy to see that she was aching and ready to leave with him. I also spotted Sal who was nearby dancing with a new woman.

Everyone was having success tonight, everyone except myself. I knew that eventually everyone would realize this. Outside of Robert, no one would have any sympathy towards my end result. Then again, I wasn't looking for sympathy. I decided to head to the bar to spend the rest of the night until they were ready to leave. The bar area was beginning to thin out. Everyone, even the most self-conscious of dancers, had made their way out onto the dance floor. I took a seat at the bar and waited for the barkeep to make her way over. Her arrival was simultaneous with the waitress who had been hit on by Robert earlier. I placed an order and then turned to the waitress. "Hey you, what seems to be the problem? You don't seem very happy." I gave her a smile, her attention towards me seemed genuine. "I'm okay, just a little off tonight," I assured her. "Well. You need to get out on the dance floor! It's really going on out there tonight." I looked back on the dance floor; it was no longer inviting. There was a slight opening to where the waitress would be able see Robert working his magic. I tried to turn her attention back towards me but she had already seen him. "Well it looks as if your buddy is having a good time tonight." The barkeep made her way back as the waitress was finishing her statement. I knew she was disappointed to see the kind of guy Robert and the others truly were. "Did you tell him I was looking for him or did you get the opportunity to ask him about the corner bar tonight?" She looked at me with optimism that I hadn't. "No, not yet." Her reaction was with mixed emotion. I took a drink as she continued to watch Robert in action. "Well that's good, just forget what I had said if you would, there has been a change of plans. You don't need to tell him anything." She looked at me and forced a smile. I reached out and put my hand on her shoulder. "Honey, you can do much better, trust me." She looked at me with a new respect thinking that I had just defended her honor over such a great friend of mine. "You are too sweet, well listen, maybe someday, I'll catch up with you down at the corner?" she gave me a smile as she walked away. Her walk no longer as charismatic. I turned back to the bar, took a big drink and took in the new scenery.

I finished my beer and ordered another, although, at this point I could have gone without. I looked around the bar and found Stephen with his hand extended with a twenty-dollar bill in an attempt to gain a barkeep's attention. He ordered five beers and waited. As he stood there he began to look at the whisky they offered behind the bar. He looked to be contemplating shots. He then began to look the bar over and its patrons. He finally looked on down and saw me sitting there. He gave me a smirk, shook his head and then, once he had his beer he walked over and put one in front of me. "Well, you made that easy enough, what the fuck are you doing over here sitting by yourself, looking all down on your luck?" Stephen was drunk as he struggled to keep his balance. "I'm fine, just taking a moment to get a breather, thanks for the beer." Stephen looked me up and down, doubting every word that I was saying. "Listen, you need to be out there gathering some honeys! Even fucking Sal is out there in between naps, hooking up with some skanks!" Stephen paused to laugh at his own comment. "Now lick your wounds and get back out there!" Stephen gave me a smile which I returned. "I will, just going to finish this beer." Stephen looked at me and arched his eyebrow before shaking his head and stumbling back towards the dance floor. I watched him as he made his way to the others. Each of the guys seeming more inebriated than the other.

As the time passed, I began to talk to some of the fellow drunks perched at the bar. In doing so, I never made it back to the dance floor. Soon the floor started to thin out, I saw the waitress taking her apron off, she saw me and gave me a smile and a soft wave. I could easily see the guys now on the floor, their dancing had come to a stop as they stood there exchanging numbers with the women they had been dancing with. Soon the DJ called last call. The waitress walked by and let her hand drape across my arm that rested on the bar to say goodbye. She made her way towards the door. Robert saw her as she passed, he attempted to holler at her, which provoked her to pick up her pace and continue towards the exit. Her mannerisms made him aware that she chose to ignore him. Robert looked to see if he would be able to catch her before she got out the door but knew in the condition he was in that any attempt would be futile. As the women walking away with smiles on their faces and false hope that these guys were unlike all the other men that they had encountered in the last month or so in these clubs, the guys made their way over to the bar and joined me. "Hey Tristan, what the fuck have you been doing? I lost you out on the floor." Robert slurred as he put his arm around my shoulder. "He has been up here sulking most of the night," Stephen said with a smirk on his face. "Say it isn't so, Tristan, I know you hooked up some honeys tonight." Robert massaged my shoulders as he looked at me with a sympathetic smile. "Hey, are we going to get one more round before we head out or are you boys going to suck one another off on the bar top?" Stephen said as Hal smiled, shaking his head. "Don't be jealous, baby, I'll have you bent over out there in the van, you can be sure of that!" Robert gave him a wink. Stephen looked at him and shook his head, he called over to the barkeep who paid no attention to his calls as she talked to one of the patrons. "Did you talk to that waitress, Tristan? Did she say anything?" Robert slurred with optimism. "She spoke to me a couple of times earlier, just in passing. The last time we spoke, she said she was heading home." Robert looked at me as if I was holding back on him. "She didn't say anything at all about me?" Robert was in disbelief. "No, I really didn't get much time to talk to her, she was pretty busy." Before Robert could say anything else Stephen shouted, "What the fuck ever!" This grabbed everyone's attention as we looked over and saw the barkeep walk away from Stephen with a smile on her face. Stephen had been turned down for his last round since last call was over with. Stephen and the rest made their way over. "Let's get the fuck out of this dive, they aren't going to serve us anymore." Robert and the others looked disappointed although they all knew that they didn't need any more.

As we left, it was obvious that I was the best to drive us home. Robert walked ahead of us, all his stumbling made Stephen sober enough to recognize it as well. "Hey boss, why don't you let someone else drive home? How are you, Tristan, you know this area the best, are you fucked up at all?" Robert looked at Stephen as if he was insulted. "I'm good, I can drive if you like," I offered. "I'll be fine, I just got to get a little food in me. Is there any place around here still open to where we can grab some grub?" Hal and Sal jumped into the conversation to try and coerce Robert to give up the keys. Robert ignored their request and continued his persistence on getting something to eat as he made his way to the driver's side door. His ignoring of everyone's plea caused mutual looks of disgust. We all got in the car and sat there as Robert fumbled through the keys. Once the car was started we headed across the street to the nearest fast food restaurant to get some food.

Robert worked the woman at the drive-thru as if she was one of the women on the dance floor. His flirtation while ordering was trumped by Hal's as he placed his order. Sal ordered quietly to the point that Robert had to repeat it. Stephen took my order and then gave her his best flirtation while he ordered to see if he could win the woman over; it had become a friendly competition. As we pulled up to the window everyone greatly anticipated some beautiful young woman making her way to the drive-thru window. Instead, they had a middle-aged, obese woman that approached the window with a smile on her face. The car erupted in laughter except Robert and myself. As she headed back to get his change and the food, Robert turned and snapped at Stephen and the rest. "That was complete bullshit, heartless. I swear to God, if I have spit on my burger I will be beating all your asses." Hal, who sat directly behind him, grabbed Robert by both shoulders and massaged them "Calm down there, big boy, look at them shoulders all tensed. You are getting too worked up on us!" Hal finished by leaning up and kissing Robert on the neck which brought a smile to his face. "So what the hell happened to you tonight, Tristan, was the game just off a bit?" Robert, who was now calmed down, asked. "I don't know, I had a good time, talked to some women, danced with a few. I guess I just wasn't drunk enough to settle for any of the pigs like Stephen was working." The comment brought laughter throughout the van. Stephen even looked back at me and nodded as he smiled. "Yes sir, I was hanging with a pig tonight, a couple of them, but my ball sack is about a pound lighter too! You might want to be careful where you are sitting there Tristan, just in case she didn't swallow it all!" Once again the guys laughed as Robert gave Stephen a high five. "So how about you, Hal, you seemed to disappear for a little while, what did you do with that Honey?" Hal looked out his window with his hand against his chin, chewing on his nails. He looked as if he was going to opt not to respond to the questioning, when he turned to us all. "Well boys, take a deep inhale. Do you smell it? I'd let you all smell my shaft if you can't but I might offend the petite little old lady in the drive-thru if I did." Once again the guys busted out laughing. Stephen leaned back and gave Hal a high five. At that moment, the woman came back to the window with our order. Robert thanked her kindly in an effort to console her after everyone had laughed at her expense earlier. Stephen impatiently ripped the bags out of Robert's hands and started rummaging through it to find his order. Robert reached over and regained control of the bag from Stephen which brought Stephen to yell "Fucker" with a french fry hanging halfway out of his mouth. After Robert had all of his order in his lap, Stephen took the bag and went to hand it back to Hal. "What the fuck, are you fucking serious?" Stephen stopped in the middle of handing the bag over, looking at Sal. I hadn't noticed but Sal had his head tilted back completely passed out. "What's the deal?" Robert asked with his mouth full as he pulled away from the restaurant and tried to focus on the road, completely unaware of why Stephen was going off. "Fucking Sal is passed out again! He was just sitting there watching Hal and I talk a few moments ago." Robert laughed, "I've tried to tell you that he has narcolepsy. It may have yet to be diagnosed but I tell ya, that boy has it." Stephen shook his head in disbelief as he looked at Sal. "Oh well, I say we pass his food around and eat it, there is no sense in letting it go to waste." Robert looked at Stephen with a dirty look. In return, Stephen looked as if he was clueless on why he had earned the dirty look. "You're not going to do anything with that boy's food, we'll wake his ass up when we get home." Stephen looked at Robert blankly. "You have known me long enough to know that I wasn't being serious, so don't go making me out to be some kind of prick." Stephen said in his own defense. Robert just shook his head and continued to drive. The rest of the ride home was for the most part quiet. Everyone opted to feed their drunken state rather than indulge in slurred conversations. Once we pulled into the house, Stephen and Robert hopped out of the car and walked straight over to the bushes to piss while Hal shook Sal's arm until Sal finally woke up. Robert and Stephen cheered on Sal as he made his way past them towards the house. Everyone else followed behind Stephen as he overtook Sal and led us through the house quietly until we were able to get downstairs.

As soon as everyone was downstairs, Robert and Hal glanced towards one another then raced to the couch, Hal leaped onto the couch first, followed quickly by Robert who pounced on him. This quickly escalated to a wrestling match between the two for ownership. Sal walked quietly passed the two of them and took a seat and untied his shoes. I sat in the recliner and began to eat my food while being entertained by the wrestling match, a match in which Robert's strength was finally victorious over Hal's speed. Stephen sat on the other recliner and reclined it all the way back and let out a sigh of relief. Everyone settled in with Robert on one end of the coach with his legs propped up on the coffee table, Hal mimicked him on the other side of the couch which left Sal sitting in the middle with little space to maneuver. Stephen, who had been sitting there with his eyes half closed, opened them up and surveyed everyone's sleeping accommodations. "You boys can move that coffee table if you like and pull that out into a bed," Stephen offered as he yawned and stretched across the recliner. "We'll be all right, we have plenty of room and Sal here will fall asleep at any moment doesn't matter if he is sitting, laying or standing up," Robert said as he nudged Sal, who was concentrating on eating. "Speaking of Sal, what the hell happened to you tonight? You were hooked up with a couple of honeys and the next thing you know, you drop them both and hooked up with some old bat that I thought was my grandmother?" Stephen said with a big smile on his face as he lay there with his eyes closed. "She wasn't that old, she was sophisticated," Sal mumbled in a soft voice while eating his sandwich. "No offense, Sal, but that old lady was a fucking fossil!" Hal jumped in with a smile. "It is what it is. She wasn't that old. Besides, she was better looking than the pigs you all were landing!" Sal defended himself, the whole while never raising his voice. "I bet you in the morning I won't be pissing razor blades either." This brought laughter to everyone. "I'm not trying to be an asshole or anything I was just wondering how in the hell did you go from them honeys to my Aunt Gertrude?" Stephen continued to keep his eyes closed, his words getting heavier as he spoke. After a few seconds, Stephen realized that Sal had yet to answer him, he slowly brought his eyes into focus and then looked over at Sal, who had his head completely back and his mouth wide open as he slept, some of his food was still on the coffee table. "Unfucking believable," Stephen said as he lay there and slowly closed his eyes. Stephen said no more as he began to snore a few moments later, Hal was the next one to fall asleep. Robert and I talked for a little bit, which was nothing more than drunken rambling that was difficult to decipher. The next thing I know I was waking up.

I woke up before anyone else had wakened. I tried to gather myself and then my belongings and head upstairs. Stephen began to shift as I walked by and with eyes fighting to open whispered that he would be calling me a bit later. I said nothing as I headed out the door quietly, escaping without being noticed by anyone else. I spent the drive home trying to think of a way to get back out tonight. Once again, it would be an all-nighter. I thought about the night before, the opportunities or should I say, the lack of. I thought about the guys, the fun and the new opportunities that presented themselves tonight, if we could get out early enough to head to Columbus. The only con was a big one. There was no way my mother was going to approve of me being out all night, two nights, back to back. The thought of even attempting to talk to her about it made me full of anxiety. I pulled into the house. My mother was already gone, probably at work, possibly the grocery store. I opted to pass the couch which was typically my place of sanctuary and headed upstairs to avoid my mother once she did arrive home. The last thing I needed was for her to walk in, smell the beer that still lingered and cause an issue. I fell asleep shortly after my head found the pillow. I awakened later to the phone ringing. I looked over at the clock and it was already past one. I rarely slept in; I continued to lay there as the phone rang expecting my mother to answer it at any moment. As the phone continued to ring, it became obvious that my mother hadn't made it home yet.

As I lay there, I realized that this was the night that my mother usually went out. Now there was a window of opportunity when it came for me to get out of the house. Although leaving her a note that I wouldn't be coming home would guarantee that I would feel the full brunt of her wrath once we saw each other again. It would still provide the opportunity to get out of the house without the initial confrontation. I jumped up, went to the kitchen to feed what was left of my hangover and to get a shower. I was almost done with my lunch when the front door opened and my mother called for my help. I walked around the corner to see some groceries laying on the front room floor with more on the front porch. I grabbed the bags, took them to the kitchen and returned. As I walked out the front door, I could see that my mother wasn't in the best of moods, so I continued bringing in the groceries and avoiding eye contact with her. I headed back to the kitchen and began to put away the groceries, my mother joined me and spoke not a word until the proper opportunity presented itself and then she got straight to the point. "Well, did you have fun last night?" she asked in a labored voice. I paused knowing that the trap was laid. "It wasn't too bad, I guess you could say we had a good time." She kept her head down, not once looking even close to my direction. "Well I didn't get a call from the police station so I guess that's a good thing." Her tone was becoming more and more confrontational. "Well, remember, you told me not to call

COME WATCH THE NIGHTTIME BREATHE

if and when I was arrested." My attempt of humor didn't work. "Well, you don't need to be out all night, there is nothing good going on out there once the sun sets." She spoke from experience as she had seen her share prior to having children. I kept quiet and finished putting the groceries away. "I bought some beer. I'll be gone tonight. You can drink here and if I don't get home too late, I'll have one with you if there is any left." And there it was. I wasn't going to touch that comment, she was searching. I just nodded my head, thanked her and said okay. She waited for a few moments to give me the opportunity to say something else. Instead, I ended up heading into the living room to lay back down since taking a shower could possibly tip my mother off on my plans. Besides, the night was going to be a long one, I could use the rest. I grabbed the phone, placed it on the ground, next to the couch so I would be able to answer it before my mother in case it was Stephen. My mother came in and sat down, paying no mind to the phone as she turned on the television for nothing more than some background noise and began to shuffle the cards for a game of solitaire. The fact that she had yet to have a beer led me to believe that she might be gone for quite a while tonight. I rolled over, turning my back to her and the rest of the world to get some rest.

I woke up on the second ring of the phone, my mother was beginning to get up when I told her I would get it. Still in the midst of incoherence, I got up from the couch to answer it, forgetting it was laying besides me. The manner in which I raced around to find the phone caught my mother's attention, the way I took the phone into the other room once I found and answered it ensured an interrogation. It was Stephen on the other line. "You aren't fucking sleeping still are you?" Stephen yelled into the phone. "Not at all, what is going on?" Stephen sat there for a second mumbling to one of the guys in the background about how I was still sleeping and then turned his attention back to me. "Well, we're going to Columbus, if you are interested. Just don't be showing up here at eight o'clock expecting to sit around drinking half the night. We wasted last night on your ass doing that, we won't be doing that again." I looked up at the clock, it was closing in on four. "I see, so when were you thinking?" I tried to whisper to avoid my mother from hearing. "We want to be on the road by eight thirty or nine at the latest so you will have to plan accordingly. We found a place called 'Hot Shots' that is a straight shot on the highway to Columbus, are you familiar with it?" It was becoming harder and harder to try and talk, I knew my mother was trying to hear what was being said. "I believe so, it should work." Stephen sat there for a moment, trying to figure out what I was actually trying to say. "Well, we researched the area and found quite a few clubs, so we figured if one doesn't work we'll have plenty of time to hit the others and still have a quick turnaround home." I couldn't help but think of the area they were referring to, I had been there plenty of times, although never in the club. The area was becoming more and more shady with the kind of people that lived there, I imagined it would spill over into the area clubs as well. Tonight would be an interesting night indeed. "That works," I said, my response time was taking longer and longer. Stephen knew something was up and yet by my tone he just couldn't figure it out. "Okay, well you know the situation, don't have us leave your ass down here by being late, understand?" Stephens's delivery made me wonder if he had already started drinking. "I totally understand, don't worry about me, it'll be fine." Stephen once more paused and then said alright as he hung up the phone. I walked back into the room and placed the phone down quietly and then took my seat on the couch and awaited my mother's interrogation.

We both sat there and watched television, the look on her face told me that she could go off at any moment, I looked for a way to intervene but couldn't come up with anything. Once it came, it came quickly. "Who was that?" she asked without looking up. "Just Stephen, he was talking about last night." She put the last of her cards down on the coffee table a little harder than the rest and then looked over at me with a disgusting look. "Don't even tell me that he wants you to go out again tonight." I looked at her as if I was shocked that she could even conjure up such a crazy idea. "What would make you think that?" It was the best that I could come up with, I was hoping that the tone would sell the defense. "Well, why else would you take the call in the other room?" She looked at me, waiting for the best lie I could give her. "I just thought that I would be respectful and take it into the other room so you could enjoy your card game and show without the interruption." She just looked at me. Her expression spoke more than anything she could have ever said. It was an expression that no one wants to see their parent display. It was filled with disappointment, whether reflecting the way she had raised me or the way that I had grown up was uncertain, but didn't matter. I sat there and waited for her to say something but it never came. Instead she looked up at the clock and began another game of solitaire. At the game's conclusion, she got up and headed to the bathroom and started the shower, she was in the bathroom for a good half an hour. I looked up at the clock and watched the time pass by quickly. I still needed to get a shower and get a couple of drinks in me before I headed over to Stephen's. She opened the door of the bathroom and made her way out to the kitchen very slowly. I looked up at the clock, I still had some time to play with. There was no way I could go to the shower while she was still here, it was too late in the day now to take a shower for any other reason than to go out. Instead, I headed into the kitchen to see what was going on. She sat at the end of the table with a cigarette in her hand, looking in the purse with the other. She placed a twenty on the table. "Here is some money for pizza, don't spend it all." I thanked her but it fell on deaf ears, she finished her cigarette and then walked past me to head to her bedroom to get changed. I grabbed a beer, sat down and waited for her to leave. The time continued to pass me by quickly. It was closing in on six o'clock and three beers later when she came out and grabbed her purse to leave. "You better be careful if you end up going anywhere tonight. I'll be home by eleven, I'll see you then." She looked at me with a glare that told me that she was completely aware of what I was doing. I told her goodbye and then waited for her car to pass the house so I could head into the shower.

Chapter XI

By the time I finished showering and getting ready, it had just passed seven. I knew that all the guys would be well on their way to a drunken state and probably wondering if and when I would be getting there. I went out to the kitchen, wrote a quick note to try and limit my mother's concerns, then grabbed a beer and headed out. I pulled into their drive as it closed in on eight o'clock. Dick opened the door and let me in. "The guys were about to leave, you just made it," he said as he passed through the kitchen and headed into another room. I was instantly greeted by Hal and Robert. Sal was sitting down with a drink in his hand. Stephen just stared at me and shook his head, I could tell that he was disgusted with me. "I told you not to get here late. We're almost ready to go, you might want to grab a beer." I walked over to the refrigerator and grabbed a beer, I looked around the counter, there was beer cans everywhere. By the looks of everyone, no one was feeling any pain. "So Tristan, you ready to go out and get some honeys tonight?" Robert asked as he held his beer up towards me. "Yeah, don't be acting all depressed and what not tonight. No one wants to see that shit," Stephen made sure to add. "I'm ready to let loose," I said in an energetic tone and a smile as I returned the gesture to Robert and ignored what Stephen was mumbling about.

We finished our beers, grabbed another one for the road and then headed out the door. We all found our way to the same seats as the night before. Robert looked worse for wear as he whipped the car out of the driveway and headed towards the highway. "Hey there, Chief, watch what the fuck you are doing there, I would like to make it to Columbus in one piece!" Stephen gave him a dirty look. "Oh just relax, you have nothing to worry about," Robert said with a slight slur and a big smile as he opened his beer and took a big swallow. "I'm being serious," Stephen grumbled. "I am too," Robert retorted. Uncertain if this was the normal behavior between the two, I looked over at Hal and Sal. However, they didn't seem to be phased by it as Sal rested his eyes and Hal worked his gum in between drinks. I figured that this bickering had been going on quite a bit today and would most likely continue deep into the night. Stephen and Robert exchanged a few more glances before Stephen shook his head, turned on the radio, reached into the glove box and grabbed a tape out of it. As the jazz began to blast, everyone seemed too loosen up.

By the time we pulled into the parking lot of the club it was closing in on ten o'clock. The club dwarfed the clubs we had in Newark, and was filling up nicely for how early it was. Hal seemed to become a little antsy as he watched some of the women pass. "Now that is what I am talking about!" Stephen said with an ornery tone. "Good call on the club there, Alice," Hal said as he took his last drink. "Yes, yes, the fun is about to begin!" Robert said as he continued to look for a parking spot. "Now Sal, try and keep yourself under control tonight, you wild man you!" Stephen said as he looked in the mirror to make sure he looked good before going in. "Hey, keep it down there, Sal is trying to get some sleep," Hal nudged Sal as he said it. Sal responded with a shake of the head and a smile. Once parked, no one wasted any time to get out of the van and head to the club, Stephen went through all the rules and regulations for us to abide by, Robert had drifted back and walked along side of me, shaking his head in disbelief as he listened. I could see by Robert's mannerisms that my concerns with the two of them were legitimate. Stephen made his way into the club by storming through both doors. If this wasn't theatrical enough, he paused and spread his arms out and took in the atmosphere. This gained the attention of those around us. As everyone turned their attention back to what they had been previously doing, we looked around. The setup of the club was different than most. There was red carpet that led you up a couple stairs and into one of the two bars that they had. The bar was furnished with double the seating, double the amount of drinks that Parkinson's had. To the left was an area that bordered the whole dance floor with tables. If you went down a couple of steps, then turned and went down a few more, you entered the dance floor. The dance floor was considerably lower than the area in which people could sit around. It gave the resemblance of an ancient coliseum. Stephen loved it. "I can sit up here and just pick one honey after another that I am going to work!" Stephen walked up to the bar and got us all a round of drinks, as he turned back around, he smiled "What do you all think? This should make it easy for all the honeys tonight!" I wasn't sure what kind of drunken gibberish Stephen was talking until Robert began laughing and nudged me. I looked over at Robert who redirected me towards Stephen and pointed down. There stood Stephen, with his zipper down and the head of his cock hanging out as he handed us all our beers.

Once the beers were out of his hands, he casually walked over to a table where two women were sitting. We all stood there with a smile as we watched Stephen try and work his magic. The women were completely oblivious that Stephen had his cock out. "You know, Stephen is probably going to get us all killed tonight, you're aware of that, right?" Robert leaned over and whispered to me. Robert ended the sentence with a small chuckle but I could tell that he had some concern and justifiably so. For someone who didn't want to fight and refused to have anyone else's back he was definitely fooling around in the wrong kind of club. Hal, who didn't seem entertained by Stephen, continued to survey the club. This came to an abrupt end as he spotted a young woman alone and smile at us as he walked away. Sal turned his back to us all and found himself a spot at the bar in which he could stand and take in the surroundings while enjoying his beer. Robert continued to stand alongside me while he drank. We finished our beers and I ordered us a couple more, I was beginning to feel the pressure of Robert's company. I wanted to make sure he had a good night, especially with the uncertainty on how much longer they would all be staying. I leaned over and was ready to ask him if he wanted to scope out the dance floor when Stephen and Hal made their way back to the bar. "What's up son, no luck?" Robert teased Stephen. By now Stephen had his pants zipped back up and was pulling a cigarette out of his pocket. After he was done lighting it he shoved his free hand down the front of his pants, took a long drag from the cigarette and then placed the cigarette snug between his two fingers that were down his pants. "When you go to meet someone and offer to shake their hands and they have their hands full and resort to doing this to free up a hand to shake, it's probably a good idea to count your losses and move on!" Everyone busted out in laughter, this was the worst I had seen Stephen when it came to being drunk and how he was acting and the night was just getting started. Robert reached down and took Stephen's cigarette and took a big drag prior to putting it back down in the grip of his fingers which brought everyone back to laughter once more. "Son, you just don't have the game established, let Tristan and I show you boys how it is done." Robert brushed Stephen's shoulder as he passed, I followed Robert as Stephen looked at Robert and just shook his head. We headed down to the dance floor where we looked for opportunities to dance. There were plenty of women dancing with one another, Robert nodded towards a couple of women who were smiling at us and we headed over and began to dance. It wasn't long before Stephen and Hal made their way down and began dancing nearby with a couple of blondes.

We danced for a while with the women but could sense with the little conversing that we had with them that it wasn't going to go anywhere. We moved onto another couple of women and danced another song till our drinks were out. I looked over at Hal and Stephen, they were running low as well. Stephen motioned for me to grab them both a beer. Robert and I gradually danced our way away from the women and off the dance floor and headed back to the bar. The two of us walked up on Sal, who seemed content with where he stood. Sal smiled at us as we approached, all seemed well. "What is going on there, Stud? Are you waiting for the women to come to you or just waiting for the right moment to go on the hunt?" Robert asked him as he draped his arm lazily over his shoulders. Sal looked up at Robert and smiled, took a drink and looked as if he wasn't sure whether to answer or not. "I'm heading over to the dance floor shortly, just giving you boys the opportunity to warm it up for me." Robert smiled and ordered us all a round of drinks. I scoped out the bar and found nothing of interest. I thanked Robert for the beer, grabbed Stephen and Hal's and made my way towards the dance floor. Stephen and Hal had drifted from one another. I made my way over to Stephen who arched his eyebrows at me and winked in recognition of the attractive woman he was about to land. I couldn't help but feel for her as I walked away and headed to Hal. I found Hal with a real beauty, she was tall and slender with a gorgeous face. You could tell by the energy she expelled that she was completely into him, any attempt for her to conceal her interest failed within her body movements, in the way she smiled at him. If only she knew. Then again, there was a good chance that she did and was content. I made the exchange of a full beer for the empty and moved on. I looked around for Robert to see if he had made his way to the dance floor, but couldn't find him. I eventually walked back towards the bar to see if he was still there and found him with Sal beginning to walk my way. "There you are, we were just heading onto the dance floor, you coming?" Robert looked like he might have had to coerce Sal into finally getting up and away from the bar. "You know, I need to find a bathroom and then I think I'll check the place out. I'll grab us all a round here in a bit and then I'll meet you all down on the dance floor." Robert nodded with a smile and some noticeable doubt on whether or not I would make it down and then continued on.

I made my way around the bar looking for a restroom that I never found. I eventually had to ask one of the many waitresses going to and from the bar. When I came back, I decided to head up and sit at an empty table that overlooked the dance floor to view all the potentials and to see how the guys were doing. The dance floor was filling up with beautiful women everywhere, hooking up was not going to be an issue. I finished my beer and took a look around to find the guys before going to the bar to grab them all a beer. Hal was up against his woman, leaning in and whispering in her ear. She played the game well, laughing and pushing him away only to have him pull her in even closer and repeat the process. Taking this in from afar, it was hard to recognize who the real victim was in the game they were playing. Sal wasn't too far away and had hooked himself up with a good looking older woman, it was the most active that I had seen Sal since we had been out, he was aggressive and she seemed to be receptive to his advances. I looked over to the other side of the floor to find Robert dancing within a group of women. This provided an easy opportunity to join him and share his wealth once I had drinks. Stephen was still dancing with the woman from earlier. They were getting closer to one another, he was stealing a page out of Hal's book and was getting similar results. However, there seemed to be other women in this mix. A couple of women stood off to the side dancing with one another. However, they weren't dancing as much as they were keeping their eyes on the woman that Stephen was with, which made me wonder what was going on. Soon the two women began to talk amongst one another and began giving disgusted looks towards Stephen and his lady friend. I kept an eye on them all. Once they turned to where their left side faced me I realized that the two women who were talking both had wedding rings on. I tried to catch the hand of the woman who was dancing with Stephen but her hand wasn't in view. Eventually she turned to where I could see her left hand. There was no ring on her finger although I was too far away to see if there was a tan line. Stephen looked too drunk to be paying attention or even care.

I headed over to the bar to grab a round of beers. The bar was the fullest it had been since we arrived. I waited for quite a while before I was served. Once I was waited on, the barkeep got caught up with other orders from a waitress. A good ten minutes passed before I was able to get my drinks and head off to the dance floor. I headed to the area where Stephen was. However, Stephen and the woman were gone. I looked over and saw Robert who was completely unaware of Stephen or anybody else's where-abouts. His attention was directed to the women he was dancing with. I looked around and saw the two women who had been observing Stephen and their friend dancing, they were both talking, possibly arguing with one another. I could see that whatever was going on, it wasn't good. I decided to take Sal and Hal their rounds before heading over to Robert to not only give him his round but fill him in on the situation. As I left Hal and Sal, I could see that the two women were still talking and looking around. They were obviously upset and looked concerned. I made it to Robert who was excited to see me "Tristan! What is up! Jump in with me!" I handed Robert his beer and leaned over to talk to him. The music was loud and he couldn't hear anything I was trying to say. He just kept dancing and smiling. I went ahead and turned towards one of the women he was dancing with and danced until the song ended. Once the song came to an end, I leaned back over towards Robert and told him that I needed to talk to him. The look on his face told me right away that he knew something was up and more than likely it was with Stephen. The look also confirmed that he didn't care. "This can't wait? I'm about to land us both some honeys for the night!" The women were attractive and by the way they were interacting with Robert I knew he was right. "It's probably best we don't wait. I'll try and make it quick." Robert looked at me with a grimace, he weighed out the options and then excused himself from the women with a promise that he would return shortly.

We headed over close to where the two women that I had been observing stood. I nodded towards the two of them in which Robert looked and acknowledged me. "Those two women there are friends of the woman that Stephen is with." Robert looked them up and down then leaned over towards me. "Tristan, there is nothing wrong with the women I have for us. Besides, these two have big ass rocks on their fingers, I don't fuck with married women. That's not my style, it's none of our style. We've always joked about it but we never play out on it." Robert unintentionally opened the door and I didn't hesitate to jump in. "That is what I was wanting to talk to you about. Stephen and the woman he was with disappeared, as soon as they did, these two women became irate. I have a pretty good feeling that the woman Stephen is with is married." Robert looked as if what I was saying was sobering, not to mention concerning. "Stephen may be drunk but he is pretty good at being able to read a woman. Even the pigs who take their ring off. Stephen wouldn't step down to that level and fool around with a woman who is married. Tristan, take a look around. This is honey central! There are way too many hot women here to waste your time on a married woman." I nodded my head in agreement, I wanted to believe Robert but the way the women were acting told me a different story. "I'm not doubting what you are saying. Something just isn't right." Robert looked frustrated. "Listen, Stephen is a big boy. Let's not blow it with the honeys we are dancing with. We can ask Stephen when he shows himself again." I agreed.

We made our way back towards the women. However, they were no longer to be seen. Robert dropped his hands in frustration to his sides. "Are you fucking serious?" Robert looked at me in disbelief. "I'm sorry." Robert just stared at me for a moment and then smiled. "Let's not worry about it, the night is still young, there are plenty of honeys here that we can conquer." We looked around the area but almost all the women had found someone to dance with. Robert finished his beer and then leaned over. "Listen, let's go to the bar. We'll grab some beers and then hit the other side to see what is up." I nodded and followed him to the bar. We stood there and waited for the barkeep. I decided that while Robert faced the bar I would stand with my back to the bar and keep an eye on the door and the arrival of Stephen. Robert grabbed our beers, handed me mine and motioned for us to head to the other side. As we started to walk, the door opened and Stephen walked into the club with a drunken air of accomplishment and confidence. He looked around, and then moved forward and headed to the bar. Soon after, the door opened back up and the woman he had danced with came in. The two of them once again took on the role of complete strangers. She turned and walked quickly in the direction of her friends.

I nudged Robert and nodded towards Stephen. Robert looked over at him about the same time that Stephen looked and noticed us. He walked up to us with a smile. "What's going on boys? You having fun yet?" Robert gave him the once over and then with a smile began his interrogation. "What happened to you? We tried to find you on the dance floor and you were nowhere to be seen." Stephen gave him a look as if he been caught with his hand in the cookie jar. "Funny you ask, remember that woman I was dancing with? Well we ended up heading out to the van." Stephen wasn't up to his typical boasting self which threw a red flag up to Robert instantly. "Okay, and?" Stephen looked at us both and then sighed. "Nothing really, she got out there and had her panties down and I was about ready to drive it home when I noticed she had a fucking tan line on her ring finger. I looked at her and said well that's fucking nice. She tried to tell me how it wasn't a big deal, that her and her man were on the outs. I told her to get her fucking clothes on. She kept on being persistent so I ended up letting the skank suck on my boy for a while. Nothing big, no mess, she swallowed like a champ." Stephen smiled as he awaited the two of us to recognize his accomplishment. Robert just looked at him and then down to the ground. He shook his head in disbelief. "Are you fucking serious?" Stephen looked at him confused. "Yeah, what's the big deal, it's not like I fucked her." Robert looked back at him with a glare. "I'll tell you what the big deal is, you went against your own rule that you preach and teach everyone else. That pig that you hooked up with has a couple friends that are here, they both are married as well so I am sure they all know one another's husbands. They were all kinds of bent out of shape when they couldn't find the two of you." Stephen slowly developed a look of concern which he tried to shake off as fast as it had appeared. "It's not a big deal, if it wasn't my cock she was blowing on, it would have been someone else's. Besides, she said her and her husband is on the outs" Robert just shook his head. "You just don't fucking understand do you? Is that what you're going to say when her husband comes in here with his buddies and beats all of our asses? You fucking sicken me man." Stephen looked at him with a look of disbelief. "Just relax, it isn't going to happen. You're fucking drunk or something. Let me go and get a beer and we'll all go out on the floor with Hal and Sal and get some honeys!" Robert looked over at me and then back to Stephen. "I say fuck this place, let's go somewhere where it is going to be safe or just head home, either way, I am fine with it. I just don't want to stay here anymore." Stephen looked at Robert in amazement. "No, fuck that, we've been wanting to come up here all this time, there is no reason to head elsewhere and we aren't leaving this early. There's all kind of honeys here, nothing is going to happen, trust me." Robert said nothing as he looked Stephen up and down, shaking his head. The tension was now being felt by those standing around us.

The moment of silence was even tenser than the conversation that had preceded. The two of them stood there staring at one another. Robert took a deep breath, exhaled. "You know what, go ahead and stay, I'm fucking leaving. Tristan, if you want you can stick around, if you don't want to, you can head out with me." Stephen looked at him in disbelief. "What the fuck are you talking about? You aren't going home, besides no one else is going to be ready to go, what are you going to do, taxi it?" Stephen was calling what he thought to be a bluff. Robert looked at him, shook his head in disbelief and then walked away. Stephen looked at me with a smirk on his face. "Are you fucking serious, did that just happen?" I looked at Stephen who was completely lost on why Robert would be acting that way. "Yeah, he is serious. Go ahead and grab yourself a beer, I'll go talk to Robert, try and calm him down and see what I can figure out." Stephen just looked at me and then shook his head in disbelief and made his way to the bar.

I headed back down onto the dance floor, I began to look for Robert, as I looked around, I noticed the woman that Stephen had hooked up with standing off to the side with her friends. They were in a deep conversation. The woman seemed to be trying to plead her case. As she moved her hand, I noticed that her wedding ring was on her hand for both of her friends to see. Her friends continued to scold her to the point in which they were drawing attention. I realized that Robert was probably right on what the outcome was going to be. I continued to look around and found Robert as he walked away from Hal and made his way over to Sal. By the time I made my way through the crowd, he was shaking his head and walking away from Sal and off the dance floor. I caught up with him and put my hand on his shoulder. "So what exactly is going on?" I asked, although I was already pretty certain of what the answer was going to be. "They don't want to fucking go, they think I am fucking drunk and need to relax. I'm telling you what, Stephen fucked up. I don't want to be around him tonight. I am going to figure some way of getting home even if it means hitchhiking. You can do what you want. Either way, I am out of here." Robert was drunk, I knew that if there was no way of his friends calming him down or getting him to change his mind that there would be no reason for me to try. Besides, with what I had just witnessed with the woman Stephen hooked up with and the other two, I didn't really want to stick around. "I'll go ahead and head home with you but let me go and see if I can get Stephen to change his mind. You would still be up for us going somewhere else tonight as long as it wasn't here?" If it was ten minutes ago there might have been a chance. However, Robert was only becoming more irate. "No, I just want to get back down to Newark, I'll be honest with you, I am done with his stupid shit tonight, I don't want to be around him." I nodded my head in agreement. "Okay, just give me a minute or two and I'll be back." Robert nodded his head. I walked away and headed back to the bar. I had no clue how we were going to get home if Stephen refused to leave, a taxi would be too expensive. As I approached the bar, I found Stephen with a beer in hand looking like a desolate cowboy. I leaned up against him and he perked up. "Well, what the fuck is going on? Did you calm his ass down?" Stephen looked at me with concern. "No, he is wanting to go home, I told him that if you didn't want to go, I would go with him, that way we get him home safely." Stephen just looked at me in disbelief and shook his head. "Are you two really fucking serious? I'm not leaving here over something this petty. So you guys are going to head back down to Newark? How?" I had no clue myself. "I don't know." Stephen looked to be weighing everything out in his mind and then reached down in his pocket. "It's like whatever, if he wants to go, then so be it, here." Stephen handed me a twenty dollar bill for a taxi. That wouldn't pay for even half of the trip. "I'll give it to him, thanks." I began to walk away. "Hey Tristan, you two be safe. We'll meet you back home tonight, if anything changes just let me know, okay?" I nodded. "You make sure you stay safe," I said as I turned around and headed back to try and find Robert. He was no longer where I had left him.

I went and looked around the club and found Robert off to the side of the dance floor talking to a couple of women. Perhaps he had a change of mind. Neither of the women looked as if they would be of interest to Robert. The one he was focused on was short, maybe five foot two, a brunette with short hair. Although she had a cute face, she had a train wreck for a body. She looked to be in her mid-twenties. The woman next to her was possibly an inch taller, also a brunette, a little longer hair with curls, she was also heavy, with way to much makeup on. I wasn't sure why out of all the women Robert could have chosen to work on that he decided to go after these two. He had a smile on his face and seemed to be coming out of his mood so I wasn't going to complain. As he spoke, he looked up and saw me heading his way, he looked over at the women, said something and they both turned and looked at me. As they looked at me, Robert gave me a wink. Robert introduced me with a big smile "Ladies, here is the man of the hour that I spoke to you about, Tristan. Tristan, this here is Laura and her friend Marie." The women smiled and offered their hands. I could tell by Marie's smile and handshake that she was the one that was going to be hooking up with me. She had the longer hair of the two. I was drunk but not drunk enough to know that something wasn't right. I looked at Robert trying to use my eye contact to let him know we needed to talk. It didn't work. "Ladies, let's hit the dance floor," Robert said as he put his arm around the base of Laura's back and gently moved her onto the floor. Marie and I followed. I stood alongside Robert as we danced. The hook up was odd enough that it made the people around us stare wondering the same thing I was wondering and that is "why are they with them?" Robert leaned over towards me as the song was starting to end and said, "Follow my lead." Robert was loud with how drunk he was and how loud the music was. I wondered if the women were onto Robert or at least had heard what he had said, they continued to smile at us as we finished out the dance. Robert led us off the dance floor and reached deep into his pocket. "Tristan, go ahead and get us another round and get these two ladies anything they want." The women weren't used to this sort of attention and with it came some curious looks between the two of them. At first they declined the drink, but Robert persisted. As I walked away, I wondered what Robert was up to. I made my way to the bar. Stephen was still there having a drink. He watched me as I approached, gave me a small smirk and looked around to see if Robert was with me. "What's going on? Is Robert staying?" I could tell this had been weighing on Stephen considerably. "I really don't know, he just hooked up with a couple of women and asked me to go get us all drinks so I am not sure if he plans on staying or if he wanted to have one last round." Stephen nodded his head and then shrugged his shoulders as

COME WATCH THE NIGHTTIME BREATHE

if he didn't care. "I see, well, let me know what is going on when you figure it out." Stephen turned his back towards the bar and continued to drink. Once again, I had to wait for the bartender for quite a while before I was finally waited on. I grabbed the drinks and assured Stephen that I would let him know as soon as possible and headed off to find Robert and the two women. As soon as I rounded the corner, I found them, which was not a difficult task since they stood out amongst the rest. Robert gave me a big smile and a wink. Once I returned, we headed over to a table to drink. The two women excused themselves and headed to the restroom. Once they were out of sight, I looked over at Robert to see what exactly was going on. He was already shaking his head in disbelief of the situation we were in as well. He dropped his head and began to laugh, he took a moment, took off his glasses and rubbed his eyes almost violently as if he was trying to make this all go away. Once he placed his glasses back on he looked up at me with a smile. "Robert, what the hell are you doing? I don't know how drunk you are but these women are nowhere remotely close to our league!" Robert looked at me as if he was surprised I would even say something of the sort. "Are you fucking serious, Tristan? I fucking know that. These women give a whole new meaning to the term Coyote ugly!" I became more confused. "Then what in the hell are you trying to do?" Robert put his arm around me and patted me on the shoulder. "What does it look like I'm doing? I'm getting us a ride home, that's what I am doing. Nothing more, nothing less. Then again, a few more drinks and who knows, we may be up for more!" For a moment, I thought Robert had lost his mind. "Robert, we are almost thirty miles from home, there is no way you are going to get two women who have just met us and who have been drinking to take us all the way home, just for them to turn back around and head back to Columbus." Robert just smiled "How about this, not only will they be taking us home but we won't even have to have to pay them for the ride!" I just shook my head at Robert. "You my friend are completely out of your mind!" Robert just continued to smile, his patting of my shoulder became more of a massage. "You think? We'll see and you can thank me later." Robert seemed confident; unfortunately, he was also drunk.

The women headed back over towards us. They greeted us with smiles as Robert handed them both their drinks. "So what do you women say, drink up and then head to Newark? It's early enough, we could make last call somewhere." I looked over at Robert who had a big smile on his face. He had already secured the ride home while I must have been at the bar. Marie must have been the driver as she took a drink and nodded with a smile on her face. We finished our drinks as we tried to share some small talk over the music. Robert looked at the women and asked if they mind if the two of us went to the restroom before we headed out. They agreed and we walked away. Once we were out of their sight, Robert looked back and then looked at me. "Listen, we have a way home, it's not costing us a penny. It doesn't really matter what they think they're going to get out of this, they're both pigs, just have a drink with them when we get down to Newark and we'll call it a night." I looked at him as we entered the restroom. "How in the hell did you pull that off?" Robert just laughed. It's all about charm you see, a little friendly persuasion. I might end up making the car stink a little bit on the way home, I don't recommend for you to look back at us, it might not be something you want to see." Robert raised his eyebrows at me with a smile. "Actually, we may want to hurry up and head back there before the two of them disappear on us." Robert finished up and waited on me. "Go ahead, I need to stop and tell Stephen that we have a ride, he gave us twenty dollars for a taxi and asked me to let him know what we were going to do." Robert looked me up and down as I finished. "Okay, you tell that shit bag that we have a ride, just don't tell him who with, as for that twenty, that just bought us all a round down in Newark. Do you know of any decent places to hit that isn't too far out?" Robert had it all planned, I could tell he was well rehearsed. "Yes, there are a couple places." Robert nodded. "Okay, I am going to go catch our rides, you hurry up and tell him what is up, just be quick, I want to get out of here well before he sees us leaving and who we leave with." I nodded my head, Robert headed out the door as if he was trying to escape a fire.

I made my way over to Stephen, he was now joined by Sal. Stephen saw me as I approached and noticed that Robert wasn't with me. He looked as if he was now well aware of his crime. "So no Robert?" Stephen looked over my shoulder to see if he may be coming at any moment. "No, he is going to head home, I am going to go ahead and go with him. So we will meet you at the house as planned earlier." I could tell with my announcement that Stephen was disappointed and still in disbelief. Sal looked at us both blankly, it was obvious that he was unaware of what was going on. "Yes, I guess so. We are going to hit a couple more places once Hal comes back in with the honey he took outside." I nodded my head. "Just be careful, alright?" Stephen returned to his cocky self. "You two be careful, we will be fine." As I went to walk away Sal looked at Stephen for answers, Stephen told him that he would tell him in a minute. I walked around the corner and found Robert standing with the women, laughing, his charm was on overdrive. As he caught sight of me he nodded and gave me a smile as if he was grateful that I saved him from anymore alone time with Marie and Laura. I couldn't believe that the two weren't completely aware that they were both being used. Then again, something told me that they were aware, that this was the most attention they had received coming here and were willing to give us a ride home with the hopes something might happen.

We walked out to their car, Laura and Robert got in the back, Marie and I got in the front. As we pulled out I saw Hal who must have come out to try and intervene making his way back towards the bar; he was by himself. I looked back at Robert to see if he had seen Hal. However, Robert was already closing in on Laura as he began to lean in, whispering in her ear which caused her to giggle. I knew it was only a moment before the heavy breathing and the steaming of the windows would begin. Marie looked in the rearview mirror at the two of them and then leaned over and turned on some music. As she pulled out of the parking lot, I sat their quietly, looking out the passenger's side window at the scenery until it became nothing more than a blur. I could still hear the two of them moving around in the back seat, the uneasiness in the air was building quickly. I looked over at Marie and could tell that the music alone wasn't distracting her enough either. She looked at me and smiled "So Tristan, what is it again that you do?" It was the standard question one would use when they were running out of options and hoping that a conversation would take them to a better place. "I currently work at a carpet and flooring shop in Newark while contemplating what is next." She looked at me as if she was hoping for a thirty-minute description to keep her eyes from wandering to the rearview mirror. "I see and how exactly did you and Robert meet?" She said "Robert" loud enough in hopes to grab his attention but it didn't work. "Well, Robert is friends with Stephen, one of the guys we were with earlier. It is Stephens's brother who owns the store." I could see through the corner of my eyes Robert's hand drifting all over the place. "Well that's interesting. Do you all come to Columbus a lot or just on the weekends?" Marie was becoming more uncomfortable with each question she asked. She was stabbing away at a conversation that had no substance. "Well, this is the first weekend that we all have been together. Almost everyone is from Cincinnati so I just became acquainted with Robert and the guys this week." Marie looked over at me and nodded, she then leaned over and turned the music up a little louder as the commotion in the back seat increased. "So, I've been to Newark plenty of times, where exactly are we going to go?" Marie was now staring wide eyed out the windshield trying to keep her focus on the road. "I was thinking about going to the corner. There are a few different bars there that we can hit. We have to go to the Manor at the end of the night which is kind of nice since it will be on the way back home for you." Marie looked over at me just long enough to give me a small smile and then turned her head and attention back to the road as she picked up speed in hopes of getting to Newark and putting this drive behind us. I glimpsed back through the rearview mirror and as the two of them shifted around I was pretty sure that Robert had managed to get his cock out of his pants. I turned my attention back to the music, a smile appeared on my face.

Chapter XII

We made it into Newark and as we slowed down to get off the highway, Robert perked up and acted as if nothing at all had happened. The musk in the air confirmed that something had. "We are in Newark already? That was pretty quick," Robert said in a casual tone. Laura jumped in quickly behind him as she tried to catch her breath. "So where exactly are we going to go?" I looked back at the two of them, Robert looked at me with a big smile while Laura tried to avoid eye contact. "I figured we would all go to the Corner, it is late enough so the Corner should be happening." Marie turned the music down "Laura, we'll have just one or two and then take them home and head back to Columbus." Laura nodded her head and looked out the window. We pulled into the Corner to find the area busier than even I had expected. There were patrons outside wandering back and forth between the three bars. The corner bars were a notorious strip of three bars in the city, infamously named for its location on a corner of a busy intersection. The bar I preferred "Anthony's" was directly on the corner and had been around since the end of World War II, making it the oldest of the three. If you had lived in the city or even visited for a short time, you had hit the Corner bars. Anthony's was known for its classic 50s style décor and memorabilia. You were greeted as soon as you walked into the door with a long winding bar on your right and a long line of booths to your left. After the long line of booths which came to an end coinciding with the end of the bar, there was an additional open room with tables scattered throughout the area, the ladies' restroom, a jukebox next to the men's bathroom and a hallway which led to an additional room where billiards were and a stage for music. The bar pulled in a wide range of patrons and served as a great starting spot or an ending place on the weekends. It was also a nice laidback hangout throughout the week. We found a parking spot and made our way inside. The bar wasn't as bad as the parking lot seemed to be. I found ourselves a booth and made my way over to the bar to order us all a round of drinks.

As I headed back to the booth, Maria and Laura excused themselves to the restroom. Robert watched over my shoulder until they disappeared behind the bathroom door and then busted out laughing. "Holy shit, Tristan! That whole way down here was a fucking train wreck if you know what I'm saying!" Robert took a big drink of his beer to try and forget. "You didn't hold back at all did you?" I asked him as he busted out once more in laughter. "Hey, we got ourselves a ride home, didn't we? Now what you are going to do on your end is totally up to you, it's not like it matters once we get dropped off, you know?" Robert perked up and quit talking as he smiled over my shoulder to Laura and Marie as they made their way back from the bathroom.

The situation became uncomfortable. It became obvious that the trip to the restroom had not been a pleasant one, most likely a scolding for Laura. Everyone was quiet, looking at one another, smiling, drinking, with nothing to say. They were here for a reason, they knew it and as a result I could see them starting to despise us for it. Especially Laura knew deep down that she had given up way too much, way too soon with nothing in return. I looked for something to say, some way of making what time we had left enjoyable. "So, you say you girls visit Newark often?" I asked in desperation. Laura just sat there looking at Marie for the opportunity to get up and leave us there. Marie looked over at me with a smile. "I've been to Newark a lot, just not to hang out on a weekend. It just doesn't compare." Marie was trying to be nice. "I totally understand that, well I do want to thank you both for bringing us back to Newark. I only wish there was a way to repay you." Roberts's eyes widened from my comment as he gave me a smile. "Don't worry about it, I have a big heart. I'm curious though, what exactly happened for the two of you to just get up and leave your friends in Columbus?" Robert took a quick drink and then took lead of the conversation. "Well you see, our friends were being assholes. Well at least one of them was. Enough was enough." Marie looked unsatisfied with the answer. Robert continued. "You see, I go back with these boys for years. Tristan here is the newbie. The boys and I have certain guidelines we follow when we go out and about. The guidelines take on an all new meaning when we go out in areas that we are unfamiliar with. My one friend, the one I have known the longest, has always followed these guidelines, tonight he ignored them all which put us all at risk. I wasn't going to stand there and watch him bring our night to a close in what I will just refer to as catastrophic proportions." Robert's vague description heightened the girl's attention to find out more. "I guess I don't understand?" Laura spoke up with hopes that Robert would enlighten her. "There really isn't anything to understand, the guy is an asshole, you two were fortunate enough to make acquaintance with the best two of the bunch." Robert gave Laura a smile and slipped his hand under the table which brought a smile to Laura and a new kind of interest. I looked at Robert wondering what in the hell he was trying to do. He had left it in my hands with what all I decided to do with Marie but he was now setting the bar pretty high. I looked for a way to tell him to back it up but didn't want to risk a blind poke under the table that might miss its mark and notify the wrong person. Marie looked over at me with an awkward smile. She was beginning to hope for something similar, I wasn't as drunk as Robert and looked for a way out of the situation. I found that way through last call that was bellowed throughout the bar. I played it off as if I was disappointed. As I began to stand up, I asked the girls if they would like one last drink. Robert interjected before anyone could say anything and told me to grab us all a round. Marie passed since she had to drive home. I went up to the bar, grabbed us drinks and headed back, I caught a glimpse of Robert's hand that was working its way up and down Laura's leg. Laura tried her best to play it off but was losing control quickly. As I made my way back to the booth, I reached out with both of their beers and had them take them from my hand instead of placing them on the table just to get them to give it a break.

With beer in hand, Robert found a renewed focus and enjoyed each drink a little more than the previous. Laura sat there and took small sips, keeping her eyes on Robert hoping she could get him to pick up where he had left off. Marie grabbed her purse and threw it over her shoulder. She looked at me and gave me a courteous smile. She was trying her best to be friendly but it was obvious she wanted to get us home and head back to Columbus. I hurried my beer along which put me over the top for the night. Robert recognized that the night needed to end and finished his beer. I stood up and Marie followed. Laura was the only one taking her time, she looked at us in disappointment. "I am sorry, I'm just a really slow drinker." Robert stood up and stretched then looked down and grabbed the beer out of Laura's hand and finished the beer with one mighty tilt of the head. "There you go, sugar, we don't want the barkeep to come around and collect your beer before you have time to drink it." Laura looked at Robert in amazement. Marie was pressing against my feet so I walked towards the door. Once Laura realized that she wasn't going to get the attention she wanted, she got up and caught up with the rest of us as we headed out. Robert made his way next to me and leaned in, "Do you think we should have them take us somewhere to eat?" Robert gave me a big smile and busted out laughing. "No, I think we have been lucky enough as it is, we shouldn't press it." Robert looked me up and down. "You are probably right." We continued out to the car, Laura was now grabbing Robert's arm for support, Marie looked at me, her once courteous smile seemed now forced

The drive home was very similar to the drive from Columbus to Newark. Robert and Laura breathed heavy in between giggles while Marie and I looked for something to talk about or something to distract us. The heavy breathing brought a mixture of beer and musk up to the front seat that let Marie and I know that we needed to get home as soon as possible. I navigated Marie as she took through the streets like a getaway car. I was amazed that we didn't get pulled over this late at night driving as fast as we were. We pulled into Dick and Jeanine's driveway, I breathed a sigh of relief that we had beat the van home. I turned my head sideways and let Robert know we were home. He looked up, let out a rehearsed coughed as he zipped up his pants to try and reduce the amount of embarrassment Laura would feel. "This is an unbelievable neighborhood!" Laura said as she tried to get her breathing under control. "I have to admit, I didn't know a neighborhood like this existed in Newark," Marie added. "So Robert, this is where you live?" Robert was already reaching for the door handle. "No my dear, this is where I am staying for the time being, I will be heading back to Cincinnati soon, very soon." Laura reached for Robert and barely grazed his hand prior to him opening up his door, and leaning into my window, blocking me from being able to escape. "I seriously want to thank the two of you for going out of your way to bring us back to Newark, very much obliged." Laura looked as if she had just lost her best friend. "Well hold on there, I'll walk up to the door with you," Laura said in desperation. Robert smiled and headed off. Laura ran around the car almost falling as she attempted to catch up with Robert who picked up his pace the best he could without it looking too obvious. Soon it was just the two of us and the tension in the air became insurmountable. We sat there and both stared ahead. Neither of us knowing what to do. Finally as I looked over towards her it was she that took it upon herself to break the tension. "Listen Tristan, I know this is awkward. I don't want you to feel like you owe me anything. I understand." She looked at me with a smile. The night of drinking and the little bit of lighting in the car brought out an attraction that I had previously overlooked. "I know that, I do appreciate all that you and Laura did for us. We would have been lost without you two. I am sorry if Robert made you feel a bit awkward. I'm sure it wasn't in his attention." Marie smiled. "I'm not worried about it, Laura seemed to enjoy herself." We both laughed. "Can I give you some money for gas?" Marie looked at me as if I had insulted her. "Don't be silly, you bought us both drinks. However, you can tell me how to get the hell out of here when we leave so the two of us can get back to Columbus." I reached over and put my hand on her hand and then looked for a pen. "What are you looking for?" she smiled as she caught on quickly. "I was looking for my pen and a piece of paper that I typically carry but seem to have forgotten or misplaced it" She gave me a smile. "I'm not drunk Tristan, you can just tell me, I won't forget." She saw that I continued to look, she reached down in her purse and handed me a pen and a napkin. "I wasn't wanting pen and paper to write directions." I wrote down my name and number and handed it to her which brought a smile to her face. She took her pen back and returned the favor. "I had a nice night, Tristan, it was fun getting to know the two of you. I'm a bit old fashioned, so you will probably have to call on me first." I gave her a smile. Deep down, we both knew that unless by chance, the two of us would never meet again. I leaned over and gave her a kiss, as I pulled away I could sense that her lips desired more, I reached out and put my hand on her arm and pulled her in for a second, longer kiss. We pulled away softly, slowly. I gave her a smile. "I had a nice time as well. I do appreciate what all you have done for Robert and myself. I am sure we will be talking soon." Marie smiled and nodded. She knew it was all a charade. Once I told Marie how to find her way to the highway she smiled. "Thank you, Tristan, could you tell Laura to get back here unless she wants to try and find a ride home tonight?" I reached out one last time and grabbed her hand and then let go slowly as I opened the door and got out. "I can do that. Thanks Marie, please have a safe trip back to Columbus." I took one last look at Marie who gave me a smile, this smile was a little more forced than the previous ones which was understandable. She had been used. She could at least take some consolation that she had been saved a little dignity in comparison to Laura who by my calculation should be close to finishing off Robert as I headed towards the house.

I cleared my throat as I walked closer towards the door. I caught a glimpse of Robert and Laura who were standing off to the side of the steps talking. Laura was trying to secure another night out while Robert looked pained to still be standing there. He was trying his best to be nice. However, sooner or later his drunkenness would prevail. He saw me as I approached and gave me a look as if he needed to be saved. "Are you two still talking?" I said as I approached them. Laura was caught off guard and gave me a stare that assured me that my timing was off. "We were just saying goodbye." Robert said with a voice filled with exhaustion. "That is probably a good idea, Marie wanted me to tell you that if you wanted a ride back to Columbus that you might want to get out to the car." Robert gave me a smile knowing that he was about to be saved. "I see," Laura said coldly. She reached down in her purse, all the while Robert began to move his way around her to get in alignment with the front door. She reached out as he passed and handed him a piece of paper with her phone number. "Give me a call?" she said desperately as she leaned up for a kiss. "Yeah, sure. I can do that." Robert wasn't enthused. He leaned down and met her eager lips for a small peck and continued to walk past her. Laura looked disappointed. She stood there and watched Robert as he headed to the door, not knowing if she should say anything else and if so, what. Robert made his way past me quickly and stumbled up the steps and through the door. I looked at Laura who continued to stand there even with Robert being gone. "Hey, I want to thank you for getting us home tonight. Please be safe on the way home and could you thank Marie again for me?" Laura never made eye contact with me. "No problem." She began to walk away dejected. I started for the steps when she stopped and turned around. "Tell Robert to give me a call sometime." She gave me a smile and then walked away. I assured her that I would as I watched her from the front door until she was out of sight and I heard the car pull off.

I walked into the house and found Robert raiding the cupboards. He turned and busted out laughing once we made eye contact. "Was that some crazy shit or what?" He asked as he threw some potato chips into his mouth. "That was definitely some crazy shit. Not sure exactly how we pulled it off, but we made it home safe and sound!" Robert nodded with agreement as he chewed quickly so he could swallow and rejoin the conversation. "The fact is, not much worse for wear! My fingers smell like the shit stall of a tuna boat and my cock is a bit beat up, but we made it! How about you? You were out in her car for a pretty long time!" Robert headed towards the refrigerator and looked for more food and something to drink. "Marie was really nice. You raised the bar quite high, higher than I cared to reach. However, I gave her a couple kisses goodbye and talked for a while before we exchanged phone numbers." Robert nodded as he pulled out some deli meat and bread to make a sandwich and searched around until he found a couple of beers tucked away behind the produce. "Ha ha! Look at what I found us, my boy!" Robert showed the two beers he had found as if it was a lost treasure. "By the way, the trashcan is over there, you can throw that number away just as I did mine." Robert gave me a wink. He made his sandwich, piling the meat on until the bag was practically empty, he looked over and tossed me what was left and then smiled as he grabbed the sandwich and the two beers and headed towards the basement.

Chapter XIII

By the time I made my way downstairs with sandwich in hand, I found Robert with his shoes off, his legs kicked up on the coffee table and finishing the last of his sandwich. He took a big drink of his beer and looked over as I took a seat in the recliner. "Now that hit the spot! So Tristan, the way I look at it, as the bars close, the boys will most likely grab a bite to eat in Columbus, where there are more options. With that in mind, they will sit around, sober up while they eat and discuss the night prior to heading home." Robert spoke like a field general as he walked step by step through what was left of his soldier's night prior to their return from the battlefield "This leaves us plenty of time to finish our beer and go to sleep before the guys get back. I don't know about you, but I am in no mood to deal with any of them tonight." I could tell there was much more to be said, so I simply nodded in agreement. Robert continued, "You know, we never had much time to talk. Then again, we haven't had any alone time. Since we now have some time, and the room to ourselves, I must say, I'm intrigued." Robert paused long enough to allow me the time to look over with curiosity. "Tell me your story, Tristan." The request was vague, I said nothing as I continued to look over, awaiting more. Robert obliged, "You are an interesting cat. I recognized that the moment we met. So tell me, who in the hell are you? Now mind you, before you sort through your answer, this conversation is between us and the four walls and that is where it will remain." Robert brought the statement to a close with a reassuring smile as he raised his beer towards me and took a drink.

Still uncertain on what he was truly wanting to know, how much to expose and where to begin, I took a drink of my beer, then as I parted my lips, I allowed the first words that seemed most eager to escape me to come out. "I guess you would say that I'm an old soul, yet a free spirit that is a bit lost, looking for his way home." My answer unintentionally left as much mystery as Robert's question. Robert leaned back, allowing my response to resonate. Then with a sigh, he went through his hair with his hands, pausing as if he was considering pulling his hair out before leaving his hair in a mess as he went down over his face, before finally folding his arms and allowing them to rest on his stomach. He then turned and stared at me as if he had been short changed. "Bravo, my boy, well scripted. So how many people have you fed that line to?" We looked at one another, he cast a stare that was eager for more, while my stare searched for more guidance. "So you took the high road with your response which is typical. However, you my friend, are by no means typical. You can rest assured that I am here to buy, just not the shit you are currently trying to sell. Now, how about we venture off that high road and venture down the path less traveled. After all, that is your style, is it not?" Robert smiled which I reciprocated. "I assure you what I stated, although vague is accurate. If you want me to elaborate more, I would say that as I am coming of age, I am less content with what is deemed the norm. By no means do I consider myself a rebel, which similar minds, individuals may be cast as, and I falsely stereotyped as. You see, there is something within me that just won't allow what I feel to be complacency. I know there is so much more out there. I want that, I need that and I demand it." I paused long enough to ensure that Robert was following. Robert repositioned himself, now sitting at the edge of his seat, smiling, engaged. "Yes, yes, I see that, it is in your eyes. So what exactly is it that you are seeking or have you yet to figure it out?" I took a deep breath which was then released as a frustrating sigh. "I seek much more than the American dream. Although the American dream has always been cliché, In time, it has simply become too cliché, diluted. I seek enlightenment, I seek the meaning of life? The meaning of my life? You see, where most people's search is driven out of curiosity, mine goes far beyond that. My search is driven by the demons from within, as a result, it is a necessity. Without it, I feel as if I will lose my sanity or at least what is left of it. With this much on the table, why do I feel as if I am looking for answers to questions that have yet to be asked?" I could see that my tone had become one of frustration by the expression on Robert's face.

A silence filled the room. Robert glanced over at me, then the clock before letting out a long sigh and returning his attention back towards me. This time he looked into my eyes, his stare was piercing and with purpose. "I follow you, Tristan. If for no other reason, because we all are search- ing, seeking. The difference between you and myself and most others is that your search is much more intense, which supports what you stated." Robert stopped momentarily so I could confirm that I comprehended the obviousness in which he spoke. I nodded and he continued. "I guess when I started this conversation, when I told you that you were an interesting cat, I could have, I should have elaborated more. You see, the day we were introduced and I stared into those eyes, I saw something which you may typically prefer to hide. I saw within those eyes a story to be told. I saw a mystery and a bit of madness. Perhaps there is more madness than I initially observed, if so, you hide it well. You stated that you fear you may lose your sanity or what is left of it if you fail to find that which you seek. However, I feel that it is the madness that is the force, the fuel that drives you and your search. Is that enough to help you find what you seek? I don't know." Once again silence filled the air. I thought of what Robert said. "Perhaps" was all that I could say which seemed to be more than enough to allow Robert to continue. "What I will share, you already know. Nonetheless, I will state this, I feel comfortable in saying that every human on this earth questions their existence, their purpose. It goes back to Buddha, even before. Buddha attained enlightenment, yet hesitated when it came to teaching. There was so much to teach yet only so much he could impart. The journey is long, with many paths. As a result his teachings can lead you down a path, but it will be up to you whether you stay on that path for its entirety or stray. I feel that most take different paths to find their meaning, their purpose, or possibly unbeknownst to them, take a wrong turn somewhere along the way and became complacent. I feel the perfect example of this was the Beat generation. Always looking for some type of conformity as non-conformists. And that is you, Tristan. You are a modern day beatnik and there is nothing wrong with that. As for myself, Stephen and the others, we fall in a similar category to what I mentioned. We are men of simplicity, we were born and raised in the city that we will most likely spend the rest of our lives and die in. We get up, we go to work, we make enough to get by and have enough left over to go out and have fun. We still have our ventures, they are just a bit more contained. The day will come where we will settle down, perhaps get married, perhaps have a family and we will be content with that. Now, I don't know what the future will bring for you, not sure whether your search will yield success. However, I wish you the best of luck and Godspeed. Now, since the likelihood of us crossing paths again will be in the hands of fate. I want to say the following. As you search so diligently be mindful not to get lost. I fear that one day you could look back and realize that in your search to find the meaning of life that you forgot to live." A concerned smile appeared on Robert's face as he waited for a response. His words burrowed deep into my mind, my soul. "I appreciate everything that you said." And with that response, the conversation that still had substance, inadvertently came to an end.

I looked up at the clock and realized that Stephen and the others could be walking in the door at any moment. I finished my beer and positioned myself to fall asleep although I was no longer tired. Robert turned on the television more or less for some background noise as he stared at the television blankly and let out a drawn out yawn. "Are you still pissed off at Stephen?" I asked a question in which I already knew the answer but I wanted to spark up some conversation before Robert fell asleep and left me to fend for myself. The question broke Robert's trance-like state as he looked over at me with a smirk and shook his head in disappointment. "Man, you don't even know! Stephen has really been trying me. This isn't anything new. However, lately I have been struggling to deal with it. Perhaps it is not him, perhaps it is me. Nonetheless, I'll be glad to get back home and not deal with his shit for a while." That was the first time that I had heard the confirmation that Robert and the guys were indeed heading back home. "You guys are about to head home?" I asked as I finished the sandwich I had neglected during the previous conversation and turned my attention towards my beer. "We hope to leave as early as next weekend. Don't get me wrong, I'm sure we will be back sometime. We didn't think we would be here past this weekend but Dick still needs us to help out and we all were able to work things out at home so we could stick around." Robert went back to looking at the television. I let the news settle in and then took another drink of my beer. I went to continue the conversation when Robert perked up. "Did you hear that?" Robert asked as he listened attentively. "Hear what?" I asked. "I think I just heard the van pull in." I leaned up in my recliner and listened. A couple of doors shut and some drunken voices could be heard slurring as they made their way to the door. "It's Stephen and the boys, I'm not going to deal with it, just tell them I'm asleep," Robert whispered as he lay down, turning his back to me and played make believe. I could hear the guys enter the house, Stephen shushing them as they laughed and conversed loudly amongst one another. I tried to finish my beer and close my eyes but they were already stumbling down the stairs towards me.

Stephen led the way into the basement and leaned down as he walked past to make sure my eyes weren't closed. Once he saw that I was still awake he gave me a smirk. "I see you were able to find my nightcap. When did you guys get home?" Hal and Sal made their way past me and sat down. Both of them were quite drunk and fumbled their way through taking off their shoes to settle in. "I'm not sure, half hour maybe an hour." Stephen looked unsatisfied with my answer. "Is Robert passed out or just not talking?" Stephen looked over at him with a dirty look and then turned his attention back towards me. "He passed out a little while ago." Stephen looked at me as if he didn't believe me. "Is he still pissed off at me?" I wasn't sure how to answer it, I was drunk, I wanted to go to sleep, didn't want to get in the middle of it any more than I already was but could tell by Stephen's glare that he was going to be persistent until he got an answer. "I think he is calming down a bit, I would just let it go." Stephen looked down at him and shook his head. "He has no reason to be pissed. Oh well, what did you guys end up doing? How did you get home? Did you taxi it?" Stephen had less concern, more curiosity on how we finished our night. "We were going to get a taxi but then Robert met a couple women who knew their way around Newark and he ended up sweet talking them into taking us home." Hal looked up

178

as I finished the comment. "Was that the two pigs I saw you guys in the parking lot with?" Hal asked as he smiled and winked at me. "Yes, they were the ones." Stephen looked at me unamused. "So you didn't need the twenty dollars after all? Well, you might as well fork it over." Stephen extended his hand as if it was the last twenty dollars he possessed. I looked for a way out. "I gave the women twenty dollars for taking us home." Stephen dropped his hand in disgust. "You're telling me, you got two pigs to take you home and then gave them twenty dollars? Did you get your dick dirty or at least some stink on your fingers? They would have probably been happy with that, no need to give them my money." Stephen's voice was getting louder. He walked over to the other recliner and sat down to take off his shoes. I thought that possibly the conversation was over and we would all be retiring when Stephen tossed his first shoe and started back up. "So Robert gets pissed off for no fucking reason whatsoever and then takes my fucking twenty dollars and burns through it like it's nobody's business. That is pretty fucking awesome if you ask me." At this point Robert turned his head towards us and slurred. "Let it fucking go, Stephen, just let it go." Robert's comment surprised them all. Stephen looked at me as he stood up as if I had betrayed him by telling him that Robert was passed out and then turned his attention towards Robert. "You have absolutely no reason to be pissed off at me, Robert. I did exactly what you have done a million times over." Robert turned his body towards us all more, so he could be heard. "No, no I haven't. Don't even start to compare me with your poor ass standards." Robert's face turned red. Stephen looked at him and smirked. "Whatever makes you feel better, Robert." Stephen seemed lost for words. "First off, I don't have to say anything to make myself feel better, I have morals. For seconds, you need to step away from me and go sit down before you really piss me off." The room became quiet, the tension was thickening. Robert was becoming more and more agitated, Stephen stood there defiantly, not about to step down in front of all his friends. Everyone sat there in silence, not knowing what to say, what to do, feeling uncomfortable.

A couple moments passed which seemed like an eternity when Hal finally reached over and smacked Robert on his ass. "Settle down there, tiger, no reason to show your stripes." Hal worked his gum as he gave Robert a smile and a wink. The diversion seemed to work as Robert gave Hal a smile. The tension although still strong seemed to be slowly lifting from the room. Stephen paused for a moment, then after shaking his head and letting out a long sigh, headed upstairs. Once he made it up the final step, Robert settled completely down. He mimicked Stephen under his breath as he shook his head, sighed and then closed his eyes. Everyone else in the room acted as if nothing had happened and began getting ready to go to sleep. I decided to close my eyes with hopes of passing out before Stephen made it back downstairs.

Chapter XIV

The next morning when I woke up everyone was sprawled out throughout the room. I knew I had a long day ahead of me once I saw my mother so I decided to work my way through the maze of bodies carefully, trying my best to be as quiet as possible and keep from waking anyone up. I was successful as I made my way up the stairs and out the door. I drove home half hungover and half-drunk trying to figure out the best way of dealing with my mother's scorn once I walked in the door. I had pressed my luck extremely hard this weekend, something I wouldn't be able to continue doing if I had any hopes of continuing to live there. I did the proverbial holding of my breath as I made my way up the street in fear that my clothes might already be packed and sitting on the front porch for me to collect. I caught a break, not only was the front porch clear of my belongings, my mother's car wasn't there. I looked at my watch and realized that she was at church, which was something else that she would hold against me for missing. Once church ended she would more than likely go to the Sunday social where the parishioners had coffee and donuts and spent an hour or so conversing with one another. She would then make a quick stop to the grocery store before returning home to start preparing our traditional Sunday dinner. I pulled in, made my way inside, went to the kitchen and found my note that I had left her, looking as if it hadn't been touched. I grabbed something to drink and a bite to eat and headed upstairs in an effort to avoid her.

I turned on some music, laid back in bed and ate a sandwich while leafing through a few pages of Rimbaud. I eventually fell asleep as I read, when I woke up I could hear the familiar voices of my family and the aroma of Sunday dinner cooking. I looked over at the clock it was closing in on 4:00 p.m. I had successfully wasted a whole Sunday morning and afternoon sleeping off the previous night's drama. I continued to lay there, listening to the voices of my sisters, at least two of the three had arrived. The more present, the more likely my mother wouldn't risk ruining the dinner with an argument. I was more than capable of dealing with dirty looks, it was the actual confrontation I could do without. I waited till it was closing in on five before I got up and began to make my way to the door. Just as I grabbed the doorknob my mother approached the steps and yelled, "Dinner is ready, are you going to come down and join us or were you just going to sleep all day?" I grimaced as I opened the door. I looked down the steps and found her looking back up at me. She gave me a glare. "Was it that big of a night? Do you need to sleep it off?" she mumbled as she walked away. The conversation was rhetorical, or at least I played it to be.

I made my way into the kitchen and found all my siblings there with their children. They all looked at me with judgmental stares, assuring me that they had heard my mother's ranting. The table was full which gave me the opportunity to grab some food and go into the living room to eat while avoiding more stares. I sat there alone, ate in peace and planned an after dinner walk strategically around my sisters' departure to buy a little more time before any argument could take place. That evening, I wandered the streets aimlessly as did my mind. However, my mind was allowed to do so without the voices that usually torment me. I couldn't help but question, why? I have been searching to find myself, my meaning. Was I heading in that direction with the life I was leading? This was the most peaceful I had felt in quite some time and yet, there must be more. I came back home to find my mother out in the kitchen, cigarette smoke lingered in the air with the sounds of her playing solitaire. I kept to myself in the front room, turning some music on low and kicked my legs up on the couch. I lay there and listened to the music, reliving the weekend with the boys until I eventually drifted off. When I awoke, I was surprised that the house was dark except in the living room. The phone never woke me up, my mother never woke me up. The fact that she had retired for the night was probably for the best. I quietly got ready for bed and called it a night.

The next day as I got ready for work I began to wonder what the atmosphere was going to be like. Had Robert and Stephen resolved their issues, would there be tension, would Judith and the rest hound me to know what exactly was going on? I pulled into work and noticed that only Jeanine and Dick were at the shop along with Judith and Ann. I walked in and went straight back to work to avoid any questions about the weekend. I seem to pass the staff without being noticed. I grabbed my job order and began to work. The day was uneventful and without the presence of Stephen or any of the guys from Cincinnati until just prior to leaving. That was when Stephen made his way back. It never ceased to amaze me at how good Stephen was at playing off the events of the weekend and to be able to focus on his profession. He came back and worked alongside me. Once we were done with all the cuts he took a moment before I left for the day to go over what we would be working on this week when the time permitted. We went over to the other warehouse. Once we were completely away from anyone possibly being able to hear us, he started in. "So, what did you think about the weekend?" Stephen asked as he was obviously still disturbed on how the weekend went. "You know honestly, I didn't. The weekend has been put to rest." Stephen wasn't about to let the conversation end like that. "Do you think that maybe Robert was a little fucked up and that he went over the deep end just a little?" Stephen was looking for support. "I really don't know, you guys have hung out for so long, you have your own rules. I just think that Robert was upset that you took a chance that could have caused problems for all of us by night's end. I think he was upset because he cares, you know?" Stephen wasn't buying it. "I think he was pissed because I was hooking up and he wasn't having any luck, oh well." Stephen was doing his best to reinforce the decisions that he made over the weekend. "Well, what is going on with Robert and the guys? I haven't seen them all day?" Stephen kind of shrugged his shoulders. He took a moment and then turned towards me. "I guess Robert got a phone call Sunday morning, he needed to head back to Cincinnati so the rest of the guys went as well to take care of some loose ends. They said they would be back mid-week but I don't know if they will or not. If they do, Robert probably won't come back. He is like that. When he gets pissed off at someone, it can take him a week or two to bounce back." I nodded my head. "I'm sure he'll be back, you guys have been through a lot, this is nothing." Stephen looked at me and smirked. "Robert can be pretty stubborn, we've had some pretty bad fights in the past. I don't know, I guess we'll see." I could tell that Stephen was still upset about the argument. We finished the day without talking, the silence was confirmation that Stephen was preoccupied with the reassessment of what all took place over the weekend.

The week was uneventful, the absence of Robert, Hal and Sal kept Stephen pretty much to himself. The whole business was quiet. Stephen and I, when we did have a chance to work, did so in silence. Wednesday came and went without any of the guys arriving. Stephen spent most of the time with Dick that day. I worked hard to get the back warehouse where Stephen wanted it. It was Thursday morning when Robert, Hal and Sal arrived. Their arrival livened the place up for Dick and Jeanine. Stephen and Robert still acted a little tense with one another but they were able to co-exist. It was Friday afternoon when Dick came back to check on us. "Look at you all! Very impressive. You better be careful, Tristan, I think these boys may be after your job!" Dick looked at me and gave me a smile. "You don't have to worry about us, Tristan, we have to be heading home soon. Your job is safe," Robert looked over and reassured me. Roberts's announcement turned the heads of Stephen and Dick. It wasn't to anyone's surprise that the guys were going to be heading back to Cincinnati, it was more of a surprise that the time had come so soon. "When do you think you guys are going to be heading out?" Dick asked in a curious tone. "Hal and Sal need to be heading out Sunday. I could possibly come back and go one more week," Robert said. "I see, well if that is the case and there is nothing that I can do to keep you guys can do to stick around, then we should all go out before you leave." Dick's comment brought an ornery smile to Hal and caught the curiosity of both Robert and Stephen. "Really? Your old lady is going to unlock the chains and let you run with the bad boys for a night?" Hal asked as he reached out and jabbed at Dick's ribs. "Shit, my wife has no lock and key over me, I go out when I want," Dick said with confidence as Robert raised a doubtful eyebrow towards him. "Shit, whatever," Stephen said with a smirk which got Dick to look over. "What's wrong, don't think you can hang with your big brother?" Stephen smirked. "I have no fear or concerns on that, I just don't know if you can run with the young dogs,"

Stephen said with confidence. Dick looked over towards Sal and I who had yet to partake in the conversation. "What do you think, Tristan, you think this old dog can run with the young pups?" I was unable to answer before Stephen jumped in. "Shit, he's not the one to ask, hell, he can't run with us ether." The stakes were growing. "You hear that, Tristan? They have no faith in either of us. I'll tell you what, we'll call the bluff. Let's get it going tonight! Tristan, get out of here and go get ready, meet us over at the house around eight thirty, eight o'clock if you want to get off to an early start and have some beers before we leave." Without saying a word, I was committed to going out with all the guys, this time with the boss as well. I began dreading what was to come of the evening before I even headed home. Not to mention, I was going to have yet again, my hands full with my mother as I tried to devise a plan that would let me get out for the night.

The only thing I could come up with as I pulled into my house was to be forward with my mother and tell her that it was the boss's idea for us all to go out. Possibly play the whole "final get together for the boys" card. I walked in and found my mother in the front room, having a beer and looking at me as if she already correlated Friday nights and me leaving. I was surprised with how passive she was when I told her about the plans. Whether she completely understood or had completely given up I wasn't certain. All she ended up saying is that I better get something to eat before I left and to go get a shower so I didn't end up making any of them wait. Although there was some definite tension when it came to me going out with my boss and the guys, I couldn't have asked for a better start to the night with the little bit of resistance I felt from my mother. Yet, there was a part of me that stood there feeling worse than if there would have been resistance. I watched my mother as she resumed her game of solitaire. I realized at that moment that this woman was all I had, meant everything to me. I realized that deep down, her acceptance, her approval was not only something I wanted but needed. As the weight of my stare began to bare down on her she paused and looked up at me. For a moment, without saying a word, I felt as if she understood. "You better get going," she said in a soft tone. I nodded and walked away. I headed to the kitchen, made myself something to eat and then got in the shower, trying to get everything done before she had the opportunity to drink a couple more and possibly become more difficult. I made my way out of the shower, got dressed and headed into the living room. My mother was still sitting there with the beer cans and cigarette butts accumulating besides her. The only thing she said as I came in was that Stephen had called and wanted to know if I had left and if not, how much longer she thought I would be. I told her that I wasn't going to call him back. Instead, I would just head out. This provided no time at all for her to have second thoughts or voice her concerns. It also would keep the guilt I was already feeling a chance to strengthen and become insurmountable to overcome. I told her that going out with them would probably result with me being out for the entire night. She answered in a labored tone that she had already figured that, to be careful and try not to make too much of an ass out of myself in front of my boss. I made her a promise that I wouldn't. A promise that we both knew I would most likely break. I thanked her for reasons outside of the obvious and headed out the door.

As I made my way across town, I began to think of the night that awaited us all. I was uncertain if it had ever leaked out to Dick that there had been some issues between Stephen and Robert. If so, would they be resolved, could the two of them make an exception with their differences and actually enjoy what would probably be their last weekend out and even more rare, a weekend in which they would be able to hang out with Dick? The fact that Dick was going out with us for the first time also sparked my curiosity and raised some questions. First, how would Dick interact with everyone once he had an excessive amount of alcohol in him? Second, how would he act with me when drinking in excess and his real feelings towards me surfaced? My curiosity grew more and more on my way there as did excitement and some anxiety. As I pulled in, the anxiety worsened. I made it there early which seemed to shock the whole crew as Dick opened the door with a big smile as if I was a long lost friend that had found my way to his doorstep. He called out my name in a drunken slur to the guys, who cheered as I walked through the doorway. Upon entering the kitchen, I was greeted with a mountain of empty cans forming on the table and around the sink which had far surpassed any amount that I could recall on the other nights. Everyone was laughing, even the tension between Stephen and Robert seemed somewhat controlled. Dick handed me a beer; I had a lot of catching up to do which was reaffirmed by Hal who patted me on the back. I decided to take a step back, take in the activities more so as a spectator and observe the interactions between Stephen and Robert. Dick for the most part played the role of storyteller as he shared one story after another about the follies between the guys and him that had occurred in the not so distant past and some of his own adventures that had similarities to the ones that Stephen and the guys had experienced. Each story became epic as the others shared their perspectives and eventually ended with a roar of laughter. The stories continued and so did the drinking until Dick realized we were running low on beer and the time to head out was drawing near.

Chapter XV

The plan to possibly go to Columbus came to an abrupt end when everyone declined getting behind the wheel to get us there as a result of the amount of alcohol everyone had gone through. As everyone congregated outside of the van, Dick decided to drive. As we left the manor, Stephen suggested that we hit Truman's first since we had yet to go there as a group. This was the prelude to telling everyone about his experience there, an experience that was heightened by as much fabrication as it was actual events. Stephen looked at me and smiled as he carried on. I wasn't sure if the smile was there for me to reinforce his tale or if he was buying into his own storytelling and the smile was coincidental. Either way, I shared the smile and listened to the tale unfold with a newfound interest. The stories continued until we pulled into the parking lot, then a silence filled the air, silence caused by disappointment. The place wasn't completely bare but empty enough to draw some concerns from the guys. As I previously stated when Stephen and I first visited the bar, I assured them all that it was still somewhat early and that the club would be happening shortly. Everyone took turns looking at one another with expressions of uncertainty. Then, with reluctance, some collected sighs, and nowhere else to go, Dick turned off the van. We all got out and slowly made our way towards the bar with a walk similar to a prisoner making his way down death row.

Once inside, Robert and the others paused, looked around and took in the atmosphere. Stephen asked them to find us a good place for us all to congregate and then motioned for me to follow him. The two of us made our way to the bar. As we approached the bar, Stephen nudged me as he saw the barmaid he had previously spoken to. At first she came over and gave Stephen the cold shoulder, treating him in a manner so professional that it came across as fake almost rehearsed for this exact moment. Stephen saw right through it immediately, gave me a smirk as she turned her back to us and then gave her the same treatment when she returned with our drinks. Stephen paid her and left her a nice tip which made her eyes widen as she fought back the smile that tried to surface. Stephen paid no mind, said nothing as he gathered up what he could and slowly began to walk away. While I grabbed the rest I noticed that the barkeep kept an eye on Stephen as he left. Her effort had not only failed, but in her failure it showed not only Stephen but anyone that had observed their interaction how weak she was. Stephen had her in the palm of his hand. We rounded the corner of the bar, making our way towards the dance floor to find the guys. Once we were out of sight from the barmaid Stephen turned his head towards me and began to boast. "She is so into me, she doesn't even realize it. It's only a question of if and when I tear her to shreds." All I could do was smile while I nodded in agreement. Stephen was already off and running.

The guys motioned us over to a corner right off the entrance of the dance floor. It was dark in the corner; you could make out figures but couldn't tell who was who until you were upon them. It was the perfect place to bring your woman, where you could practically get away with anything without being noticed or the perfect place to hide from someone if you were trying to shake them momentarily to work some other woman. Stephen immediately congratulated Hal and Robert for being the masterminds behind the location. The guys stood there for a moment, surveyed the floor simultaneously and tilted back their bottles of beer in sync with one another. Once they put down their bottles, they headed onto the dance floor. The ratio of women to men was yet to be a desirable one so I stayed behind and continued to observe the women as they walked in the door. I hadn't noticed at first but Dick had stayed behind as well and stood there with drink in hand, watching the guys go out and make their way towards the few women that were lingering around in packs. Packs that were meant to protect one another in situations like these now actually served more as an invitation. As I took a drink I noticed Dick slowly inching towards me. Once he closed in enough to converse he leaned in and asked, "What are you doing here? Get out there with the guys and dance." I looked at Dick, his eyes were becoming lazy, his face was red and the slur more and more noticeable. "I usually like to let the guys get settled in first. Besides, the pickings are slim right now. I'll get out there in the next beer or so, it'll open up a little by then. What about you Dick? Why aren't you out there with them?" Dick tilted his head and gave me a smirk as if he was surprised that I would even think about asking such a thing. "Those days are far behind me. Don't forget, Junior, I am a married man. I don't think my pregnant wife would be too happy with me if I was out there dancing with some skank." Dick's answer seemed more targeted towards self-reassurance than it was as an actual statement based off of facts. I nodded my head in understanding, but I wasn't buying anything that he was selling. I turned my attention back to the floor, hoping it would bring the casual conversation that turned awkward to an end which proved to be successful. By the time I was halfway through my bottle, Dick had finished off his drink and with a nudge asked if I was ready for another. I nodded my head and watched him walk away. The night was going to be interesting.

By the time Dick returned. All the guys were with women and were on the dance floor. The dance floor was becoming crowded and the area around it was filling up as well. Dick worked his way through the crowd, handing me my beer with a lazy smile. "I had my doubts, we all did, but this place is really starting to happen!" Dick turned his attention to the dance floor to try and find the guys. "Yes it is, this is turning out to be a good night." Dick was oblivious to what I had just said as he continued to look around; soon he busted out laughing. He shook his head in disbelief and then looked around a bit more. Once again, he busted out laughing. "Come here, Tristan, you have to see this!" I walked over towards him as he took in what he was seeing like a proud father. "Look out there at Hal and Sal! They are working them women in circles, Sal is priceless, look at him letting loose with that broad!" I looked around anxiously to find Sal. He had always been conservative. Getting the opportunity to actually see him work his magic was priceless. I finally found the two of them. Dick was drunk but he was accurate with what he was witnessing. Sal was actually the center of attention on the dance floor. His improvisation had the crowd staring but his confidence also had them acknowledging, appreciating him. Dick was loving it as he busted out laughing once more. Hal was doing everything he could to keep up with Sal and yet keep his calm, cool composure. Behind them was Robert and Stephen who were teamed up with a couple of women that were attractive and well dressed. Robert and Stephen's attention had shifted from the women to Sal as they took it in with a big smile and cheered him on. It was nice to see Robert and Stephen coexisting once more. Dick was getting antsy; he was easy to read. As I saw him glance over at me in an inconspicuous manner, I could tell that he suddenly didn't want me there, that I was keeping him from going onto the dance floor and having the kind of night he truly desired and probably thought he deserved. "Hey Tristan, why don't you go and get the guys a round of drinks." This time Dick's tone and body language were more like it had been at work. He handed me a twenty, I nodded and made my way to the bar.

The bar had also become crowded and as a result there was another barkeep assisting the patrons. Any opportunity to chat with the barkeep that Stephen was working came to an end as I was greeted with the help. As I waited for the order to arrive, the barkeep that was playing cat and mouse with Stephen noticed me and smiled. She took a moment to survey the bar and then glanced back over for a moment before returning to all the out-stretched hands that waited for her attention. I quickly grabbed the beers as they were placed on the bar and made my way back to the dance floor. I first spotted Stephen and Robert, I handed them their beers just in time as they looked as if they were becoming a bit desperate for a replacement. Robert leaned over and asked where Dick was. I told him the situation. He just frowned and shook his head. Stephen had a disgusted look on his face as he overheard what I had said. "You tell his lame ass to get out here and dance with us. It's just dancing, it's not like he has to hop in bed with any of these women." I nodded in agreement and then made my way over to Hal and Sal. Hal took the beer and gave me a wink as his mouth continued working his gum without rest. I handed Sal his beer, he smiled and took the beer, immediately turning his attention back to the woman he was dancing with. It was good to finally see Sal in the manner that everyone had talked about in the last couple weeks. He had a glow about him, he was confident and it showed. The woman he was dancing with was by far the best looking in comparison to the women that the other guys had. I went to make my way back to Dick, who I noticed was keeping an eye on me as I came back. As I neared the end of the dance floor I noticed a woman who looked familiar and made my way over to her. When I came closer to her I realized it was not who I had expected. However, she had noticed me and had smiled, so I continued on over and took advantage of the set up. We stood there and spoke for a few moments. It was hard to hear her over the music and the crowd. The one thing that I did determine was that she wasn't here with anyone. We mingled for a while and shared laughs. She seemed to laugh with every sentence I spoke whether it was a funny comment or not which confirmed her interest and proved to be somewhat annoying. It wasn't long before I became tired of it all and excused myself to the restroom. I took a few extra moments in the restroom hoping someone else would have decided to give her some attention before I returned. As I exited, she was still standing alone but with her attention turned to the dance floor. I made my way past her quickly, certain that she called out to me. I continued on and made my way back to where Dick was.

When I got back to our table, Dick was gone. I didn't think much of it. My beer was running low and I figured at the pace he was drinking he would be found at the bar. After a few glances on the dance floor I realized that he hadn't made it to the bar, he was out there, off to the side of Stephen and Robert dancing. I was unsure of who his partner was, or if he had a partner. There was a group of women in his vicinity dancing with one another, from where he stood he could claim any of them or play it safe and dance alone. I watched him for a moment and then made my way up to the bar to grab us all some beers. The barmaid worked her way over and looked around the vicinity I was in to see if Stephen had made his way up with me. She looked a bit disappointed when she realized I had come up alone. "So, where is your friend at?" forgetting that I was a paying customer looking for a round of beers. "Oh, he is with his brother and some of their friends down on the dance floor." She looked at me with a face of disgust as if she was being cheated on. However, she wouldn't allow this news to deter her "So, what are you guys getting into tonight?" I found it hard to feel sorry for someone who is naïve by choice and my tone showed it. "We're going to have another round or two here and then probably go to Parkinson's. Then again, everyone is pretty ripped so I'm really not sure if we will hit Parkinson's or just get something to eat and call it a night." I was weary to answer her. I could see it in her look that she was bound and determined to hang out with Stephen tonight. With the way Stephen was and the fact that his brother was with him this would be bad news for her if they did hook up. "Okay, I'll grab you guys a round. Just do me a favor if you would." I pretended not to hear her as she stalled for a moment and then walked away to get the round of drinks. The bar was still growing in crowd, which left her with little time to converse. She came back and placed the beers on the bar. Unfortunately, she hadn't forgotten. "Hey, do me a favor." I looked around the bar at all the patrons that were waiting to help her recognize how busy she was and then grabbed my beers and nodded my head. "If he doesn't make his way back up here to grab another round and you all end up leaving, come up here and let me know what you guys are going to do. I get off early and I wouldn't mind hanging out tonight." I looked at her and smiled, she was desperate, her voice was desperate, her actions were desperate, and her plea was desperate. "I can do that," I assured her. She smiled as she turned her back to me and went back to work. I looked at her as she walked away, she had a nice tight little body for having a child. Her face was extremely cute, she deserved much better than what awaited her.

I made my way down with no intentions of taking the beers out onto the floor, nor with any intention of telling Stephen what the barmaid was wanting me to say. Instead, I made my way over to the corner and put all the beers on the table and surveyed the room. This was possibly the most crowded I had ever seen the club; it was hard to track down the guys. Eventually, one by one I began to find them. Sal was still going at it with determination although he was starting to look a little tired. Hal was getting more personable with his dance partner off to the side of Sal as he paused from dancing to lean over and kiss. Robert and Stephen had moved a little deeper away from the lighted floor with their dance partners. Dick had now maneuvered to one particular, an attractive blonde that actually looked a little like Jeanine. His conditioned had worsened, he had let his guard completely down and worse yet, he looked as if he could pass out at any moment. I stood there and watched him as he struggled to maintain balance. The blonde he was with looked totally engaged with him and blind to the ring on his left hand. No one out of the group paid any attention to him as they were all caught up in their own situations. Robert was the first to make his way over, he gave me a big smile as he approached. "Tristan, what the hell are you doing? Why aren't you out on the dance floor." I handed him a new beer, he winked at me in appreciation before taking a big swallow. "I just made my way back from the bar with the drinks. Is everyone on the dance floor?" I asked the question that I was already aware of the answer to. "You know what, I think so. Sal and Hal have it going on, so does Stephen. I lost Dick, I wasn't sure if maybe he headed off to the bar or to the restroom." I pointed out in the direction where Dick was. Robert roared in laughter. "He is fucking wasted! Look at that boy go!" Stephen approached the table as Robert continued to watch Dick on the dance floor, he looked over to see what we were looking at and gave us both a smile as I handed him his beer. "Isn't that something? Old Dick, cutting the rug!" No one seemed too concerned about Dick on the dance floor, instead the conversation was based on their own escapades. "Hey Tristan, did you grab these beers?" Stephen asked. "Yes, just got back a few moments ago." I knew where he was going with this conversation before it even got started. Stephen nodded his head, took a drink and then studied the beer for a moment. "Did the hottie up there ask about me" Stephen looked at me like he was taking part in an interrogation. "She did, didn't she?" Stephen said with confidence before I could answer. "She was really busy, so I didn't take much time to talk to her." Stephen nodded his head. "So, in other words, she asked about me." I could tell in his tone that whether he got the answer he wanted from me or not, he was going to be heading up there to talk to her. There was no reason to delay the inevitable. "She asked where you were." Stephen's facial expression became concerned. "You didn't tell her I was fucking around with some pig did you?" I looked at him with a look of disbelief. "No, I just told her you were on the dance floor with your friends, nothing else." Stephen nodded his head as if he accepted the answer but still had doubt on whether or not I was telling him the truth.

Hal and Sal made their way through the dance floor and over to the table. That left only Dick out on the floor to fend for himself. By his smile and interaction, he was doing quite well. Hal and Sal took turns sharing their tales of the dance floor while the other caught up with his drinking. As the storytelling came to an end, Hal looked around the group. "Where the hell is Dick at?" he asked with a big smile, somewhat certain he knew what the answer would be. Stephen pointed out onto the floor, Hal looked around, chewing his gum as he looked and then stopped. With a smile, he turned back towards Stephen and Robert before busting out laughing. "Look at the boy go!" he said as he gave Robert a high five. The group looked on and laughed. Robert reached over and put his empty on the table while grabbing Dick's beer. "Doesn't look like he'll be needing this anytime soon." Stephen looked at Robert and shook his head. "Are you fucking serous? Well, I guess I can go and get us another round." This couldn't have played into Stephen's hands any better. This gave him the perfect opportunity to go up and talk to the barmaid. "Don't get all worked up there, Chief, I can go get us a round. Besides, it is my turn to buy." Hal caught Stephen as he was beginning to walk away. "No, don't worry about it, I've got this one. You can get the next one when we head over to Parkinson's." Stephen assured him as he realized the threat Hal presented and walked away quickly to avoid any more interruptions. As Stephen approached the bar and was about to lose sight of us he took one last look over at us to make sure that no one had decided to follow him and then proceeded on to the bar. Stephen and his actual intentions weren't hard to figure out. The guys looked at one another and shared a smile. I looked around for a few moments, attempted to listen to the guys as they told their tales before deciding to head to the restroom.

As I left the restroom, I passed the bar and found Stephen leaning over the bar top. He was met by the barmaid at the midway point. I watched Stephen as he attempted to seduce her with his charm and his unique vocabulary. The rest of the bar seemed nonexistent to the two of them as they continued to converse. I walked up and stood to the foreground of Stephen. The barmaid never looked up and had yet to grab the order. I stood there observed and waited. Soon the moment became too awkward. As I stepped closer to Stephen and reached out to tap him on the shoulder I caught the eye of the barkeep which in return startled Stephen. As he turned around he gave me his trademark smile. I didn't have to say anything as he turned around and placed an order, she gave him a wink and walked away. She quickly grabbed the order and brought the beers over to the bar. He scooted them towards me and grabbed one for himself. I paused for a moment not knowing whether I should say something about heading over to Parkinson's or not. I could tell by the way they were talking that he was in there, so I grabbed the beers and walked away. As I headed back down towards the dance floor I was met by Hal and Robert who were wondering what exactly was going on and what was taking us so long. I handed them their beers and continued towards our table, this seemed to calm Hal's curiosity as he turned and followed me. However, Robert continued to make his way towards the bar. When Hal and I arrived at the table, Dick was standing there with sweat on his brow and a big smile on his face, he reached over rather clumsily and grabbed a beer from me. He took a drink and asked where Stephen was. I chose not to answer and turned my back to him as I took a drink of my beer and surveyed the dance floor. I caught a glimpse of a couple attractive girls standing in the corner alone. I observed them for a few moments and then decided to head over to them solo. As I made my way across the floor I caught a glimpse of Stephen and Robert as they made their way back down from the bar. Stephen had a smirk on his face and Robert was jawing towards him. It seemed as if the two of them had decided to revisit their typical Stephen and Robert bickering. Stephen saw me as he headed down and nodded for me to come back to the table. I had just made it within a few feet of the women, they had taken notice, which was confirmed with a friendly smile. The lighting as I approached did not disappoint as the two were still attractive. I paused momentarily, they both seemed interested to meet me but I couldn't pass on an opportunity to get out of this bar and head to Parkinson's where even more women would be there for the choosing. I turned casually around and headed to the table.

Chapter XVI

It didn't take long for us once we were over at the table to finish our drinks and head out the door. The guys were wanting to try another scene as bad as I was. Dick was in no condition to drive which was confirmed by the others as he made his way to the driver's side door. All the persistence in the world would have fallen on deaf ears as he proceeded to get in and start the car. This resulted in a quiet ride to Parkinson's as everyone allowed Dick to focus on the road. As we pulled into Parkinson's we were all relieved to see that the crowd was even larger than that at Truman's. The guys and I made our way out of the van on a mission, a mission driven with drunken confidence. Stephen and Robert led the way, Dick struggled to keep up as he was well past his limit. This brought a form of entertainment for the guys once we had arrived safely as they watched and laughed. The plan was to stay together, find a table and then divide and conquer. However, that plan was abruptly aborted as soon as the guys paid their cover and entered the club.

The club was happening, beautiful women packed the dance floor, spilling out onto the area surrounding it, dancing with drinks in hand wherever there was a place to move. The sparkle in Robert's eye was matched by the others except Stephen who looked as if he regretted the coercing he did at Truman's with the barmaid. She would be coming soon to hang out which would definitely wreak havoc on any possibility of Stephen hooking up with someone else. I surveyed the club and saw a group of women that looked good for the taking, I turned to find Robert and bring the ladies to the group's attention but he and the others had already walked off. I looked around the tables leading to the bar to see if I could spot any of the guys but had no luck. I made my way up to the bar working my way through the crowd. The bartenders were slammed, running from patron to patron overlooking those who had been there for a while to the ones who held their money out the furthest.

Once I placed my order, I turned my attention to the dance floor. It didn't take long before I saw Hal dancing. Alongside him were Robert and Stephen, who was working quick in an effort to land someone prior to his barmaid's arrival. As usual, Sal was nowhere to be seen. I looked around the floor a couple times over before I saw Dick who had found a dance partner. After watching Dick for a few moments, I found Sal who was standing away from the floor talking to a woman who was more focused on sipping her drink and looking around the dance floor than engaging in conversation. I turned back to the bar and waited on my drink. The barkeep continued to take orders as she made her way back in my direction and placed someone else's bottle of beer down before me. Not wanting to wait for the actual beer I ordered, I laid my money down, grabbed the beer and walked away. I decided to walk around the perimeter of the dance floor to look around for someone that would attract my interest. By the time I was passing the pool tables, I found two women standing in the corner, yet standing out amongst the rest. The taller of the two grabbed my attention and as our eyes met, her smiled confirmed that I had captured her attention as well. I made my way over. Both women greeted me with a warm hello and a smile. Now, standing much closer, I realized the woman I was attracted to resembled my perception of an angel. She stood around five foot six, very slender, what shape she possessed was well hidden in her loose dress and sweater that hung loosely from her shoulders. Her hair, dirty blonde, was unkempt, her face was pale, thin and well defined. Her lips were also thin but appeared much fuller with her sloppy application of bright red lipstick. Her nose was small but distinctive with its shape which brought more accent to her beautiful green eyes, eyes that fought to show themselves through the bangs that flowed freely down past her forehead and worked their way towards her cheeks. She had a bohemian look about her which was an instant attraction, her style separated her from the rest but not in a screaming "look at me" sort of way. She gave me a forced smile as she diverted her eyes momentarily from mine in order to keep her mystery unsolved. However, this remained only for a moment before she found herself looking once more at me. She attempted unsuccessfully to block her smile by taking a quick sip of her glass of wine. I caught a glimpse of her friend as she rolled her once inviting eyes in disgust that I had turned my attention towards her friend. I knew that my opportunity would be short lived if the two of them had any kind of alliance so I began to converse in an effort to lure her interest my way and to make her departure more of a challenge "How are you ladies doing tonight?" my poor attempt to keep both women occupied came up unsuccessful as the brunette looked at me and with no response, turned her attention to the dance floor. "We aren't too bad, how about yourself?" the blonde's voice was soft, sensuous, it brought a contradiction to her appearance. "Not too bad at all, quite a night here. Have you ladies been here for very long?" the ability to converse was limited with the amount of people around and the music which was the loudest I had yet to recall. She seemed well aware of this as she leaned in to answer me. The smell of body oil and her sweet sweat filled my nose and left me desiring more. "It does seem crowded, this is actually our first time here, we just got here a little while ago, not sure how long we will be staying." This comment brought a smile to her friend as I realized that she was listening. "I see, so you two aren't from around here?" I asked with much intrigue in an attempt to keep her put. "So is it that noticeable?" she said with a smile then continued before I could answer. "We go to college locally, but no, we are not from around this area." This provided the explanation on her unique style in comparison to the others in the club. "I see, so you are attending Denison, I reckon?" She gave me a smile and nodded her head as she took another sip of her wine. "Yes, how did you know?" she said as she lowered her glass. "It's a great college in a small town, people come from all over to attend and those who are not locals tend to stand out." She looked up and winked. "I see. So you are from around here, because you stand out." The conversation was developing and so was the interest. "Actually, I am." The answer didn't seem to amuse her, she nodded her head and we experienced the first awkward moment of silence as she continued to nod as she turned her stare towards the dance floor.

Her friend saw the opening and leaned over towards us. "Hey, I'm ready for another drink, are you wanting to continue to hang out here or do you want to check out some other clubs while the night is still some-what young?" The blonde looked around, looked at me with a smile and then looked over at her friend. "Why don't you go grab us one more drink and then we will head out after that." This didn't bring any solace to the brunette as she took a moment to just stare at her with a disappointing look on her face and then slowly drifted off towards the bar. This is where I needed Robert or Hal to step in and occupy the brunette while I worked the blonde. The blonde had decided to roll the dice once more with her new company and I needed to make the most of it. However, there was no one to be seen in the area and I couldn't afford to leave her side. I could only hope that the line at the bar was long enough to provide a little more time with her to see where this may go.

We both leaned towards one another to engage ourselves in conversation once more. Then upon acknowledgement of one another's intention we both took the time to wait on the other to start. I motioned for her to take the lead and with a smile she asked, "So, do you go to college?" she ended the sentence slowly, as if it was incomplete. She studied me, looking as if she was replaying the conversation in her mind. Then jumped back in before I could answer. "I am sorry, I just realized that I don't believe you have told me your name." I looked at her for a moment, thinking about the conversation we had and realized that she was correct, we hadn't. "I apologize, my name is Tristan." She reached out with her free hand. "It is very nice meeting you, Tristan, my name is Teresa." She placed her hand softly in mine and allowed me to control the greeting. As I released her hand, I felt her slowly, reluctantly dragging her hand back to her side, each inch of her hand that passed through mine seemed to linger longer than the last. I struggled to pick up where the conversation had left off. Her lips were enticing, she bit down on her bottom lip for a moment as she smiled, fully aware that I was gazing at them. I wanted to lean over, to lift her head towards mine and taste her lips. However the timing wasn't there. I continued to look at her, then remembered where the conversation had left off. "I am not in college currently. Although I have been contemplating it." She nodded her head, she seemed as if she was disappointed. I wasn't sure if she was upset that I wasn't in college or that I hadn't pursued with my initial intentions of taking a kiss from her. "So, Tristan, as I said earlier, you stand out amongst the rest, I immediately realized this when I first saw you. So tell me, who in the hell are you?" she inquired intuitively. I felt as if this was a make or break kind of question in our early encounter. I was caught off guard, not knowing what to say. The conversation that Robert and I had the other night raced through my mind. There wasn't enough time to explore this question but I also knew that stating that I worked in a warehouse of a floor covering store wasn't going to be sufficient. Knowing that she was attending one of the more renowned art schools in the area, I could always throw in my writing and poetry as a consolation or leave out the flooring store altogether and see where my love for art took me. "I'm a local boy, currently work local, and looking for my way out. Once I do enroll in college whether locally or preferably away from here, I plan to pursue my interest in writing and poetry." There was so much more to say, but the time we had would not allow it. Her eyes lit up as she gave me a smile. "A writer, eh? Very nice, I can definitely see that. I like your ambitions. So tell me, Tristan, who are you here with tonight?" she asked with curiosity, the tone made me feel that she was hoping I would say I came alone. "Some of the guys from my job and I are out tonight." The fact that I didn't mention a significant other brought color to her cheeks as she nodded. "So what about you? Is it just you and your friend?" Her smile faded as I finished asking and she realized her current situation. "Yes, her name is Veronica. We go to college together. She actually drove us here, she is a bit more familiar with the area." I knew now why she had quit smiling. She was at the mercy of Veronica who was already becoming restless. My predicament became more extreme as I looked over and saw Veronica making her way quickly back from the bar. We had one more drink to share prior to them leaving and unfortunately, I didn't see Veronica leaving Teresa again once she made her way back.

Veronica came over and handed Teresa a glass of wine. Veronica had appeared to have been working her drink while she was on her way back as her glass was half empty. Teresa tipped her glass towards my bottle, we tapped them together and took a drink. She gave me a smile and arched her eyebrows. I could only imagine if any of the thoughts I had going on in my mind were thoughts that she shared. Teresa wasn't a backseat kind of woman. Although I wanted to make her, I knew that she was one who deserved better and demanded more. I went to say something to her when Veronica jumped in. "So what are you thinking?" Teresa looked at her blankly for a moment. "You don't like it here?" Veronica had barely allowed Teresa to finish before she said, "No." Veronica was well aware of what was starting to happen and had no intentions of being the third wheel. "I am not familiar with this area so I guess it is up to you," Teresa said. Veronica smiled at me with this acknowledgement that she indeed was victorious. "I hear there is a nice little club right down the road called Truman's, we could go there and then head back towards college if nothing is going on and stop in a pub or two in that area." Veronica saying Truman's practically destroyed any chances of myself getting to know Teresa any better and yet it did bring a small chance of intercepting their plans. The guys would never go for us heading back to Truman's and yet, I might be able to persuade Teresa and Veronica to stay here since we had just left there. "What do you think, Tristan? Are you interested in maybe meeting up with us over at Truman's?" I could tell that Teresa was beginning to want what I was wanting which brought a look of disgust on Veronica's face. "Actually, the guys and I just came from there. The place was a little dead for our liking." Teresa looked over to Veronica as she heard this. "Did you hear that? The place is dead, we might as well hang out here for a little while." We both knew that there was little chance of persuading Veronica. "This place is too crowded, I was hoping Truman's is a little dead, more room to dance, easier to talk." We both looked at one another in acknowledgement that this night was coming to an end. Teresa took a drink as I finished mine.

Veronica kept an eye on Teresa with each swallow she took. As she took her last drink of wine, Veronica searched for her keys. "Are you ready to head out?" Veronica's persistence earned a disgusted look from Teresa. "I suppose." Teresa put her glass down on a table and looked at me with a smile. "Tristan, it was so nice meeting you. If you happen to change your mind, we'll be at Truman's for a while." I took ahold of her hand and smiled. "The same goes for you, once the two of you become bored with the scene over there, come back over, the next glass of vino is on me. We can get to know one another a little better." Teresa gave me a small wink of approval. "That sounds like a plan." We had no time for an awkward moment or goodbye, Veronica was becoming inpatient and leaned towards her. "Let's go." She said in a muffled but intense voice." Teresa began to turn away. "It was nice meeting you." She said again as she gave me one last smile, hesitated for a moment and then walked off. She walked off slowly as if she was hoping I would say something or intervene. I watched her as she weaved her way in and out of the crowd. As she was engulfed by the crowd I realized that I hadn't attempted to get her number. Now I understood the reasoning behind her hesitating as she left. I began to work my way into the crowd, looking for a way to get through, looking for a way to at least catch a glimpse of her until I could find my way back to her. To yell would be pointless with the noise from the crowd and the music. I continued on, bumping shoulders and squeezing between couples trying to dance. Every opening I found was quickly lost within the emerging crowd.

Moments like these are all about timing and time was something I was running out of. I couldn't help but ponder the correlation between time and the hand of fate which brought forth a sad smile as I continued to push my way through the crowd until I could see the exit. There was no sign of Teresa or Veronica. I was getting to the end of the dance floor when I received a tug on my shirt, I turned quickly hoping to find Teresa, and instead I found Stephen. "Where the fuck have you been?" Stephen asked as he fought to keep his eyes open, his face drooping from the drunkenness, each word slurred as he struggled to complete the sentence. The same question entered my mind. "I was towards the back. Have you seen a cute blonde with long, messy hair walk by with a brunette?" Stephen was unaware of anything I had just said as he looked me up and down. "Listen, I think that bartender is going to be showing up here at any moment, I need you to find her before she finds me and keep her occupied. I'm about to take one of these skanks out to the van for a few." I looked over Stephen's shoulder but couldn't find any woman that seemed to be awaiting his company. "I'll be right back, I have to find someone real quick." Stephen looked at me in disgust. "Fuck her, don't worry about her, there are other skanks in here to hook up with. Will you help me out or what?" Stephens's lack of consideration only worsened with the involvement of women and drink. "Find one of the other guys, where is Robert, where is your brother at?" Stephen's look only worsened. "Fuck, I don't know, I'm not their babysitter." I pulled away from Stephen's grasp and began to walk away. "I understand that and I understand that I am not yours. I'll be back in a moment." Although with the noise surrounding us there was no way of Stephen hearing me, he dropped his arms in disappointment as he watched me leave. I made my way through the rest of the crowd and over to the exit, I took one last look around the club, there was no sight of Teresa or Veronica although I caught a glimpse of Sal and Dick as the two of them danced with a couple of women. I walked out the door, numerous cars were at the exit of the parking lot, and several cars were pulling out of their parking space and heading towards the exit. I realized that in one of those cars, Teresa sat, probably arguing her case with Veronica on why they should stay at Parkinson's. Of course, this argument would fall on deaf ears. I could only wonder whether she realized that we had forgotten to exchange numbers. I watched as each car left until no more remained at the exit and then headed back inside.

I made my way over to the bar where I saw the familiar face of the barmaid from Truman's as she stood with drink in hand surveying the dance floor. I attempted to walk behind her and over to the bar without her noticing me but was unsuccessful as she yelled, "Hey you!" as I passed. I continued to walk pretending not to hear her but she watched me until I came to a stop and then walked over. "Hey you! I yelled at you over there as you passed me but you must not have heard me." She smiled as if she was well aware that I had purposely ignored her. "I'm sorry, I must not have." She nodded as she took a drink. "So, where is Stephen at?" She cut right to the chase and asked. I looked at her, she was too eager to see him, the tone in her voice, her smile, her eyes, her gestures, the scent of freshly applied perfume, it all spelled desperation. Stephen would pounce on her without a second thought, use her and send her home to her child. I didn't want to blow him out of the water with what he was really doing. However, I didn't want to stand there and help him with his quest knowing the end results. "You know, I'm not quite sure. We all kind of scattered once we came in, I was back in the back doing my own thing. Once I grab another beer, I'm going to go looking for him." She looked at me with studying eyes trying to figure if I was telling the truth or not. "You're more than welcome to join me if you would like?" I took a chance making this offer, I didn't want her with me, helping her find Stephen was the last thing I wanted to do. The offer was to ease her mind and it seemed to do so. "No, that's okay, I think I am going to look for a couple of friends who wandered off, maybe dance. Maybe I will bump into him out on the dance floor. Could you tell him that I'm here if and when you see him?" I gave her a smile and reassured her I would. She returned the smile and walked away.

I looked at my watch as I waited for the barkeep to make her way over to me. It was closing in on one o'clock. I no longer wanted to be here. Truman's usually closed earlier than most the bars in the area. I couldn't imagine them being open for more than another half hour. I ordered a beer and then decided I would try and get the guys together and see if they wanted to head over there as a group or at least find someone to go with me. It took quite a while before I found Sal. He had taken a break from dancing and was now standing in the far corner, conversing with the same woman he was with earlier. Knowing that Sal wouldn't be leaving that spot I headed around the perimeter of the dance floor. I knew where Dick, Stephen and Robert were, I just needed to find Hal. I had almost walked the complete dance floor when I noticed Hal. He was standing off to the side of the others, all of them laughing, dancing and showing no pain. I made my way over to them; Robert was my best bet. He gave me a big smile once he saw me. "Where the hell have you been, Tristan, we thought that maybe you had walked home or something?" I leaned in on Robert and tried to ask him. It was too loud and he was unable to hear me. The second time I leaned in, Dick and Stephen become curious and leaned in. "What in the hell are you doing, Tristan? Are you and Robert necking?" Dick smiled as he slurred out the sentence. I looked at Dick, who was already losing his interest in a response as he began to turn his attention back to the woman he had been dancing with. "Hey, what the fuck are you doing?" Stephen asked in a bitter tone, I could see his curiosity wasn't going anywhere as he stood there waiting for a response. "Nothing, I was just seeing if Robert wanted to head back to Truman's. If no one else wants to go, we could pick you guys up when they call last call." Robert looked indecisive, he turned and looked at Stephen as if he was looking for guidance. "Fuck that, we just left there. This place is closing in what, an hour? By the time you get over there it would be time to leave. Besides, you would actually fuck with Robert's game because you don't want to be here any longer?" Robert looked at me as if he was still contemplating possibly taking me over. I looked down at my watch; it was almost one thirty. "Don't worry about it," I said realizing arguing would prove to be pointless and walked away.

I went back to the front of the dance floor and stood there as I drank my beer. Stephen had already put the conversation behind him as he and Dick resumed their dancing. Robert who had been by far my best bet to possibly help me looked over a few different times, a couple times he shook his head with a look of disbelief on how the others had acted. However, I knew that was as far as I was going to get. I decided that although, I was on my last beer and last call would be announced soon that I would look around to see if there were any others to pass my time with. By this time, almost all the women had hooked up for the rest of the night. Those who hadn't had either left or were heading to the exits. As I looked around I found the barkeep from Truman's, her search for Stephen had come to an abrupt stop with the guy she was on the dance floor with. The two of them seemed comfortable as they began dancing up against one another. They moved closer and closer to Stephens's area. I couldn't believe that she had yet to see him but then again, she might have and this might have been a deliberate gesture to get his attention. Either way, Stephen, if he had seen her, wasn't concerned as he continued to lean on his dancing partner.

Last call was called and with it a scramble to both the exit and the bar as patrons tried to beat the traffic out of the parking lot and others attempted to get that last round in. The women that were dancing with the guys said their goodbyes. Robert headed over to the bar. Stephen's attempt to talk the women into staying for one last drink fell on deaf ears as they shared hugs and phone numbers before they headed out. Stephen stopped in the center of the dance floor and began to look around the club. With both arms thrown into the air with uncertainty he shouted, "Where is Sal?" Stephen's question could be heard with the thinning out of the club. The others laughed as they realized the night had passed by once more in typical fashion without Sal being present. I made my way back towards the group. "He is over in the far corner talking to some woman." The guys looked over and saw Sal emerging from the shadows with a smile on his face. As he caught a glimpse of us and made his way over, Robert appeared with a last round of drinks for us all. No one in the group needed another drink but no one refused.

The storytelling began with the first drink and grew stronger as we headed out the door and made our way to the van. Once we reached the van, Robert surveyed the situation in the parking lot to ensure no cops were around and then turned towards Stephen to find out what he wanted to do about eating. "Let's just make it simple, head across the street to the drive-thru. I need to get home and get to bed. I am a wreck!" Dick said in a slurred voice as he jumped in the conversation before Stephen had the chance to answer. Stephen nodded in agreement and we headed over to the drive-thru. The ordering was chaotic, everyone screaming at the same time, ordering way more than they could possibly eat. Once Stephen placed his order he said he was done for the night and climbed from the front seat to the back. Dick maneuvered his way up to the front. We moved past the window to wait on the order. The van was filled with drunken silence while everyone anticipated the arrival of the food. Then suddenly Hal broke the silence as he turned towards Sal. "So what the hell, happened to you tonight, Sal? I figured I would ask you before you fell asleep." This brought laughter from the rest of the guys as they turned their attention to Sal who was indeed about to fall asleep. "Nothing really." Sal answered in a lazy voice. "Do you think?" Stephen said as he reached over and tried to grab Sal's knee. "Well, you know what I mean. I met a few women, danced a little. However, just before closing, I met me a little honey and we hit it off pretty well and took our business back to a darkened corner for a bit." Hal then turned his attention to Dick. "What about you, Dick, look at you! Showing all us young pups how the big dog hunts! You know you may want to lighten those pockets a bit, lose all the phone numbers you collected before we get home. If you like, you can pass them over to me. Well except for the girl with the beard, that one you can toss" Dick smiled. "I don't know what you guys are talking about. Hal, you were the wild man!" Dick diverted the conversation. Stephen looked back at me as Dick finished his sentence. "Hey, Tristan, tonight stays between us, you understand?" The van became quiet as everyone turned their attention towards me. I wasn't sure the reasoning behind the comment. I didn't know if it was typical Stephen trying to throw his weight around or if he actual had concerns. Either way, there had never been any reason to suspect me of saying anything to anyone, that wasn't one of my traits. Although the comment didn't deserve a response, I broke the awkward silence. "You don't need to worry about me." We exchanged glares. Stephen continued to stare at me with no success in achieving any kind of intimidation. "I'm just saying," Stephen added. Robert looked back to interrupt the two of us prior to it escalating but as he did, Dick pointed that the food was ready. Robert grabbed each bag, took a quick peak in each one and upon realizing they weren't his, he tossed them back towards the back. Upon the last bag being passed around, Robert looked back and asked if everyone had their food. Everyone answered except Sal, who was fast asleep with his head tilted back with the only unclaimed bag resting on his lap.

We drove off and headed home. Everyone focused on their eating until Robert looked in the rearview mirror in an effort to find me and asked. "What was going on with you, Tristan? Why did you want to go back to Truman's?" Everyone took a moment from their eating to await an answer.

"I met a woman, had a great connection. She was there with her roommate and her roommate was wanting to get out of there and was persistent until they left. It wasn't until they were out of sight that I realized I forgot to get her number. She said they were heading to Truman's." Robert frowned as if he sympathized, the van was quiet for a moment until Dick spoke up. "Rookie!" The van busted out in laughter. "No, I'm just kidding, Tristan." Dick smiled back at me. "No, he isn't kidding," Stephen said as he arched his eyebrows and smiled. Stephen had been on my nerves since the night began. "Yes, it's all about executing. Too bad for your failure with the bar-keep from Truman's tonight. She looked really good away from the bar." Stephen stopped eating his sandwich in mid bite. "What the fuck are you talking about, she never showed." I realized that Stephen was too drunk to even realize that she was dancing less than ten feet away from him. "Yes she showed, she was practically beside you dancing at the very end of the night. She probably didn't want to bother you while you were dancing with that pig." Stephen stared at me waiting to see if I was just busting his chops. Once he realized I wasn't, he looked for something to say. "It's not a big deal, I'll hook back up with the skank tomorrow over lunch before we head back home." It was the first time that I had heard him mention home. Until then, I was unaware that plans had changed and he was heading back when the others did. I looked at him to continue but instead he went back to eating.

We were getting closer to Dick's house; the van had become quiet. There were a few more references about heading home between Dick and Robert up front as they were conversing in a more sober, somber tone, although it was too hard to understand what they were actually saying. I looked over at Sal who continued to sleep with his food untouched, Hal had his head turned to the window, I couldn't tell if he was awake or not. Stephen lay on his side on the floor with a half-eaten hamburger hanging out of his mouth. As we pulled into the driveway, Dick looked back to wake everyone up, he found Stephen with the hamburger and brought it to everyone's attention as he turned to awaken him. The laughter woke Stephen who said nothing but smiled as he finished the burger and sat up. We made our way into the house, I stood back and waited for Robert to catch up with me. "So you are all heading home tomorrow?" I asked in a lower voice to avoid anyone else joining in the conversation. "Yeah, Hal and Sal are needing to be home by Sunday. My leaving wasn't planned. I was going to stay another week or so. However, the shop is caught up enough, so we are going to leave tomorrow after work. Stephen is heading out just for the day, he will be back by Monday. I think he will be sticking around for a couple more weeks." Robert patted me on my shoulder as we made our way into the house and down the steps. Once we were downstairs, everyone was drunk and tired and seemed to keep to themselves. Sal sat down and began to eat, Robert, Stephen, Hal and myself got ready for bed and found places to sleep.

Chapter XVII

I woke up the next morning early. Everyone else was still out of it and there was no noise coming from the upstairs yet. I got dressed and began to make my way out when I saw Hal shift. He looked up at me, smiled and put his head back down. I walked over and told him to have a safe trip home and I would see him soon. He smiled and shook hands and returned the well wishes. Our discussion woke up Robert. I made my way over, shook hands, thanked him for everything and then asked him if he would say something to Sal for me once he woke up since I knew that any effort to wake him would be unsuccessful. He gave me a smile and nodded. "You take care of yourself. Once I am back we'll take over this town," Robert said in a whisper. "I am looking forward to it," I said as I turned and made my way to the steps. As I placed my foot on the first step, I paused for a moment as a feeling came over me, a feeling best described as uncertainty. I took one last look at the boys from Cincinnati, smiled and left. I headed home still a bit drunk from the night before. I replayed the evening and the other times we had the chance to go out in my head. They has showed me what the nights had to offer, had brought me into their world, allowed me to live in it and for that I was thankful. I had no regrets other than it came to an end far too soon. Although promises and plans had been made for the near future, something they intended on doing, I knew that last evening would be the last time that we would all get together again as a group.

I went home and successfully avoided my mother and headed straight upstairs to sleep it off. Without having to work on Saturdays, the day was spent as a day of recovery. I kept to myself, taking time to go downstairs only to grab food, drink and to go out for an evening walk. On Sunday, I woke up in the middle of the afternoon and made my way downstairs. I was surprised to see my mother keep to herself. I had spent all of Saturday around the house, and although I had been out all night on Friday, there was an understanding that I wouldn't be home. Yet, she still seemed upset. Perhaps she was getting an overwhelming feeling that she was no longer in control of me and that trouble lurked around the corner. I walked in the kitchen and found her cooking. I looked through the refrigerator when she surprised me by speaking. "We are having dinner at five. You don't need to be eating before then, unless you were looking for a beer. You will probably want to go and get a shower before everyone gets here and get dressed somewhat decent." Although her conversation with me was one-sided and direct, I was glad that she took the time to talk to me. I gave her a smile which went unnoticed and headed into the bathroom to shower. By the time I was out of the shower, all the family had arrived and it was closing in on the time for us to have dinner. I made most of my conversation during dinner, which was nothing more than small talk.

When I returned to work on Monday, I was surprised to find the warehouse empty. Stephen was typically there awaiting my arrival to go over the weekend that was. Instead I was greeted by Dick moments later who had come back with a worklist in hand and was back to being all business. However, something seemed off. There was tension as he stood there, surveying the worklist before handing it over to me. Perhaps it was the fact that Stephen had yet to arrive. Perhaps it was his behavior during our night out and the guilt he was experiencing or the uncertainty of what all I had witnessed and remembered that was causing his peculiar behavior. He continued to stand there in silence and the silence was creating more and more awkwardness between the two of us until I could no longer deal with it. "So, is Stephen running late?" Dick continued to stand there in silence, looking blankly at the list. Moments passed with no response which began to make me to wonder if he was even aware I had asked him a question. As I began to ask him again he turned and interjected. "He had a couple of things come up. He called and said he will be here by mid-week." Dick said nothing else. After a few more moments, he handed me the list and walked away.

The week progressed without incident. Without Stephen's presence, everyone stayed busy, I rarely saw Dick besides in the morning as we were all getting our day started. That changed on Wednesday as the day began to age and there were still no signs of Stephen. Dick made his way back. He seemed to be in much better spirits than on Monday. "So what is going on, Rookie, you about done?" He asked in a tone that was similar to the tone he used when speaking with the boys from Cincinnati. "Yes, just finishing up." Dick nodded as he walked over to the jobs I had completed, surveyed them with hand on chin before nodding and making his way back over. "Not too bad, if I must say so." He gave me a wink. "It has been a busy week," I said with hopes to getting to the presence or lack of from Stephen. "Yeah, it doesn't help when you are shorthanded." Dick had inadvertently opened the door. "Speaking of, where is our help? I thought Stephen was going to be back today." Dick nodded. "That was the plan. However, I just got off the phone with him. I guess things are taking a bit longer than expected, he said he will be back sometime on Friday. He wanted me to tell you to not plan on anything Friday night, he wants the three of us to head out to the locals and see what we can get into." Dick looked at me with a smile. I could see that his night out with all of us last weekend had caused him to want more, need more. "I can do that," I said for no other reason than to appease Dick. In reality, I couldn't help but be cautious when considering going out with Dick. Partially from my mother's concerns and forewarning. "Good, good. Well, you know the protocol. Be at my place by eight or shortly after if you want to drink prior to us heading out." I nodded, once acknowledged, Dick smiled and walked away.

Morning and afternoon passed on Friday and there was still no presence of Stephen. Nonetheless, I gave it little thought. Dick had not stated whether he would return in the morning for his work shift or when. I couldn't help but hope that his arrival may be delayed which would give me a way out of the night ahead. As the day came to a close, the door opened and Dick appeared. "You heading out?" he asked as I was approaching. I nodded. "Alright, get yourself ready. I am needing a night after this week. Come thirsty. Stephen will be buying after what he has put us through." Any hopes I had of not going out were now out the window as I smiled and nodded. "I will see you at eight. Try and not be late okay?" I nodded as I continued on my way out. I glanced into the office as I left to see if Stephen was there; he was not. As I made my way to my car, there was no sign of his car. Perhaps he was at their house. Perhaps he had yet to arrive, and perhaps there was still hope of him not returning. It was a slim hope, but hope that I held. For some reason, the thought of going out with the

Messmer brothers without the company of the others was not appealing, not to mention the problems it was sure to cause with my mother and I as I would once again be out for the entire night

I waited until the last possible moment to get ready and still make it over to Dick's on time before I made my way to the shower. It wasn't long after I had left the bathroom and dressed that my mother approached me. "So you are going out again?" she asked. "Yeah, Dick and his brother wanted me to join them." She said nothing as she shook her head and walked away. There was nothing I could say to ease her concerns, lighten her mood. So I avoided further conversation, finished up getting ready, then waited until the last possible moment before heading out the door. When I arrived, I was greeted by Dick with beer in hand. As I made my way around the corner and into the kitchen there was no Stephen. I turned and looked at Dick who was closing the refrigerator door with two beers in hand, he placed one before me and opened it. "Where is Stephen?" I couldn't help but ask. "This is it, just you and I tonight," he attempted to say with enthusiasm. Each word that he spoke weighed on my shoulders. "What happened to Stephen?" I asked before I took my first drink of beer. "He called about a half an hour ago to say that him and the boys were about to get into something so he would just be back on Sunday. I called over to your house to let you know but you had already left." I took another drink as I realized that if I had only waited for a couple more minutes before leaving that this could have all been avoided. "Well, we don't have to go out if you don't want to," I said hoping to bring a close to the evening by the end of the beer. Dick gave me a disgusted look. "Nonsense, you're already here. Besides, we don't need Stephen to have a good time." I could tell by Dick's tone that deep down he really didn't want to go out. "Seriously, we don't have to go. I am completely fine," I continued to try and convince him. "Listen that is not the way I work. We made plans; we are going to stick with them. Listen, let's do this. Let's finish this six pack and head out for a while. If there isn't anything happening, we will call it a night early. How does that sound?" Knowing this was the best option I was going to be offered, I raised my beer in agreement and took a drink.

Chapter XVIII

There was little conversation between the two of us while we drank. What little conversation there was, seemed to focus on his brother, the boys from Cincinnati and their adventures while being here. I could see with Dick's bachelor days behind him, his reminiscing of these said days, the escapades his brother and the guys still partook in was all he had left. This allowed a fear to set in that chilled me as I realized I never wanted to be in Dick's situation. Here he stood, a successful owner of a business, yet to see thirty. He was married to a beautiful wife who adored him, with a child on the way, living in one of finest houses in the city. He would most likely never endure a true struggle again. He was the epitome of the American dream and yet, it wasn't hard to look into those eyes, to look past those eyes and realize how miserable he truly was. As the conversation faded we found ourselves standing in an awkward silence, trying to get through the rest of the six pack as fast as possible so we could get on the road. The car ride was much the same, Dick worked the radio, going back and forth between songs before he became frustrated, gave up and turned it back off. Dick let out a long sigh, said nothing else as he drove quickly to our destination. He never said anything about where we should go or where we were going which caused me to think that this was already determined far before we ever got in the car and most likely before I ever step foot into his house. I sat there, staring out the window, with each turn he made it seem more and more apparent that we were heading to the corner. Once we were parked, Dick surveyed the parking lot. "Doesn't look like much is happening. Then again, it is still early, I'm sure it will liven up." I looked at my watch as we made our way to the doors, it had yet to reach ten. The bar wouldn't liven up for a couple more hours. Hopefully by that time, we would have brought the night to a close.

Once we were inside, Dick looked around the bar that was practically empty before turning his attention towards my way. Well, it doesn't look like we will have any problems finding a seat. Why don't you grab us a booth, I will grab us a round. Dick headed to the bar, I headed to the closest booth. Once seated I turned my attention back to Dick who seemed out of sorts. His posture, his mannerisms, his tone, his stare. Something was wrong, something that I couldn't quite grasp. Dick made his way back, took his seat across from me and fiddled around with the label of his beer as he stared at it blankly. As I sat there, observing the peculiar behavior in between my drinks I couldn't help but wonder why he was so persistent on getting out when he was off his game. After a couple long sighs he looked over at me, then perked up in his seat, I realized that I was about to find out the reasoning behind his peculiar ways. "So what do you think?" he asked, intentionally leaving it vague to allow me to run with it. Typically I tread cautiously, almost strategically to avoid opening the wrong door. However, the night was already wearing on me so I addressed him to avoid the dragging out the conversation any longer than it needed. "That depends on what you are referring to." Dick nodded in appreciation to the response. "Good enough, let me rephrase. So you are my employee, I am your boss. However, I feel with the arrival of my brother, the last few weeks, especially last weekend, we are a bit farther along than that. Would you agree?" I studied Dick, his comment and nodded. "Yes, we have gotten to know each other a bit more outside of the professional basis, correct." Dick's eyes lit up as if my response was perfect to proceed with the conversation he was hoping to have. "So let me ask you. Although you're young, have you considered what lies ahead for you? What is next?" The question caused me to smile as I understood where the conversation was going. It was more or less the same question that Robert had asked me, the same question that Teresa had asked me, it was simply phrased in a different way and although the question was the same, my answer continued to evolve. There was a part of me that wanted to avoid the rest of the set up and get to the point. However, I decided to entertain the conversation, let it run its course and in doing so, get drunk on his dime.

I repositioned myself in the booth as if I was preparing for a speech. I then grabbed the beer and finished it. I placed the empty down in a manner that I knew would draw his attention. As I looked over at the bar Dick spoke up. "I'll grab us another round." Dick got up and headed to the bar quickly as if he didn't want to lose his train of thought with our pending conversation. While Dick waited at the bar, I thought of the similar conversation that Robert and I had, knowing although similar, the end result was to be different. As Dick returned, I decided to approach the question a bit differently than I had with Robert. "You know, you are right, I am young. Sure, like everyone else my age, I have dreams. To escape the hometown. Yet, still reside in smalltown USA. However, that is where my dream differs from the norm. Where most dreams typically are based around a wife, family, a nice home surrounded by a white picket fence while working a nine to five that we hopefully like. Most want to succeed enough to shine at our high school reunions. However, am I not to be the one within the whispers of my peers as they say, 'Wow, look at Tristan Wallace, he made it, he escaped. Who would have ever thought?' You see, as I stated earlier, I am by no means the norm." I paused for a moment to take a long drink of my beer and then looked over at Dick who was waiting for my response to resume, I obliged. "I find myself trying to find balance. Although I find myself looking forward to the future, the mystery of what it holds, I am also trying to live in the moment, enjoy the moment." I paused again to take a drink. I looked over at Dick who confirmed with his repositioning in the booth that he was becoming inpatient. "So are you telling me you don't have any kind of plans, any kind of dreams?" I looked at Dick with a mouth full of beer and shook my head before swallowing. "Of course, I have plans. I have plenty of plans. I want to experience life; mine, as well as others. I want to be on the road soon, and explore. In doing so I may find myself or at least lose myself for a while. Does this make any sense to you or better yet, does this answer your question?" I turned my attention to Dick, who looked as if he was still absorbing everything I had said and looking for the correct way to respond. The anticipation became awkward, I grabbed my beer and finished it as I turned my attention to the door opening and a group of people walking in.

Dick turned and watched the same group of people make their way to a booth. With their arrival we knew this was just the beginning. Soon, any hopes of bringing this conversation to its conclusion wound be gone. Dick laid a five on the table. "Go ahead and grab us a round, I am going to go to the restroom." Dick got up; I could see as he made his way to the restroom that he was digesting every word I had stated. I made my way up to way bar, surveyed my surroundings and placed my order. By the time he made his way back to the booth I was already well into the bottle, Dick took notice and smiled. "It looks like you learned quickly from Stephen and the boys." Dick raised his beer towards me, took a long drink and continued. "To get back to our conversation. You know, I hear what you are saying, I get it and to each their own. You seem like you're a smart kid, even wise for your age. If that is your plan, I wish you the very best. May you figure out life before life comes at you ... because it will and it will most likely come at you hard." I looked at Dick and nodded. "With that being said, this may be a bit hard for you to fathom but I really want what is best for you." Dick paused and took a drink. "You see Robert, Hal, Sal, even my brother Stephen. They had a similar plan as you and now here they are still living a life similar to what you are describing. Perhaps they took a different path than you. However, here they are, all of them in their mid-twenties, and I can pretty much assure you that they will still be where they are in their early, maybe mid-thirties. Why? Because they took those paths, found their way here and now have no direction. I just don't want to see you where they are. Do you understand?" I sat there allowing each and every word Dick said as well as the similarities with the conversation Robert and I had resonate deep within me. Dick addressed what I always knew was possible, his examples were what impacted me the most.

I nodded before finishing my beer. Dick looked at his beer which was more than halfway full and then smiled as he reached into his pocket, pulled out a five and put it on the table. "Go ahead, grab another. This conversation is not allowing me to keep up with you." I said nothing as I grabbed the five and headed to the bar. There were enough people now present to delay the barkeep from getting to me immediately. This allowed the realization to set in. Was the life that Stephen and the others are living my fate? While I stood there and pondered, the barkeep made their way over. I looked over at Dick who hadn't touched the beer since I had walked away so I ordered two for myself. As I made my way back to the booth Dick busted out laugh. "God damn son, you have been hanging out with the boys for too long." I looked over Dick's shoulder as the door opened and more people filed in. "The bar will be getting crowded shortly so I figured I better grab a couple." Dick turned and surveyed the bar. "You have a good point, perhaps I should pick up my game a bit. Besides, I can't be allowing a rookie to drink me under the table." Dick turned around, finished his beer and excused himself from the booth to head to the bar. I made my way to the bathroom.

While I was in the restroom I continued to hear the words Dick spoke. Although I was well aware that this conversation was supposed to be nothing more than a segue to what he was trying to get to and would inevitably succeed in doing, I couldn't help but analyze what all he had said. Unable to fully grasp in the current state I was reaching, I headed back to the booth to finish what we had started. Upon my return I found Dick with two beers before him smiling at me. "I couldn't let you get too far ahead of me," he said, following the statement with a laugh. I sat down, uncertain where the conversation had left. I took a long drink and looked over at him, waiting for him to take the lead. "Tristan, let me ask you this. Have you thought about college? I mean there is no way you can be content working for eight dollars an hour." I took a drink and smiled. It had taken Dick almost an hour to get to where he was wanting to go with the conversation, but he had made it. "Yes, I have given thought of college and plan on going soon, perhaps next fall." My response brought a smile to his face. "I can't tell you how glad I am to hear that," Dick stated like a proud father. I knew it was only a matter of time before he continued, before he concluded the conversation which would most likely bring an end to the night so I grabbed my beer, finished it and then grabbed the second. Dick quickly followed suit and finished his first of two.

Once he finished his beer he looked over at me, waiting to see if I had a response before he continued, I said nothing. "You know, you and Stephen really did a wonderful job getting the warehouse where I wanted it to be." He paused and waited for my acknowledgement, I nodded. "With Stephen's return and winter around the corner, the business will be slowing down." Once again Dick paused, I could see he was struggling much more with this conversation than what he had planned. I took a long drink of my beer with hopes of finishing it and having another before he continued. Dick seemed to understand as he reached into his pocket and pulled out another five. "By the time you come back, I should be ready so you might as well grab me one as well while you are up there." Dick handed me the five as I got up, I made my way over to the bar. As I stood there I began to think more about what was to come next. The realization of what was to be was sobering. I began to wonder if I should ask Dick if we could resume the conversation later so I could enjoy what was left of the night.

When I returned to the booth I could see that Dick was anxious to pick up where he had left off. I handed him his beer and took my seat and waited. "So, getting back to what I was saying. I was thinking about this earlier, talked about it to Stephen and then went over it with Jeanine. With how slow we are expecting to be and with Stephen being there we decided that we won't be needing any full-time help in the back. I would entertain keeping you on for the weekends, so you could get some hours in if that would help." Dick paused long enough for it to sink in, knowing that the four to five hours I could work on the weekend would not suffice. Dick then continued before giving me the opportunity to respond. "I know the timing is far from perfect with you stating that you're not considering college until next year. Then again, the timing on this could never be perfect. We won't move forward with this until the end of next week. This will give you some time to decide on what is best for you. I know you stated earlier that you would like to hit the road for a while, perhaps this is a blessing in disguise and will give you that time to do so before you start college." Dick smiled as if the decision he made was more beneficial than detrimental for me.

I sat there for a moment, taking in everything he had said. There was so much to say, none of it being good. I looked over at the clock on the wall, then at those around the bar, and those entering through the door. I looked back over at Dick who was forcing a smile in between drinks. "You stated I don't have to decide until later, correct?" I wanted to confirm. Dick looked at me and nodded. "Right, you don't have to make any decision tonight." I grabbed my beer and took a long drink. I was getting drunk but had a little more to go. "Can we put this conversation to an end then, enjoy what is left of the evening?" I asked. Dick looked at his watch, looked around the bar and then turned his attention back over to me. "Yes, we can do that. Unfortunately, I can't be out too much longer. I still need to get you home and make it home in one piece. However, we can have a couple more before we call it a night." We finished our beers at the same time. Dick made his way up to the bar, as he made his way back I stood up. "If you don't mind, I don't think I want to sit any longer. I think I am going to get up and mingle for a moment. The bar is filling up nicely, I would like to see what it has to offer." Dick smiled. I completely agree with you. Go ahead, I think I will head up and find a place at the bar for a while." I nodded and walked away.

I made my way to the other side of the bar for no other reason than to distance myself from him. I said hello to some familiar faces in passing, checked out a few of the women congregated together but had no desire at this time to try and work them. Instead, I made my way back to the bar and settled in. As I tried my best to salvage what was left of the night and the drunkenness that had accompanied it, I found myself looking down the bar at Dick who stood there, out of place, gazing at the men and women around him. Although you could see curiosity in his stare as his eyes came to rest on a young blonde he continued to stand there on his best behavior for he knew there was little he could do, nothing to gain, and far too much to lose, especially after what had taken place between us tonight. I continued to stand there until my beer was empty. I reached in my pocket and began to pull out a couple of dollars before I thought better of it and began to make my way back to Dick for another round. Dick saw me as I approached and quickly turned to finish what was left of his beer with hopes of leaving. "What are you thinking, you ready to hit the road?" he asked as I took my place besides him. "Actually, I was thinking one for the road." Dick looked down at his watch and then looked over at me and sighed. Whether he knew it was the last time we would be out together or if he felt bad for me, he reached into his pocket, pulled out his wallet and motioned for a bartender. "Alright, one more. Then I really have to go. You know, you can stick around for a while if you can get yourself a ride." I nodded and then turned my attention to the bartender as they approached.

Once the beers were placed before us, Dick lifted his beer towards me, I obliged and brought the beers together. After a drink he placed the beer down and an awkward silence engulfed us. We stood there, both waiting to see if there was anything worth saying or waiting for the other to start a conversation. I began to lose my interest and started to look around for something to get into or to possibly find a ride. Dick continued to drink and drink fast. As he placed his empty on the bar and looked over, I still had half a beer remaining. "What do you think?" he asked in a slurred voice and a drunken stare. I took once last look around, surveying the bar and any possibilities, before tilting the beer and finishing what was left. "I'm ready," I said as I waved goodbye at the bartender and began to make my way towards the exit. The cold evening air helped sober me up as I stepped outside and waited for Dick to join me. We made our way to the car slowly and in silence. The silence became more awkward with each step confirming that this would end up being a long ride back to his home. Once we were out of the parking lot and onto the main road, Dick began his speech. "Hey, I know you're probably mad, may even despise me right now. I do apologize. However, I assure you there is no ill intent. Perhaps one day you will look back on this and understand or even be thankful." Dick paused waiting for a response, I said nothing as I looked over at him with hopes of making eye contact. However, Dick continued to keep his eyes on the road ahead. "Tristan, if it is okay with you, I would prefer to take you home. You have put down quite a few, and I don't want you driving. Your car will be fine at my place. You can pick it up anytime tomorrow, or I can make arrangements to bring it over," Dick said. I said nothing.

Chapter XIX

Once we made it to my neighborhood, Dick slowed down. I looked over and observed him as he looked around, studying the houses and the area. I could see that he had never experienced how the other half lived. I could feel his nervous energy as it quickly began to fill the car. I began to say something but thought better of it. Instead I remained silent, allowing the nervousness to grow, finding pleasure in it. As we turned onto my road and began to approach my house, Dick took a deep breath and once more began. "I appreciate you coming out tonight. I had a good time, all things considered." Once the car came to a stop, I rolled my window partially down, got out quickly, and shut the door behind me.

I then bent down and peered through the opening of the window. "I appreciated the beer tonight. Be safe on your way home." I tapped on the roof of the car and began to walk toward my house when the sound of Dick's voice brought me to a stop. "See you on Monday?" he said with a smile although he had doubt in his voice. I stood there for a moment before smiling and continuing on. I made my way inside, paused as I shut the door, until I heard his car pass.

I realized that the cold air and the atmosphere in the car ride home had sobered me. I looked over at the clock and realized that there was still enough time to walk down to the neighborhood dive bar to have another one or two, or I could save my money and go out to the kitchen and have a couple before calling it a night. I weighed my options before I decided against both and made my way upstairs.

Before I laid down, I made my way over to the window and opened it for some much-needed fresh air. I took a deep breath as I looked into the darkness, darkness that used to terrify me as a child and continued to be feared long after childhood. Now this same darkness and the mystery within it is embraced. There is a whole other world out there. A world that is unknown, waiting to be found. I walked over and turned on some music, knowing exactly what I wanted to hear. As I laid down, a smile appeared as the horns began and the familiar music that Stephen Messmer turned me onto filled the room and made its way out the window, and flooded the street below me. My mind began to wander once more, as I looked back on our adventures. I knew that somewhere on this night in the Queen City, Stephen, Robert, and the boys were out there spitting mad game and showing off their skills as they executed the game they had mastered with reckless abandon.

In doing so, maybe, just maybe, one might mention the name Tristan Wallace, causing the others to smile, reminisce, and even wonder what adventures I may be sharing in the same night air. Perhaps it would be Robert, as he remembered the late night, drunken conversations we shared that created our bond. My thoughts then drifted to Tammy and the game she played so recklessly. Who would be the next guy who would entertain her, or was she possibly spending her nights at home, still anticipating, hoping for my call? I thought of Laura and Marie, the two girls who were kind enough to drive Robert and myself back to Newark from Columbus. I could not help but wonder if they still had hopes each time their phone would ring that we were the ones calling them, or if we had faded from their memories or had possibly been replaced by the next couple of drunkards who gave them the attention they both desired. I thought of Teresa, who I got to know only long enough to tease me, haunt me with what may have been if only the timing would have been perfect, if fate would have been favorable, if destiny would have been on our side. Perhaps we will meet again, I thought this to myself for no other reason than to provide some consolation. I knew deep down that this opportunity would be stubborn, would not present itself. That she would be one of those immortalized in the long list of "what ifs" and perhaps one day within the pages of a novel or in the lines of prose.

As my eyes began to tire, my mind drifted back to the conversation that I had with Robert and more specifically his mentioning of Buddha. Could all that I seek be within the teachings of Buddha? The Four Noble Truths, the Five Precepts? My tired mind would not allow me to explore this any deeper on this evening. Instead, my mind drifted to Dick, who would now be safely tucked away in bed, under the false security of the covers with Jeanine against him as he slept peacefully, with no remorse. In the conversation that we had, any bystander in passing would have recalled more times than not the termination of my employment as the significant topic.

Yet, I laid there reflecting, almost haunted. Not by my job, which I was losing, but by some of the questions that he had asked. "So what lies ahead for you? What is next? Are you telling me you don't have any kind of plans, any kind of dreams?" With those questions echoing through my mind, I could not help but wonder what does lie ahead for me? However, it goes much further than that. It is obvious that each person has his own unique dreams. However, when it is all said and done, is one's life based off of his own success with society's norm embroidering the his dream? When I first began to answer Dick's questions, I placed myself nicely in the aforementioned category when I stated, "I am young. Sure, like everyone else my age, I have dreams. To escape the hometown, yet still reside in small-town USA. However, that is where my dreams differed from the norm. Where most men's dreams typically are based around a wife, a family, a nice home surrounded by a white picket fence while working a nine to five that we hopefully like. We want to succeed enough to shine at our high school reunions. However, I do not want to be the one within the whispers of my peers as they say, "Wow, look at Tristan Wallace, he made it, he escaped. Who would have ever thought?"

You see, as I stated earlier, I am by no means the norm. I find myself trying to find balance, looking forward to the future, the mystery of what it holds, while also trying to live in the moment, enjoying the moment. After all, the moment is all that we have, is it not? For tomorrow is never promised. Of course, I have plans. I have plenty of plans. I want to experience life—mine, as well as others. I want to be on the road soon, and explore. In doing so, I may find myself or at least lose myself for a while. Although the second part of the answer may not be acceptable in the eyes of Dick, my peers, or society, it must suffice, at least for now.

While others may not be able to fathom the desires I have, and why they must be fulfilled, I struggle the same to understand how others do not share the same desire. I am well aware that this desire will continue to run deep within me and will not settle. So I will continue to try and figure out how one achieves this? How I will achieve this? In the end, fulfilling my desire will hopefully provide or at least guide me to my meaning, provide the wisdom, the enlightenment, and the awakening I seek. I feel that the writing is on the wall that I am standing before. I am just too far away for it to be legible. With that in mind, I took some consolation in knowing that the adventure is just beginning, if the good Lord is willing. Tomorrow would be a new day, and tomorrow night will be there waiting. With that in mind, I raised my arm, reached toward the heavens, and grasped at the unknown as a smile appeared and my eyes were slowly able to close.